Praise for Darren Coleman's books

"Darren Coleman is a super storyteller. *Don't Ever Wonder* if this book is a page-turner; it is a sizzling-hot page-burner!"
—Marissa Monteilh, author of *Hot Boyz*

"It's hot!! Darren Coleman captures sensuality and eroticism through the written word. It takes you there and has you biting your bottom lip! Three cheers for the brother!"
—Justine Love, "The Sexpert," host of *Lovetalk* and *Slowjams* (WPGC, Washington, D.C.'s number one radio station)

"Darren Coleman keeps it real. He creates outstanding characters and drama that make you want to keep turning those pages. This is *Waiting to Exhale* of the 2000s."
—Shannon Holmes, author of *B-More Careful* and *Bad Girlz*

"Darren Coleman establishes himself as one of the premier male voices of our time."
—Patty Rice, bestselling author of *Somethin' Extra* and *Reinventing the Woman*

LADIES
LISTEN UP

LADIES
LISTEN UP

Darren Coleman

AMISTAD
An Imprint of HarperCollinsPublishers

This book is a work of fiction. The characters, incidents, and dialogue are drawn from the author's imagination and are not to be construed as real. Any resemblance to actual events or persons, living or dead, is entirely coincidental.

HarperCollins books may be purchased for educational, business, or sales promotional use. For information please write: Special Markets Department, HarperCollins Publishers, 10 East 53rd Street, New York, NY 10022.

FIRST EDITION

Designed by Susan Yang

Printed on acid-free paper

Library of Congress Cataloging-in-Publication Data

Coleman, Darren.
    Ladies listen up : a novel / Darren Coleman.— 1st ed.
       p. cm.
    ISBN-13: 978-0-06-085191-0 (acid-free paper)
    ISBN-10: 0-06-085191-0
       1. African American men—Fiction. 2. Man-woman relationships—Fiction. I. Title.
PS3603.O433L34 2006
813'.6—dc22

                                                              2006040689

06 07 08 09 10 BVG/RRD 10 9 8 7 6 5 4 3 2 1

This book is dedicated to all of the educators across the land; past, present, and future.

I come from a family of teachers. So to each of you I offer a special, heartfelt thanks for shaping me.

*". . . I'll mourn forever. Shit, I got to live
with the fact that I did you wrong forever."*
—Jay-Z

LADIES
LISTEN UP

THE
BEGINNING
OF THE END

(((1)))

. . . and I Can't Get Up

You got questions he got answers. I liked the way it sounded the second I read it through my windshield. It was the slogan that was being used to pitch my new radio show. I had driven past the billboard posted on New York Avenue on my way to a Mystics game earlier in the evening. Seeing my face plastered across a sixty-foot billboard for the first time, right next to that blurb, had my head spinning, in a good way. Diego Christian, better known as Dr. C., was coming soon to WJDS, Smooth 99. My own radio show during the afternoon drive, three to seven. A brother was about to blow up. There was even talk of a book and a talk show on TV One.

I cruised through the remainder of the rush-hour traffic with Jill Scott blasting through the twelve speakers of my Range Rover, her voice soothing me like a glass of Remy VSOP. I drove calmly, like a man in no rush to go anywhere. With the windows down, it felt good to be seen in all my affluence. Call me a pretentious fool, but

I'd blown nearly every penny of my advance on the down payment for the Buckingham-blue beauty that got me eye-fucked, surprisingly, by more men than women. I remembered my friends clowning me about my *little* column for the past year, calling me the hip-hop version of Dear Abby. Now who was having the last laugh? I'd gone from teaching elementary school for thirty-five grand a year and writing my one-page advice column part-time for a thousand bucks a month to hosting my own radio show. Like Don King says: Only in America. I was gonna turn the nation's capital out first, then maybe the nation. *Who'da thought?* I grinned from ear to ear at the whole idea as I pulled into the parking garage at the MCI Center.

Six hours later I was no longer smiling. I was now simply hoping that I'd live to do the first show. What I'd thought would be a discreet outing with one of my favorite women had turned into a nightmare. She wasn't my girl, mind you. We simply shared an intellectual attraction and a physical chemistry that was too tempting to resist. We'd met at a bar four months back. Oddly enough, she'd been smoking a cigar and made it look sexy.

She'd offered me one. "It's a Cuban. This is no habit for me," she said as she lit the stogie I'd accepted. "It's just a little conversation piece."

I nodded and responded, "Well then, let's converse." Ozio's was packed and we'd found a booth in the back to sit and talk shit.

"I love your eyes," she commented. I might have heard that before but never really understood why. "They make you look so innocent, like a little boy."

4

I laughed into a smile when she said that.

"And those teeth, there's nothing like a man with a nice, sexy smile."

"Thanks, your smile is nice, too." I wasn't lying. I realized that my focus was more on her lips. She had big juicy lips like the chick Jill Jones from the UPN show *Girlfriends*. And truthfully, I had fantasized about a blow job from Toni Childs on more than one occasion.

The girl continued to compliment me on all the things about me that she found oh so wonderful. By the time she finished, my head was big as a hot-air balloon. The last thing she said almost made me spit my drink out. She leaned in after taking the cherry from her martini into those big lips. "Now, as cute as you are, if you can fuck, then we're in business."

Needless to say, we'd hit it off, in spite of the small fact that she was married.

Over the next few months I'd found out that she loved to fuck as often as possible, which turned out to be another thing that we had in common.

She also loved basketball, so this particular evening I took her to see the Washington Mystics versus the Houston Comets. We of course drove separate cars and met at our seats. Because of the hundred-plus-degree heat, she wore a pair of cutoff jean shorts and a pink wife beater. She knew her coming out half-naked like that would drive me wild—as always. We were planning to go our separate ways after the game, but as usual, after we'd fondled each other through the entire second half, she decided she had to come home with me. We barely remembered that the Mystics lost. "Just for an hour and then I'm gone," she promised.

I didn't put up any resistance.

One hour turned into three. The next thing I knew, it was one in the morning and shit was hitting the fan with the force of a bull charging toward a matador.

Usually great at thinking on my feet, I was stuck. Honestly, I was as nervous as a tick in a forest fire. My heart was beating so hard it almost leaped out of my chest with each knock. This was indeed some bullshit of my own design and I was neck-deep in it.

I could swear he was staring straight at me as if he had X-ray vision. Though I couldn't really make out the details of his frame, he reminded me of a black Mr. Clean. The nigga was at my door with a tight body shirt on. His arms were folded and the grimace on his face let me know that he wasn't going anywhere, not peacefully at least. Just as I pulled my eye from the peephole he banged again. "Open this motherfucking door. I know she's in there. If I have to kick this motherfucka down, I swear, I'm going to kill you both when I get in there."

I tipped away from the foyer and tiptoed across the hardwood back to the steps. I ran up the steps and back into the room. She was draped in a sheet, tears in her eyes. "It's him, right?"

"Yeah, I guess it would have to be your man." She had seen his pickup parked out across the street.

"Oh shit," she panted out. Her face showed the fear of someone facing the gravest of danger. "I don't know how the hell he found out."

"What difference does it make? His swole ass is down there right now about to kick the damned door down."

Her hands over her mouth, she shook her head. "Ohmigod, ohmigod."

"Yeah, exactly."

"So, what do you think we should do?" At that moment the door sounded like it was being kicked in. The booms that echoed up the steps were way too loud to be coming from a fist. Then the nonstop chimes of the doorbell began again. Even the incessant ringing gave away his intentions and served to further escalate my fears of how this was all going to turn out.

I slipped on my jeans and a pair of sneakers. Hands trembling, I was disgusted at my own fear. I breathed deep, trying to pull it together, then grabbed a T-shirt and moved to my closet. On my tiptoes I reached for, and found, a small case. When I pulled it down and popped the lid, her brows went upward. "What are you doing?" came frantically from her lips when she saw me put the clip into the weapon.

"He just threatened to kill us both. He's not playing down there."

"You can't just go down there and shoot him. Are you crazy?"

"No, but I'm not going to let him bust in here shooting and kill me."

"Hold on, think rationally," she said, panting. "I don't even think he owns a gun."

"Well, it's not like they're impossible to get if you need one for a special occasion. Like someone fucking your wife."

Just then she picked up the phone. "We just have to call the police. I'm not going to be able to go home for a few days, but—"

Before she could finish I heard a loud boom followed by the crunching of wood. Without a doubt my front door was off the hinges. The fool had just kicked in my door. I ran to the steps and looked down as he made his way in over the pieces of wood in my foyer that had formerly been my door. He looked straight ahead into the rear of my house, trying to see if we'd escaped out the back door. It probably would have been a good idea, but now it was too late. I did what I could, which was to stare down *at* him and wait for his next move.

His posture was aggressive, yet unsure. I scanned him once over and was surprised that he was a handsome enough brother. It was obvious that he was one of those types that lived in Bally's or Gold's. A broke version of LL Cool J was what he looked like. I wondered for a moment why his wife had begun the affair. As he stepped forward the glare from the moonlight hitting the steel in his hand caught my eyes. He did indeed have a gun. I looked down at my own hand, not believing that I was actually holding a loaded weapon of my own. I had never fired it at a human being and wasn't sure that I could. I was a lover, not a fighter. Now, I wasn't a sucker by any means, but I was far from a gangster. Realizing that I had the jump on him if I took it, I wished for a moment that I was one.

At that moment I wondered if I was within my bounds to shoot at him. Could I sneak down and shoot him in the back without going to jail?

I had enjoyed the sweet music that I'd made with his woman. Now it appeared time for me to pay the piper. *My life or his?* I pondered. This man had crashed down my door and had a shiny, silver revolver in his hand. I wondered if the brother was prepared to kill as he'd promised.

Just then he peered up the stairs and spotted me. As he asked the words in a deep James Earl Jones voice, my whole life passed in front of my eyes.

"Where is my wife?"

I stood there silent. I asked myself *how*. How did it come down to this? I thought about everything that I'd done from the beginning to get here. A chain of events began to play out right there as I traded stares with my lover's husband in the middle of the night.

I thought about all the things that had made me act the way I did. My upbringing, my selfish desires to have it all, right or wrong. It might have been the fact that I was so good at hiding who I really was most of the time that women were always falling in love with an illusion. From the time I was eight, nearly every woman I came in contact with called me charming.

I grew into a handsome and confident brother. I was intellectually inclined, with a strong sense of street savvy. Women loved me, not only because I knew what to say to them, but because I even knew how to listen.

It was all about to blow up in my face, though. It looked like I was headed to jail or to the morgue. I couldn't hear him talking anymore even though his lips were moving. He moved toward me and I was startled as his wife yelled out from the top of the steps.

"Pleeeease stoooop." Her voice pierced my state and almost snapped me out of my trance. My hands trembled and I thought about all the letters I'd responded to, all the advice I'd given.

I heard the words that I'd read that day play through my mind: *One day, Diego. You'll get yours.*

Then I thought about all that I had to live for. Things were going to be different for me. I *had* something to live for. As the dirt I'd done all began to flash in front of my eyes, it became so clear to me. It had never been worth it. Then just like that, I heard the boom, the echo, and then I lost my balance. It was over just like that.

As I lay on my back and closed my eyes, I thought of her.

(((2)))

Better Love

July 2004

Alicia and I had been through a lot during our whirlwind romance. Watching her approach me now, it was not hard to get caught up in how incredible it was that we'd wound up together. I had *more* than love for the woman; I held a deep admiration for her. She brought out the best in me at a time when I'd found it easy to care about only one person—myself. Until the day she'd crossed my path, I'd done nothing but blaze a trail of heartbreak and devastation in the lives of all the women I'd come across.

I remember the night we first met in front of Circuit City in Landover. I was headed into the store to grab a copy of the DVD of *Bringing Down the House*. She was leaving, with one already in her bag. She caught my attention, or rather her hips did as they swayed back and forth. As she moved past me I lifted my eyes to meet hers, and she did something that was totally atypical for a D.C. chick: she gave me a friendly, unassuming smile as she walked past. I was already grinning by that time. There was something uncanny about her looks. Her skin had a smooth radiance and I instantly noticed her full lips. She reminded me of the singer Tweet, only prettier.

Then, just as quickly, I looked down at her finger and noticed the engagement ring. It wasn't a hell of a rock by any stretch, but whoever he was, he had gotten her to wear it. Out of impulse I called out to her, "That fiancé of yours is a lucky man."

Before I could turn to continue on my path, she replied, "Somebody needs to tell him that," never breaking her stride.

The words reverberated through my mind and stopped me in my tracks. It was an invite if I'd ever heard one. I wasn't sure why but I yelled out, "Hold up." She didn't pause, but I gave chase and caught up to her as she hit the alarm to her car. Now I was standing in front of her as she had her hand on the handle to her car. "This is nice," I said, referring to the convertible Beemer she was driving.

"Thanks." She was smiling again.

I didn't waste any time. "So you mean to tell me that the brother doesn't know what he has? What could possibly be his problem?"

She laughed. "You don't know, brother. I could be the problem." She placed her bag of DVDs in the car and then folded her arms across her chest. She had small breasts but the BCBG tank top couldn't keep her nipples from making noticeable prints in her shirt.

"I somehow doubt that."

"Oh yeah, and why is that?"

I looked her into her eyes and confidently stated, "If I told you, you wouldn't even understand. In fact, you might write me off as a lunatic."

"You think?" Another smile and bright teeth were showing again. "I'm pretty open-minded. Why don't you try me?"

I smiled at her. I caught her staring directly into my mouth this time. "All right," I responded. Staring directly into her eyes, I said, "You have a kind and honest face and it's hard for you to hide your emotions." I noticed her face was now stone; she was waiting for something more. I added, "You *want* your man to do right, ya know, to appreciate you to the fullest. But even though you got the ring . . . you still ain't feeling all that you *need* from him." She was quiet for a moment. The next thing out of my mouth was "Sorry. I didn't mean—"

She interrupted me. "No, it's all good. You just took me away for a second right there."

"Yeah, well, I've been told I can do that from time to time."

Just like that, the conversation and the courtship started. It was a quarter to eight on a humid summer evening when we exchanged names. The time between the start of our conversation and the time for us to part ways seemed to fly by.

The store had been closed for forty-five minutes when we saw the employees begin filing out of the side entrance to go home. We realized that we had been talking for two full hours. I had to wonder how or why a woman who had accepted a ring from a man would stand outside and talk to a stranger until he was no longer a stranger.

She'd told me that her wedding was coming up on Labor Day weekend. I wasn't really in a relationship, just a few bodies here and there that I laid up with when the need arose, so I didn't bother mentioning my status. Finally her cell phone rang and she said, "Diego, it was so nice meeting you. A sistah gots to get home, though."

"So, this is it? I'll never see you again?"

"I don't know. I can't really see how that would be good," she almost sang.

I'd sat there talking to her for two hours and never once had it crossed my mind that she wouldn't be giving me at least a work number. At this point the ring didn't matter to me. She had mesmerized me with her soft sensuality. She was curvy and sexy, yet she didn't carry herself in an overly sexual way. Even so, I had thought more than once that she looked like she would have some good pussy. And with men, that's what the looks and the initial attraction are all about. A pretty face doesn't mean much unless you can get the chance to look down into it while thrusting away on top of a sister. If a relationship or love springs forth from that, then that's all the better, but it's not necessary for satisfaction.

"Listen, I know you had to have been feeling this good conversation the same as I have. As a matter of fact, I can't recall ever connecting like this with anyone. So unless I'm just tripping, I know you want to at *least* give me your work number." I may have sounded like I was begging if not being pushy.

She was silent and had an almost pained look on her face. She was fighting with herself. It was obvious.

"Alicia, I'll tell you what. You can just give me your work number and I'll call you there. If you decide between tonight and the time I call you that this is really a bad idea, I'll lose your number. It's obvious to me that you need someone to talk to. Someone that will listen for a change."

She half huffed, and laughed at the same time. "It's that obvious, huh?"

"You did sit out here for two hours talking to a brother."

"True dat. And you know, I could hook you up with a friend of mine. I think you'd like her. I know she'd like you. She's into you pretty-boy types."

"Oh yeah." I smirked. "I don't think *you* could handle that."

"What do you mean?"

"Suppose she and I hit it off. What would you do with the chemistry between you and me? You'd be sitting over there at the cookout with him, mad 'cause he ain't me." I laughed, but I was serious and she knew it.

"Boy, you are too much." She shook her head.

"So, what's up with that work number?"

"Why don't I just take yours and—"

I cut her off. "Won't work. You'd be too scared to do what you really want to do. I can't take that chance."

"You make it sound so drastic and serious."

"You make it sound like it ain't."

She scribbled her number down on the back of her loan officer's card. I helped her into her car and we just stared into each other's eyes; for a second it was obvious that she didn't want to leave. "It was so nice talking to you. I mean that."

"You, too."

"I'm serious. You just don't meet many men around here who know how to talk to a sister, or better yet, listen to one. I don't know what you had on your agenda before you met me, but you made me feel like there was nothing more important in the world than talking to me. Thanks."

With that, she pulled off.

I called her early Tuesday morning and asked her to stop past my crib. She said she would have to think about it first. Still, we sat on the phone and talked for half the day and she got *almost* no work done.

It turned out that she didn't come that evening, but I relented and she wound up coming the next day. It turned out that her inclinations against being alone with me were well founded. We had sat on the floor in front of my couch and talked for three hours about our dreams, hopes, and fears. We connected as time slipped away. She left her scent in my home that night and I stayed up for a couple hours thinking about her.

We wound up kissing each other gently on the lips before she sped home to her fiancé.

The next day had me filled with excitement as I spent every available minute trying to persuade her to come over again. She did. That evening we listened to Erykah Badu, Jaheim, and, ironically, Tweet, while we drank white Zinfandel. This time I canned the sensitivity and I stuck my fingers inside of her panties and massaged her pussy until she came while I sucked her tongue. She ran out of the house after telling me that she couldn't do this again. I was too dangerous, she said. Even still, she couldn't keep herself from calling from her home phone while her man was asleep upstairs.

"Diego, I don't know what it is about you. You are so confident, even a little cocky. Normally, that would turn me off and make me think that you're really insecure. Hiding behind the bravado. With you, though, it seems like you couldn't be any other way if you tried."

The next day I smiled like I had the winning lottery ticket when she showed up at my doorstep as the sun was beginning to set. We fucked like two newly released prisoners and she got a chance to see one reason why I was so confident. We fucked until we sweated buckets and there was a puddle of her juices in my bed. I didn't let her out of the bed until I felt like I had mastered her body. "Oh my gawd, it's so big," she yelled out as I stroked her out.

When I finished, her eyes gave away everything that she didn't want to say. She didn't understand why I had come into her life, then and not sooner. Her wedding was three and a half weeks away.

She was at my house nearly every day after that. I would bang her as she bent over my steps even while he called her cell phone. "I got to go. I . . . got . . . to . . . go," she'd cry out as she came all over me. The sex was intense, the conversations were deep. It felt something like love, though it couldn't have been. Three weeks later we were lying in my bed naked, sweat coating our bodies. With her head on my chest she said, "There's no way I can stop seeing you."

"What do you mean?"

"I mean even after the wedding. I can't."

I thought about the reality of it. This woman had consumed all of my time, my thoughts, for the past month, yet in a few days she was getting married to another man. I then said the only thing that I could think of. "You can't do it. You can't get married."

There was silence in my room for a moment. "It's too late. My mother and uncle have spent too much money. Maybe I can do it and just get an annulment." She was estranged from her father, but her uncle had stepped up and always taken care of her.

I shook my head in disbelief. "Nah." I thought about it then added, "Listen, maybe I'm being selfish. Maybe you should just give your marriage to him a try. But if you marry him, I can't see you anymore." I heard the words, but I knew full well there was no way I'd stop hitting it. I didn't care if she was marrying Mike Tyson; there was something about her, something more than sex, because she wasn't even in my top fifty as far as that aspect went. I simply enjoyed her, and the way she adored me filled me up in ways I'd never experienced.

She left my house that night with tears in her eyes. Standing at my door, she asked, "So you're serious? If I do this, you and I are over?"

I nodded and showed no emotion. It was the pimp in me.

Four days later, on the Saturday morning that she was supposed to be getting dressed for her wedding, she rang my phone. The night before, during the rehearsal dinner, Alicia had called off her wedding.

(((3)))

Crossing the Thin Line

Alicia was no more than twenty feet from me. I had nothing on my mind other than the fact that I was about to finally do this. Get out of the game for good and make this beautiful woman my wife. Her uncle walked her to my side, and when the pastor asked, "Who giveth this woman to be married?" he responded and released her.

The ceremony was small, with no more than seventy people in attendance. After her last fiasco, she didn't have the nerve to try for another big wedding or ask her girls to stand for her again, so she only had two bridesmaids. At her mother's insistence she had reimbursed the entire wedding party for their expenses from gowns to tux rentals, and even airfare for a couple of folks.

That was all behind her, though her mother always made it clear that she didn't approve of the way our relationship had started. Today, though, was our day, as we were getting married at the Marlboro Country Club in front of our closest friends and family. She wore a white Vera Wang wedding dress that stopped above her knees. It was cut in the front to accent the little cleavage that she did have. Our pictures were going to be beautiful. At five feet ten inches, I had half a foot on her even with the three-inch heels she wore. My tux was custom-made and hung perfectly on my 175-pound frame. I'd cut my hair short, and with the waves in it, coupled with my complexion, I even admitted that I looked a little like a young Boris Kudjo, only with a better smile. When I'd arrived, even my own mother told me I was handsome, and she gave out compliments about as freely as you'd give a kidney. It definitely made me smile.

As the ceremony went on Alicia read her vows to me first. Next, I had a little surprise for Alicia as the music began to play in the background and my best friend, Jacob Marsh, began to sing. He had a voice as good as any R&B star, and when he began to belt the notes out to Kenny Lattimore's "For You," tears welled up in her eyes. It thrilled me to be moving her in such a way. My romantic side hadn't always shone as much as it was shining at that moment. I mouthed the words *I love you* to her and the tears began to roll. She looked at me and I saw such a look of utter surprise that it startled me.

I smiled and said, "You all right, baby?"

Still there was no response as she stared right through me. Then Jacob called my name. "Dee, look." I turned around to see three women entering the room in a rush. The question *What the fuck?* slipped out of my mouth.

"What is she doing here?" Alicia yelled. She'd seen Kristen before. One night at a party, Kristen had tried to make it known to Alicia that she and I had history. Up to this minute, all Alicia knew of was the *distant* past.

Instantly I charged toward the crazy bitch. "Kristen, I don't know what you trying to do, but if you don't get out of here right now, your ass is gonna be sorry."

The room began to erupt with voices. I could hear people mumbling and asking, "What's going on?"

I was now up close on Kristen and realized that the third girl was her best friend, Gina. I didn't know the one standing right beside her, but I had slept with both Kristen and Gina, together the first time, but afterward I had crept on the regular with Gina behind Kristen's back. "Kris, I don't know what the hell you thinking coming up in here trying to start some shit, but I swear I will kill your ass for this. If you know like I do, you better turn your ass around and—"

"Fuck you and your wedding, Diego," she yelled. "Does this bitch know?"

There were oohs and aahs from the audience and by now the bridesmaids were coming over to see what was up.

"Do I know what?" I heard Alicia's voice as I turned around. She was now right behind me. The place was silent.

"Do you know that I have been fucking your man, driving your car after he drops you off at work? Oh, and that new crib that you are building—we done already christened that joint. I got the splinters in my ass to prove it."

Alicia took a deep breath as her eyebrows curled. "I don't know who you are, but I would appreciate if you would leave. Somebody call the police before I go the fuck off." Immediately someone ran out of the hall to get security.

Kristen smacked her lips. Kristen was only five-two but she looked like a a fitness instructor and she'd come ready for trouble, dressed in capris and Nike track shoes. Her hair was already in a ponytail and I was ready to take her down if she jumped at Alicia. In fact, the only reason I hadn't hauled off and slapped the shit out of her already was that there were women in attendance. Then Kristen said, "Oh, so you's a dumb bitch, huh? Diego don't love you. He don't love nobody but himself. His ass been fucking my best girl behind my back and here's a news flash. Her ass is pregnant." She pointed over at Gina, who looked like she had come against her will.

I looked over at Gina. Her stomach was indeed poking out. My head began to spin. I instantly went back to the night that the condom had busted, and my mouth dropped open.

After that, things happened so quickly. Alicia began to scream as she asked me if the things being said were true, over and over again. I felt dizzy and my stomach knotted. I had had several affairs, or fuckbuddies, while we were together, but in an effort to do right going into my marriage, I had cut them all off a month before the wedding. All except for Kristen, who swore she would be there for me forever, and never breathe a word of our affair to anyone. I guess that was until Gina told her about us.

I never imagined that these skeletons would come falling out of the closet on top of my head in a million years. "I don't believe this shit," I said under my breath. I looked back at Alicia and the look in her eyes told me that I was busted. The next thing I knew, Kristen swung at Alicia and landed an open-handed slap across her face that sounded off through the hall. I saw red and lunged at Kristen. I wrapped my hands around her neck and tried my best to choke the life out of her. The second girl, who was with her, pulled something from her bag and swung it at the back of my head. The next thing I knew, I was on the ground trying to get my vision back in focus. It turned out that the girl was a D.C. officer and she'd hit me with her foldout billy club. I'd probably suffered a mild concussion from the way I hit the floor, but the pain in my head was nothing compared to all of the destruction I'd caused.

By the time Jacob helped me to my feet, the place was in a complete uproar. A lone police officer came running, talking on his walkie-talkie, coupled with two rent-a-cops. People had obviously decided to leave the cursed affair and I saw Alicia's mother trying to comfort her a few feet away, all the while she was chanting, "I told you about him. I told you this nigga wasn't no good. It'll be okay, baby." She kept saying this to her daughter, who was near hysterical and nearly hyperventilating. "Someone call an ambulance."

"Come on. We got to get out of here," Jacob said, pulling me from the floor.

"I can't leave her like this," I shot back. I tried to move toward her. As soon as Alicia saw my face she began to scream at the top of her lungs and lost her breath.

Her mother charged me and I flinched, thinking she was about to hit me, too. I was wrong about her, but I didn't see her uncle as he threw a straight right to my cheek. "You son of a bitch" was all I heard as I stumbled to the ground. People were moving about, rushing out of the hall.

"I told you we got to bounce."

This time I listened as Jacob whisked me out the side to the limo. We climbed in, and once we had the doors closed safely behind us, he looked into my face. I could see he pitied me, but at the same time he was disgusted. "Yo, man, don't say shit," I said.

He shook his head and burst out laughing. He told the driver to take us to his place. "No, better yet, do you have another gig tonight?" he asked the driver.

"No, sir."

"How much to take us to Atlantic City?"

"How's two-fifty?"

"Make it three hundred, but take us to the liquor store first."

I said nothing. I gazed out the window thinking about the mess that was my life. Forty-five minutes later we were on I-95 headed to gamble, sipping on Hennessy.

"You know, Diego. Maybe you should look at what happened today as a clue that you need to make some changes in your life. You could write a book."

I laughed. Finally I was beginning to get a buzz from the liquor. "Yeah, right, on what? How to fuck up your life and everyone you come in contact with?"

He laughed. "Nah, you should make it on something for women on how to avoid men like you."

"Thanks, man."

"Hell, if the book is good enough, Alicia might even come back to your ass."

"Man, you're crazy as shit."

"*I'm* crazy? You just had your wedding crashed by Kristen and your soon-to-be baby's mama. Then you got your ass whipped by a sixty-year-old man, but I'm crazy."

"Man, that shit ain't funny." I half laughed to keep from feeling completely miserable. The rest of the ride up, he helped me laugh to keep from crying.

"Yo, when we get back you need to have one objective."

"What's that?"

"Damage control. I mean, shits already blown sky-high, but you just need to start trying to pass out umbrellas before it starts falling from the sky. Whatever you do, leave Alicia alone because there ain't no way you can possibly straighten this mess out."

Jacob was a true friend. He even took my cell-phone calls when it all began to blow up. My mother wanted to blast me. All she could focus on was her embarrassment. Alicia's best friend called to curse me out. Jacob fielded it all without hesitation. The only call I took was from my coworker Lisa. She was my best friend at work and a sixth-grade teacher.

"Motherfucker, you're crazy." She laughed into the phone. The next thing she said was "Aren't you glad you listened to me and didn't invite any of those assholes from work to the wedding?"

"Yes, Lisa."

"So, what are you going to do now? Are you going to be with the ghetto bitch who busted in?"

"Hell no."

"You need to kill that bitch. She's crazy."

"No doubt. Look, I'm gonna keep drinking this Henny and I'll talk to you later."

"All right. You gonna be okay?"

"Yeah, I'm cool."

Then she started laughing again. "So, are you coming to work since you aren't going on your honeymoon?"

"Fuck you." I laughed back and hung up the phone.

I told Jacob how grateful I was that he'd helped me escape, even if it was temporary. As I gazed out the windows as we cruised toward a night of gambling, my mind drifted. If I ever wrote a book, I was thinking that it would sell. People loved drama and sex. I was no writer, but for the right price, who couldn't tell the truth?

Birds of a Feather?

After seeing my world go up in flames, Jacob was determined to keep his house in order. A situation had come up and he was now willing to do the unthinkable to get *her* off of his back. Anna had gone from being his number one fan to borderline stalker. At first he'd welcomed the attention; now the junior had him way past worried. In a world where young people only tend to worship ballplayers, actors, singers, and rappers, Jacob, at first, had been truly flattered at the crush that Anna had on him. She complimented him on his clothing, his teaching, and then, eventually, his looks.

She had begun to show up in between classes just to say hello, and now that she had a car and no longer had to catch a bus home, she made it her business to stop by daily after school for a chat. It was during one of these chats that Jacob began to notice that Anna seemed a little detached from reality.

As Jacob had sat recording a few grades in his book, Anna had walked in and closed his door. "What's up?" he asked.

As she moved closer he noticed the redness in her eyes. Anna plopped down at a desk in front of him, covered her face with her hands, and proceeded to burst into tears. "Mr. Marsh, my life is over."

Jacob looked around the room as if someone else could help him, but there was no one there and in a panic he tried to console her. "Listen, it can't be that bad," he said. "Tell me what's wrong."

She explained that one of her friends had lied on her and now her popularity was plummeting. Expertly, Jacob made light of the situation and assured her that things would blow over.

After listening for a few moments, she'd smiled and told him thanks, before saying, "Well, at least I have band *and* you."

With that, Jacob swallowed and tried to figure out if Anna did indeed have a screw loose.

Jacob was the band teacher at Lyndon B. Johnson High School in Greenbelt. The school was nestled in the middle of black suburbia in the nation's wealthiest black county, Prince George's.

Of the fifteen schools in the county, Johnson was one of only two to be in the top ten academically in the state of Maryland. The grounds were immaculate, the sports teams were championship contenders year in and year out, and for both reasons, funding never seemed to be a problem. At his first teaching job out of college, working at an elementary school in the inner city, Jacob had learned how difficult it was to teach without the proper resources. Now that he was at Johnson, he was able to accomplish all of his goals. Though he was younger than all of the other music teachers at Johnson, he headed the music department and led the marching band as well. At Jacob's command, Johnson High boasted one of the top high-school bands in the country, dominating tournament after tournament.

The master's degree he'd received from Norfolk State University in music had served him well and he loved his job. Now he needed a little help from Dean, his new protégé, to ensure that the Anna situation didn't turn into a scandal.

Jacob had seen it before, a few years back, and was determined to never let what had happened to Wade Collins, a math teacher who he'd been cool with, happen to him. Wade had thrown his whole career and his marriage away by getting into a full-fledged relationship with a track star that he coached. After receiving several full-scholarship offers to top universities, she sent word that she'd only consider colleges that would bring Wade on board to coach her. Eventually her family became concerned about his influence and sent her to counseling, where she admitted the affair. Wade left the school in handcuffs.

Jacob couldn't understand the nature of a brother who would go out like that. True, some of the teenage girls were blossoming into young women overnight, but he had always looked at them as babies trying to find their way, no matter how good their firm young bodies looked in their tight jeans. Anna was no different. She was definitely a cute girl, above-average intelligence, and as far as her body went, she was definitely blessed in that department as well. Based on the physical alone, she should have easily been one of the most sought-after girls in the school. It was becoming obvious to Jacob that there had to be some problem with her personality if she was having such a rough time keeping friends.

One day, as Jacob headed out of the staff parking lot, he turned the music up in his Cadillac CTS. "Listen to that," he said to Dean, his student teacher for the semester.

"Who is it?" Dean asked loudly over the blaring music.

"Mint Condition—they're one of the best bands in the era after Earth, Wind & Fire." Jason was crooning along with the music. " '*This feeling is strong and we know it, but we gotta seeeeeee past the moooment.*' Young man, they don't make music like that anymore." A guitar solo came and Jacob took both hands off of the wheel and played his air guitar along with the music. "That's the shit right there."

Dean smiled and nodded. In his eyes, Jacob was the man. His skills as an instructor were unmatched. After going out to see him perform live with No Question, the R&B band he'd formed two years earlier just so he could have an outlet for his artistry, a couple of weeks earlier, Dean had wanted nothing other than to be just like him. Jacob was picking up on Dean's admiration and it figured to play right into his plan.

"Dean, can I tell you something off the record?"

"Sure," he said as the car pulled into the Wendy's parking lot.

"In life, sometimes you only get a few opportunities to do certain things. Because of that, you have to sometimes grab life by the balls and go for it, ya feel me? Sometimes just for the sake of having a good time, knowing that it might be your only chance ever to do it."

"Most definitely," Dean shot back.

"Well, have you ever done it?"

"Done what?"

"Jumped out there and just done something wild simply because you could?"

Dean was silent. He wasn't sure where his mentor was taking or leading him and didn't want to give a stupid answer. "Kind of."

"Well, how did it make you feel?"

Dean had no real answer because he couldn't actually recall ever going for it. "Good, I guess."

Deciding to cut to the chase, Jacob began to speak like a father talking to a son. "Good, huh? Well, let me break something down for you." Dean was staring into Jacob's face as he rolled the window down. Jacob paused from his speech long enough to give the worker his and Dean's order and then went on. "Listen, you're going to be teaching probably for many years, and I got to be honest with you: Sooner or later you're gonna be tempted."

"Tempted to . . . ?" Dean asked, sounding truly puzzled.

Jacob laughed. "Ya know. Get busy with one of the students." He paused and put a straw into his drink. "Over the years some of the young ladies are bound to take a special interest in you. I know it for a fact. You remind me a lot of myself when I was in college, and I am having the same talk with you that my mentor teacher had with me over ten years ago." He looked at his watch as he told the lie. They had fifteen minutes left for lunch. They could finish up in his car in the parking lot.

"Really?" Dean sat back and took pride in the comment about him reminding Jacob of himself.

"Hell yeah," Jacob said, "and I'll be honest with you. It's now or never." He caught Dean's attention. "Once you graduate from college and get a job in this county or the next, your chance is over. You've got to pick one of these young ladies and bang her good enough to last an eternity." Jacob almost laughed at himself for having said this.

Dean almost choked on his chicken sandwich hearing it. "Say what?"

"Yeah," Jacob said. "I just wanted you to know that you have the green light as far as I'm concerned. Of course that's strictly off the record and between you and me. But be my guest. I see the chemistry between you and what's-her-face. It's obvious she wants you bad." Dean had no idea who he was talking about and said so. "C'mon, Dean. You mean to tell me that you can't tell that Anna has a crush on you?"

Dean smiled. "You think so?" He had noticed her hanging around a lot.

"Hell yeah. Boy, she comes sniffing around all the time. Even when you're not there she stops by and ask about you. But you can never tell her I said that. I could get in trouble for that."

"Oh no. I would never repeat that."

"Good. Now listen. You've got three months left before you finish up with me and you might as well enjoy them. I'll even help you out with her. When she stops by today after school, I'll ask her if she can give you a ride back to campus since your car is in the shop. I'll tell her that I can't do it today because of an appointment. You should be man enough to handle it from there, right?"

Dean gave an approving nod. "No problem."

"All you gotta do is take her out, invite her back to your room, and maybe give her a little drink. From there, she'll be a little tipsy and so excited to be with a college guy that it should be like taking candy from a baby, ya know?"

Dean was still nodding, now with a grin on his face.

He seemed confident enough to make Jacob feel that it would be just a matter of time before he would be relieved of his problem. "Listen, there's one more thing."

"Yeah?"

"If everything works out, you can never tell her that I have any knowledge of what's going on with you two. Got it?"

"Got it."

Jacob breathed easier as he climbed out of his car. They headed back into the building. In a few hours he would put Dean to the test and, hopefully, Anna to the curb.

The day came to an end, and just as he planned, Anna walked into the band room. Jacob pulled her into the office and asked her if she could do him the favor of dropping Dean off at his room. "Anything for you, Mr. Marsh," she replied.

Jacob rushed home. He needed to clean his town house from top to bottom in case he got lucky after his date tonight with Kendra. He had been asking her out for two months. She sang with a band, from Baltimore, Heartfelt, which performed at Takoma Station from time to time. Kendra had a voice that sent chills up and down Jacob's spine every time he heard her sing.

She had agreed to make the forty-minute drive from Baltimore and have dinner with Jacob even though it was a weeknight, and he couldn't have been more excited. His hype was a little inexplicable because Kendra wasn't his usual type. She was talented and smart, but she was also hood. She'd grown up on Baltimore's notorious Edmonson Avenue. Even though she was radiant, her edges were a little rough. She was the type to wear an evening gown with thick cornrows and it was nothing for her to throw on a pair of Air Force Ones and cargo pants. She often hid the beautiful body that she had. She'd been a standout ballplayer at Dunbar High and still kept in shape.

She called for directions when she was just up the street from his crib. Jacob was already dressed and ready to impress. He had on a fresh pair of Paper Denim jeans on a crisp white button-up and a pair of Louis Vuitton sneakers. He had stopped off to see his barber, Dee, on the way home to get tightened up and was now hopeful that he would look the part of Kendra's dream date.

"What's up?" he said as he opened the front door to his town house.

"Hey, Jake," she said as she entered with a hug. "Is my car okay right there?"

"It's fine," he shot back, looking her up and down. She had surprised him. She had on a tight pair of jeans that were tucked inside of her Gucci boots and she was rocking a light suede jacket along with her trademark cornrows. "You look beautiful, as always," Jacob said. "Would you like a drink before we roll?"

"Nah, I'm good, but I could stand to use your restroom right fast."

Jacob pointed to the door and walked to the closet to grab his jacket. Five minutes later they were on their way downtown to Kinkead's for a seafood dinner. On the drive down, Jacob assured Kendra that the seafood would rival what she was used to in Baltimore. "We'll see," she shot back.

As they were headed down 295 Kendra turned to Jacob and asked, "Did you have to make a reservation for this restaurant?"

"No, why?"

She smiled. "I don't know. I don't really have a taste for seafood tonight."

Thrown off a little by her statement, he still replied, "That's cool. So what do you want? There's another spot down near Adam's Morgan that has some really good Mexican or—"

She cut him off. "Nah," she said as she turned to him and then smiled. "You know what I have a taste for?"

"What?"

"Some ribs from a carryout. Do you know where any good soul-food spots are? We could go grab some ribs and a bottle of wine, and go back to your spot. You have any DVDs?"

"I did just pick up *The Manchurian Candidate; I, Robot;* and *Collateral.*"

She laughed. "Denzel, Will, or Jamie Foxx—decisions, decisions. How about we watch them all? We could make it an all-nighter."

Jacob liked the sound of that and just like that he pressed the OnStar button on the steering wheel of his car. "This is OnStar," the voice said through his speaker.

"Yes, need the number to Levi's Carryout in Mitchellville."

"Would you like us to connect you?"

Jacob looked over at Kendra. "Do we wanna be *connected*?"

"Oh, I think connecting is gonna be a good look for us."

They both laughed and placed their order.

For the next couple of hours, Jacob said all the right things. He even did his best not to eat like a slob in front of Kendra. Ironically, she had had no problem letting him see the barbecue-sauce master-piece that she'd painted on her own face. After the first bottle of wine, Kendra became really talkative and began to really open up to Jacob.

They were seated in his basement with the fireplace burning, listening to music. They had temporarily abandoned the thought of watching a movie. "So, Jake, why is it you wanted to go out with me so bad?"

"You gotta be playing. You're beautiful."

"I'm average," she said in a playful tone.

"No, you're beautiful and you're talented. I just wanted to get to know you better."

"That's it?" she asked. Jacob shrugged his shoulders. "Well, what do you want to know?"

"What do you want to share?"

Kendra paused for a moment. It appeared she was scanning her thoughts for a reply when she leaned toward Jacob and planted a kiss on his lips. "How's that?"

"That's a good look."

She leaned in again and this time she opened her lips when they met his. Jacob couldn't believe it. He had hoped for this, but had viewed this night as more of a setup for the next date. His plans weren't the ones that mattered, though, as Kendra took over and climbed on top of him, straddling him cowgirl style.

A smile slid across Jacob's lips. He reached out to slide his hands up her shirt when his doorbell rang and startled him. "What the . . ." he said. Seconds later the chime came back to back to back.

"Someone knows you're home," she said with a smirk, before adding, "I'll be waiting," and climbed off of him. "I hope it's not your girlfriend."

"I don't have one, thank you."

"So you said."

"I'll be right back." Jacob climbed up the steps and looked out the window of his living room. He didn't see a car he recognized. The bell rang again, and peeping through the curtains, he could make out a woman's body at his door. He came down the steps and opened the door.

"Mr. Marsh," she said in a troubled tone.

"Anna, what are you doing here? How did you know where I lived?"

She stared into his face and stuttered out, "I . . . told him . . . I . . . told him . . . noooo. He wouldn't . . . stop."

"What? Who wouldn't stop?"

"Mr. . . . M-Marsh, he . . . heeee raped me. Dean raped me."

Jacob prided himself as being someone who could always come up with an answer when it counted most. He couldn't count the number of times he'd bailed his friends out of tough situations. Now it was his back that was truly up against a wall and he was sweating bricks. He spent twenty minutes trying to calm Anna down in his living room in order to get a story out of her. Kendra had heard the young girl upstairs crying and had rushed up to check out the situation. Trying not to blow his chances with Kendra, he'd introduced Anna as his niece. Otherwise he had no explanation for why one of his students, especially a young female student, was popping up at his house at eleven o'clock at night.

After she'd heard the word *rape*, it was all Jacob could do to keep Kendra from calling the police on Dean right then and there. Jacob assured her that he would take Anna to the hospital and told her that he wanted to speak to Anna alone. After she was convinced that it was family business, Kendra left, impressed by the obvious closeness between Jacob and his niece.

Jacob couldn't believe his ears as Anna described the events of the evening. She had dropped Dean off at school and he'd promised to buy her dinner and to burn a copy of a John Legend CD for her if she could come by later. She said that out of boredom she'd agreed. Once they'd gotten to his place, he invited her up and told her that they could watch a movie or listen to some music.

"I didn't think anything of it, Mr. Marsh. But once we got to his room, he offered me some wine and I told him that I didn't drink. Then he started acting a little agitated and it made me nervous, so I was about to leave, and when I put my coat on, he begged me not to go."

Jacob sat on the edge of the couch as he listened intently. Anna used Kleenex to wipe her eyes and nose occasionally as she went on. "I stayed and he put the Dave Chappelle DVD on. I was on the floor, chilling, and he was on the bed. Everything was all good, but after a couple episodes he just lost his mind and started trying to pull me up onto the bed. Then I tried to get up and leave and he wouldn't let me." Seconds later, she started crying again. Jacob was horrified and his mind was racing, but he tried to think rationally. He couldn't believe that Dean had been so foolish. He was thinking that he was going to drive out to the campus and break the young man's neck. Not only had he violated Anna, which Jacob found inexcusable, but he had jeopardized everything that Jacob had worked to build. He had blown a simple opportunity to rid Jacob of a problem.

Now it was full-scale damage control.

"Okay, listen. What do you want to do?" Jacob tried to sound calming.

She shrugged her shoulders.

"I got to tell you, Anna, I have no idea what to do either. Do you want to go to the police?" Jacob thought of Dean and what he would say once the authorities came to pick him up. He knew right then that he would deny all involvement except getting Anna to give Dean a ride home. Jacob's record in the county had been impeccable up to this point. How could he have known that Dean would be a rapist? His intentions were only to distract Anna's attention from him. He hadn't asked for a crime to be committed against the young woman.

"No, I don't want to go to the police. I can't do that. Do you realize that I would be the talk of the school? No way," she said as she sniffed and wiped. "I'll be okay. I just don't know if I can face him again. I'll drop out first."

If it meant that she would get over this situation, she wouldn't have to. "Don't worry about that. You'll never see him again. He's finished at Johnson."

She looked at Jacob with admiration. "Thank you for being here for me. I didn't know anywhere else to go."

"It's okay. But how did you know where I lived?"

"Stephanie Drexall's aunt used to live three doors down from you. She said she spent the night over one time and she saw you out front washing your car. She used to have a really big crush on you. It was all she talked about. She used to say that she was going to show up at your door one day in nothing but a trench coat and some lingerie." Anna laughed, which was a good sign she'd be okay. Jacob laughed, too, at the thought of two-hundred-and-sixty-pound Stephanie in a trench and lace at his door.

"So listen. Is there someone you want to speak to? What about your mom?"

"Oh, hellll no. She'll wanna call the police and have him prosecuted. Knowing her, she'll try to sue the county, the school, and probably even you."

The last remark shook Jacob. "Me?"

"Ya know, for having me give Dean a ride home."

Her statement chilled him and for a moment he feared that she might be playing the angles.

"Listen, Mr. Marsh, I can't go home. I'm not ready to face my mother. Is there any way that I can stay here tonight? I will stay out of your way. I'm still really shook up and I don't know what I'll slip up and say if I go around any of my phony friends."

"I'm sorry, but that would be totally inappropriate."

"But having me drive him home for you wasn't?"

5

More Sh#% Than a Little Bit

My car was on the top level of the lot. I saw Erin when she pulled up at Dave & Buster's. I hit my high beams to signal her and she pulled up right next to me. "What's good, homey?" she said with a smile.

"You, Ma," I said, smiling back at her.

"So you ready to do this? I don't want to hear any crying when I win." Erin had challenged me to a game of pool, so we agreed to meet where we could shoot some pool and have dinner. Dave & Buster's was in neighboring Montgomery County, and although it wasn't a real creep spot, it wasn't a hot spot anymore either. She had picked it, so I was guessing that she felt at ease.

We walked in and she took my hand. She seemed to be really into me, and oddly I was okay with it. In all honesty, she wasn't the first parent of one of my students whom I had slept with. She was, however, the first one that I'd enjoyed spending so much time with. Erin was a really jazzy dresser. She always looked nice, never cheap.

Tonight she had on a snug-fitting black sweater that stopped right at the top of her Arden B jeans.

I checked out her stride as she moved at a brisk pace toward the door. It was cold outside, but her walk was warming me up. As we hit the door I looked over my shoulder, saw no one running after us, and I breathed easy, feeling that the coast was clear.

We had eaten dinner twice together at my spot. One night carryout from Outback and the next time she'd cooked for me, which I really appreciated. This was the first time that we'd ventured out. As we shot pool I was beginning to wonder if she no longer cared if she got caught. That was always a dangerous point in a relationship for me. It meant the woman was toying with the idea of taking me from joyfriend to boyfriend status.

"Eight ball, side pocket," she said calmly before sinking the shot. "Okay, Diego, I thought you said you could play. What is that now—four games to one?"

"One last game. Then we can go back to my spot and you can collect your winnings."

"Oh yeah, I didn't know we were betting."

"Yeah, an orgasm for every game you win," I said, holding my stick like a cane.

"I'm up three on you already. That's a pretty tall order. You sure you can pay up?" She was smiling as I began racking up the balls.

"I got this," I shot back, and lifted the rack. "You just be sure that you can handle it."

As we played I watched her as she leaned over the table making shots. Every time she prepared to shoot, I would stick my tongue out and say, "You want the leeeeezard, leeeezard, leeeezard," as I imitated a Hispanic person.

She kept laughing and missed shots that she had been making earlier. I already owed her four orgasms, so it was critical that I win at least one more game. When we got down to nothing but the eight ball, she prepared to shoot and I walked up behind her and pressed my crotch to her ass. "I'll hit it right here on this table."

"Yeah, right," she said as she pulled the stick back to shoot.

"Okay, I got my dick out."

She turned and smiled. "Liar." She shot and made the shot, but she forgot to call her pocket, giving me the game.

"So that's four to two," I said confidently. "I don't think that will be a problem."

She placed the stick on the wall and walked over to me and reached her arms out. We embraced and I took in the smell of her perfume. Sweet-smelling perfume on a woman can be intoxicating; smelling it on a woman you strongly desire can be truly hypnotic. I closed my eyes and kissed her on the neck. I couldn't wait to get her back to my place.

On the ride home I sped around the Beltway and she was on my tail. It was ten already and she would have to get in around 1 A.M. to keep the peace. We reached my condo and hurried out of the cold. Once we got in, I threw a log on the fireplace and grabbed a bottle of wine and turned off the lights.

We talked for a quick minute about her job and how hard she was working. Then she asked, "Diego, what's going on here? I mean with us."

I wasn't sure but I answered, "I think it's just two people really enjoying one another's company and friendship."

"That's all? Just friendship . . . and sex." I was silent for a moment. "Because, Diego, I can't lie. It's becoming more for me than that. I'm starting to think about you all the time. It's real for me like that. I don't just give my body away to anyone."

"I feel you."

"I hope so."

"But what's up with you and Kenard?"

She huffed and said, "I don't know. To be honest I don't think he cares what I do. He doesn't really show any interest in Dante other than when he does something wrong. But I don't want to talk about him. I just want to ask you something that has been on my mind ever since the first time we made love."

Made love? I thought to myself. "Go ahead." I braced myself, thinking that she was going to ask about a future between us. If she did I was wondering what I would come right out and say. I really wasn't interested in a future with anyone at that point. I still had so much to accomplish on my own.

"What I want to know is this." She paused and looked into my eyes. I saw an innocence in her eyes and a searching that let me know I would have to be careful with my words. Then she asked, "Diego, have you done this before?"

Unsure of what she was talking about, I asked, "Done what?"

"Been with one of you students' moms. I just need to know if this is just something that you would do all the time . . . or if . . ." She paused again. "Or if it means something to you, too."

I looked her in the face and smiled. "Girl, you got to know this is special to me. I think of you all the time. Even if I had been with someone in a similar situation, it still wouldn't take away from this, ya know?"

"But that doesn't answer my question."

I thought before answering. "Well, the answer is no, I haven't." I lied to her.

As a matter of fact, I lied horribly. In my five years in the classroom, I'd been with somewhere close to fifteen parents. Not all of them were parents of my students. Occasionally I would meet a mom picking up a kid from kindergarten or catch a parent of an older kid leaving the office. It was always the same. I'd see them and know I had to move quickly. Sometimes it was nothing more than planting a seed to let them know I was interested. Nine times out of ten, they responded by flirting back. The school year that'd just passed had been a banner year. I'd managed to seduce, or perhaps be seduced by, all four of the mothers I'd put on my "She Can Get It" list. I had more success in the classroom than most brothers had in a nightclub.

"You sure?" she asked.

"I'm sure." I nodded. "Hand me your glass."

While I poured she got really comfortable, taking off her jeans and boots. Next her sweater came carefully over her head. "I'll be right back," I said, and dipped into my bedroom. I had decided to take the advice of my barber and try something new. He had urged me to try popping a Viagra just to see the effect that it would have on me. I definitely had no problem getting an erection. Actually, I had a problem with getting too many of them and keeping them in my pants. But Dee had told me that I would become a legend in the mind of the women I bedded under the influence of the blue diamond.

He told me that I would fuck the donkey shit out of a chick and my dick would never go down. I'd laughed at him, told him he was sick and needed Jesus. Then I took three of the pills off of him and gave him twenty bucks. "Don't take a whole one or your shit will be hard till the next afternoon," he'd promised. It was pure ego, but I fed into it anyway.

I had already chopped the pill in half and run into the bathroom to get some water to wash it down. I walked back into the living room with nothing but my underwear on. "That's what I'm talking about," Erin said with a smile.

I hit the remote to the stereo and my old-school slow-jam mix came on. Jodeci's "Freek 'n You" came on. "You like that?" I asked when I saw her head swaying to the beat.

"Yeah, that was my jam back in high school." She stood up and started snaking and grinding to the beat, looking extremely sexy as she moved. She had on a pair of gold lace tangas and a matching bra. Her stomach was cut up like she did crunches all day and night. She had her navel pierced and I was mesmerized by the diamond she had in it.

She kept dancing and pointing at me as I was sitting on the couch. I looked down at my underwear; I hadn't even realized how hard my dick had gotten. Watching her, I wondered why she and Dante's father hadn't worked out; she didn't seem like the type of girl a man would let get away. Now she was slipping through Kenard's fingers as well. She was in front of me, putting on a show, while he sat at home doing who knew what. My mind was becoming filled with thoughts of what I was going to do with her in the moments to come when she moved closer and leaned in to kiss me.

I could taste her lipstick as it melded with my lips. Her tongue brushed gently across my mouth as I parted my lips. Then she pulled back and continued to dance. This time she turned her ass to me and began to whip it back and forth. She was only a couple of feet in front of me, so I reached out for her and pulled her down onto me. She was now sitting on my lap just like a stripper preparing for a lap dance.

"Whoa," she said, feeling my erection poking her between her cheeks. "Did I do that?" she said seductively.

"Maybe," I said as I reached around and pulled her face to mine until I was kissing her hungrily. She moaned and purred as I moved from her lips to her neck. My hands found her breasts and instantly pulled her bra down, exposing her nipples to my touch.

"Oh, Diego, that feels so good. I like that," she moaned as she began to involuntarily grind against my crotch. With that, I ran my right hand down her stomach and into her panties. I felt the heat and the wetness as soon as my fingers parted her lips. "Shiiiiiiit," she said.

With the skill of a concert pianist I played her clit. One finger massaging it solo at first and then pinching it gently between two while the third rubbed it. I gave her pussy all manner of massages until she was pouring all over my fingers. Floetry's "Say Yes" was now playing softly in the background and the flame was flickering to the same rhythm I fingered her to. Suddenly she took a deep breath and her chest heaved. Immediately I felt her hands dig into my thighs and I knew that she was on her way to orgasm number one. I increased my pace and pulled on her nipples. "Ahhh, ahhhh, ooohhh, baby yeeeesssssss." She cried and whimpered for thirty seconds nonstop until she was finished.

She got up and took to her knees in front of me. She yanked my underwear down to my ankles and I stepped out of them. Then she slid out of her underwear and unclasped her bra and dropped it to the floor beside her. She stared up into my eyes as she gripped my manhood with her right hand. Her mouth was warm as she took the tip into her mouth, and when she ran her tongue across it she gave me a wicked smile followed by an "mmmmmm."

For five minutes she kissed and licked it expertly. My head was leaning back and I felt my mind drifting. My thoughts took me to erotic heights; I even visualized women who had sucked me before her. None had ever looked better doing it than Erin. As the sensations begin to rise in intensity I reached for her head and placed my hand on the back of it.

My thoughts were all over the place. *Look at you. If your man could see you now, would he call you a slut? Would he be hurt or would he have expected this from you all along? How did you learn to suck a dick like this and how many have you sucked? You could never be my woman, begging for the next man's cum in your mouth and coming home to me.*

I felt an orgasm coming as my thoughts raced all over the place. "Suck it, girl. Here it comes, don't stop." I had never cum in her mouth, but I was about to. She tried to pull away, but I grabbed her hair and held her in place as I shot into her mouth. "Yeaaaahhhhh," I said as I emptied the last drop.

When she was free she pulled back, panting as if I had choked her. She jumped up and moved to the bathroom to spit it out. Her not swallowing was very unattractive, but at least she'd tried.

I met her coming out of the bathroom and she looked down to see that my dick was still rock hard. I led her into the bedroom and she climbed onto the mattress at my direction. I went to my closet and grabbed a bag and walked back to her. Without warning, I grabbed her by her ankles and spread her legs. I swooped in and my mouth landed on her center. "Ohmigawd," she yelled out as my tongue sliced through her.

I began eating her out as if I was trying to send her out of this world. I French-kissed her vagina while my fingers palmed her ass. She didn't feel my sliding her to the edge of the bed and she didn't know what I'd reached down and grabbed until I pushed five inches of the vibrator inside of her.

"What the . . ." She tried to lift up to see what I'd done. With my free hand I pushed her chest back into the bed, and as the vibrator began to whiz at full speed she began to thrash her head back and forth. My lips were on her clit and I was fucking her with the toy simultaneously. "Eeeeeeee, uhhh, uhhhh, ohmigawd, nnnnnnooooo," she screamed out at the top of her lungs. She tried to regain control of herself for the next minute until she gave in to the sensations. Just then I felt her kicking her legs and she yelled out, "Dieeeeegoooooo, I'm . . . 'bout . . . to . . . cuuuuummmm."

More than three hours later, at 2:15 A.M., we were going at it once again. We had gone a hard two rounds earlier and dozed off only to wake up each time and start all over again. This time I was standing behind her, ramming into her like a madman. Her hair was completely sweated out, so it didn't even matter that I was using it like the reins of a horse to pull her back onto me.

Once again we could hear her phone ringing in the background but ignored it. Her man, Kenard, had blown her cell phone up all night while I'd been busy blowing her back completely out. "No more," she panted out. "I want you to hurry up and cum, pleeeeaaasssse," Erin pleaded. Her vagina was beginning to get dry from all the fucking that we'd done.

I had delivered on the four orgasms and added one more to boot. She couldn't do it anymore, she begged. I had enjoyed three strong nuts already myself and was going for my fourth. I grunted loudly as I came once more. I could feel my chest pounding as I released her finally. Like a beaten slave, she collapsed onto the bed. I had to admit I was tired, too, and I climbed onto the bed beside her.

"Don't let me fall asleep, Diego. I just need a minute to get my bearings. I have to get home."

"Okay," I remember saying as I was drifting quickly to sleep. As I stared over at her naked body I was thinking that Erin had satisfied me fully and I thought to myself that she was as close as I could imagine to being a woman I could call my girl.

The next thing I saw, my alarm clock said five-thirty in the morning. I rolled over and saw Erin lying there sleeping like a baby. There was going to be trouble.

(((6)))

Do or Die

Jacob woke at 7 A.M. to the smell of eggs and bacon. Anna had cooked and knocked at his door to wake him. "What the fuck," he said aloud as the knock had stirred him. He was in a fog and still couldn't believe that he'd allowed her to spend the night—even though she'd slept on the couch. "Just a second," he groaned through the door as his senses came to him.

He climbed out of the bed and slipped into his Levi's. He opened the door. "Damn, Mr. Marsh. I see you had your door locked. What did you think, I was gonna come in here and get you?" she said, smiling. Jacob was happy that she was fully dressed.

She handed him the tray. "Wow," he said, looking at the plate of food.

"That's nothing. You should see my lasagna." She placed his tray on the dresser and said, "Thanks for letting me stay. I'm gonna head home now."

"You sure everything will be okay at home?"

"That's a laugh. My mother hardly notices me. I'll be fine."

"Well, don't you worry about Dean. I'm going to see him today and it will be the last day he steps foot on Johnson High property."

Anna caught Jacob off guard and gave him a hug. "Thanks, Mr. Marsh."

When she pulled away he said, "Listen, Anna—"

She cut him off. "Look, Mr. Marsh. You don't have to say a thing. I know. I will not breathe a word about any of this. I know that you could get into trouble, and believe me, I just want to put the whole thing behind me, starting today." She winked at Jacob and said, "This will be our little secret."

Her words made him uneasy, but he prayed with all his heart that she meant them. Thirty seconds later, he heard her car start up and he looked out his window, hoping none of his neighbors saw her leave. Not that they would have known that she was a senior in high school who had just spent the night at her teacher's home. Nevertheless, he hoped the onetime sleepover would have no witnesses.

When my phone rang at ten minutes to seven, it startled the hell out of me. I had drifted back to sleep after Erin left and was dreaming of my ex again, and thought the call was part of a good dream. When I answered it without hesitation I called her name. I was thrilled that she'd decided to give me another chance. "Alicia, baby, what's up?"

"Diego, what did you call me?"

"Huh?" I said in a groggy voice.

"Listen up."

"Yeah."

"Diego." She yelled this time and snapped me out of it. "Wake up. This is serious."

I caught her voice. It was Erin. "I'm up. I'm up."

"I was coming in from your house, and when I got to my building that nigga was in the bushes."

"What bushes?"

"He was outside my apartment hiding in the bushes. My neighbor said he had been out there since like midnight."

I looked over at my clock. Erin had left my house almost two hours earlier. "So why you calling me now?"

"The nigga wouldn't let me go inside. He kept me in the parking lot talking to me. Hitting my head with questions that he didn't want to know the answer to."

"Yeah," I squeaked out.

"He kept asking me who I was with."

I sat up in the bed, and if I had time to pray, I would have done so before asking nervously, "You didn't say me, did you?"

"Of course not. But he did end up snatching my cell phone before he left, and if he scrolls through my call log, he may see your name and that I called you a few times today and right after I called him the last time to say I was going out. I'm not sure, but he might call you."

In my head I said it. *Oh, fuck.* I figured she was going through enough herself and I didn't want to pile it on any thicker. "So are you okay?"

"Yeah, I'm cool."

"So, what was the outcome of it all?"

"He says he knows I was fucking someone. He kept telling me he wanted to smell my pussy and dumb shit like that."

"So did he break up with you?"

"I'm not even sure. I'm going to sleep, though. I just wanted to give you a heads-up in case he calls. I'm sorry for getting you involved in this."

"Don't worry about it," I said. On the real, I was pissed. This nigga had my number and now I was trying to think of ways that I could avoid the drama.

An hour later I pulled up into the parking lot at the same time as Lisa. She greeted me with "What's up, bitch? How are you this morning?" Noticing an unusual look of anguish on my face, she changed her tone and came with, "What's wrong with you this morning? You look tired."

"Drama." I sighed. "I got it."

"I told you about them hookers." Noticing my total lack of enthusiasm for any conversation, she added, "Well, at least we don't have any students today. Get your report cards handed in and get the hell out of here."

I grunted a response and headed in to work.

A couple hours passed before Jacob had the opportunity to meet up with Dean. He'd been tied up in meetings all morning, but the whole time Jacob was obsessing over how things would go when he got the chance to confront Dean.

When they were inside Jacob's office, Jacob stepped to his student teacher as if he was talking to a thug in the streets. "Yo, man.

What the hell is wrong with you?" His voice was threatening and the look on his face was unlike anything the young man had ever seen from his instructor before.

Dean was literally in tears as Jacob delivered the news to him. He looked Jacob right in the eyes and said, "I swear I didn't rape her."

"Well, that's not what she said."

"Mr. Marsh, I did just like you told me to. She did it willingly."

Jacob stood up from his desk and walked up to Dean. "I'm going to ask you this one time. Think really hard."

Dean nodded. "Okay."

"Did she at any time tell you no or say 'stop'?"

Dean stared back into Jacob's eyes. In his heart he knew that he hadn't raped Anna. Or had he? He recalled her saying no and perhaps even "stop" a time or two amid the passion, but he hadn't forced her. As his mind replayed the session over and over, he recalled more clearly her saying the words to him as he was thrusting away; he looked down at the floor in self-disgust and that was enough for Jacob.

"Dean, you let me down. Have your program coordinator call me. I won't tell her the real reason why, but we'll have you reassigned, effective Monday. I'm sorry."

"What's going to happen?"

"Well, lucky for you, Anna doesn't want to go to the police with this and you'll still be able to graduate. As long as you don't press the issue about whether you're guilty or innocent, you should be okay. But the last thing you want to do is wind up with a Kobe situation facing you. Without his kind of money, you'd be done. Your teaching career will be over before it starts. Now, if I was you, I'd never discuss this with another living soul. It's over."

With that, Dean packed his things and left the school. Though in his mind he hadn't raped Anna, he realized that it was her word against his. As a black man in America, he was better off running with his tail tucked between his legs.

Jacob sat down at his desk and stared at the wall, in deep thought. By today he had planned to have Anna off of his scent and hot onto Dean's. Things had gone way to the left, and instead of her becoming fuckbuddies with someone else, she'd managed to get dangerously closer to him overnight.

Anna was sitting in her car drinking a Red Bull as she saw Dean leave the school with his bags in hand and his head to the ground. He walked across the parking lot and headed to the bus stop, his future in a state of sad upheaval. Anna's smile turned into a laugh as she pulled off and said to herself, "See you round, sucker."

(((7)))

Protect Ya Neck

I'd been watching my cell phone all day. Every time it rang, my heart skipped a beat and I'd think it was Erin's man Kenard. When it rang five minutes before I was ready to head out the door, immediately I dreamed up a scenario where he was going to tell me which door to come out of, where he'd be waiting with his weapon of choice. A pistol, a knife, maybe a baseball bat. As visions of me on top of his lady played through my mind, I barely looked at the screen of the phone as I hit the answer button. *I hope the bitch was worth it,* I heard him saying to me as he caught me by surprise. I shook the thoughts from my head as I answered, "Yeah."

"Yo," the voice on the other end said.

It was Jacob. "What's up, man?"

"Everything. I had the night from hell and today wasn't much better."

"You serious? I thought you had a date with what's-her-face."

"Kendra. Yeah, I did. Everything was looking lovely, too, till I got a knock at my door."

"What you mean?"

"Listen, some crazy shit went down. I need to talk to you," he said. "I'm . . . I . . . um." Jacob was stumbling out his words. "I might be in some trouble at work. I don't want to talk on the phone."

I wanted to share my own drama with Erin, but I didn't. Jacob's voice was shaking and it wasn't like him to fold under pressure. "Sure, so what time you want to hook up? Should I come scoop you?"

"That'll be cool," he responded. "I'll be home by five, so five-thirty, quarter till six."

Just then it crossed my mind that I'd told Lisa that I would escort her to a function downtown. Jacob's situation took precedence, but there was a chance I could kill two birds with one stone, "Listen, do you mind if we go have a drink in the city? Lisa's husband's company is sponsoring some reception down at the Black Caucus. He's one of the hosts and gave her some extra tickets, she asked if I would come, but she has like four extra tickets. You have to wear a jacket."

"It doesn't matter." He didn't sound thrilled, but it was clear he just needed to talk.

"Okay, I'll see you in a bit."

Five minutes after I hung up the phone, Lisa walked in my room. "Hey, Papi." She had a thousand pet names. One minute it was "bitch," the next it was "fag." She was nuts.

"Hey," I responded. "Listen, Jacob is going with us tonight. You don't mind? Do you?"

"Did you already invite him?"

"Yeah."

"Well, I guess it doesn't matter if I mind anyway. As long as you two doo-doo chasers aren't late, I don't care. What about your brother's punk ass?"

"What about him?"

"I got Lee a ticket. You asked for one last week."

"Oh yeah. I did. No wonder he called me last night."

She pursed her lips and said, "Yeah, if you weren't so busy with your whores—"

I cut her off. "Okay, I may have him just meet us down there. I have to pick up Jacob, then I'll be by to get you."

"Diego," she said.

"If you're late, I'll fuck you up. It starts at seven."

"Okay, I got you. Gimme an aspirin. I'm getting a headache."

"You better smoke some chronic, and get rid of that pressure. You been walking around here like you got a brick stuck in your ass all day."

I nodded and waved her off. "You got one or no?"

Lisa dug in her purse and tossed a bottle of Motrin at me. "There's only two left in there."

"Cool."

In the hustle of the week, Lisa's event had almost slipped my mind. Luckily, when I looked in my closet I had two suits fresh from the cleaners. I put on the tan, Donna Karan, single-buttoned, and grabbed a pair of Gucci loafers. I couldn't find a pair of socks, so I headed for the dirty-clothes hamper to dig out the pair with the least amount of funky flavor.

I sniffed three pairs before finding a set that I could live with.

I dialed Jacob's number. "I'm on the way," I said. Heading out the door, I peeped up the block a little, paranoid for no reason. Kenard had no reason to suspect that there was anything up with me and his girl. I didn't know any other teachers who stepped outside the bounds the way I routinely did. Maybe a little on-the-job romance, but parents and teachers were only supposed to get together for conferences. There was no way Kenard should have thought otherwise. As long as Erin stuck to her story, I was good.

I blasted my Lyfe Jennings CD as loud as my factory stereo would permit and rolled back the moonroof of my Beemer.

I hit the horn and Jacob walked out of his house as if he'd been waiting on the other side of the door. He was sporting a dark blue suit, a crisp white dress shirt, even a rocking white silk tie. He had a plastic cup in his hand when he opened my car door.

"You're looking real clean, bruh man."

"Yeah, well believe I look better than I feel."

"You didn't need the tie," I said, pointing to his collar. "Unless you running for Congress or some shit."

"Didn't you say formal?" I nodded. "Well, formal means wear a tie, my nigga." He shook his head in disgust with my lack of couth.

As we backed out of his driveway he spilled a few drops of his drink on his knee and said, "Damn."

"Napkins right there." He reached into the pockets on the door and began wiping the drops on his pants.

As we hit the corner to exit his parking lot, I looked out of my rearview mirror and could have sworn I saw someone climbing out from behind his bushes. I didn't say a word. *My mind is gone,* I thought. I was cutting Erin off first thing in the morning. Thoughts of getting caught up were wearing me out.

"You want some of this? I got an extra cup." He had pulled a pint of VSOP out of my inside jacket pocket.

"Yeah, that's on point." He poured a couple shots into a cup for me.

As we hit the Baltimore-Washington Parkway he went right into the drama that was unfolding for him. I couldn't believe it as he disclosed how he'd orchestrated a plan that had gone so far off course.

"Jake, man . . ." I paused. I didn't want to come down on him, but he and I always kept it real. "You too smart for that. Why didn't you just go to your principal and let him know that the kid was making you uncomfortable?"

"I can't really tell you. You never know how these things are going to turn out. I guess I wasn't really sure if I'd done anything to lead her on."

I tilted my head in confusion. "So what you sayin'? You didn't . . ."

"C'mon, Diego. Hell no. But I did let her hang around a lot. She was grading papers, cleaning the room, and just being useful. The next thing I knew, she was a friend. You know how women do."

"Yeah, but still."

We went back and forth over the details and his options. Jacob had always been there for me. He had consoled me for the last couple of months. Just listening when I felt like venting about Alicia. So I returned the favor and never even got to mention what I was going through.

In the end, my advice was going to be the same that he had just given me. "Pass out them fucking umbrellas, baby boy."

(((8)))

Knocking Opportunity's Boots

People were standing around looking important and elegant. A few men were actually in tuxes, and I could have sworn I'd seen a sister in a mink stole. There were bars set up all around and Vivian Green was performing, trying to loosen up the somewhat stiff crowd. Lisa's husband, Derrick, had gotten us a table in a prime location in the center of the ballroom, making it easy for us to people-watch. Mostly, though, I sat and listened to Jacob go on and on about the situation he faced. As I talked him through every imaginable scenario he frowned and grimaced as he focused on the worst that could happen.

Finally he came to the realization that he was going do his best to keep the whole situation under wraps. He ended up trying to relax and had enjoyed a couple glasses of cognac when Lisa showed up and asked, "What's wrong with you?"

He tried to act normal, but she sensed that he wasn't his usual upbeat self. It wasn't long before she had him opening up. Now that another person was willing to listen to him, he opened up the flood-gates of his woes. The next thing I knew, my brother, Lee, had shown up and I knew the round-table discussion was about to kick off.

It wasn't like I wasn't glad to see Lee. In fact, I'd invited him out, but truthfully, I was surprised that he'd been able to get out of the house. Ever since he'd been married, he'd become somewhat of a henpecked bitch, to put it lightly. On top of that, he was a born-again, which was cool, but he tended to get a little preachy, given the opportunity.

"Jacob's an ignorant son of a bitch," Lisa had said, laughing. "So you got the bitch raped? I don't want to hear any more of this scandalous shit." She was on her third glass of champagne.

"Jacob, you got to put this in the hands of the Lord, man. He knows your heart," Lee had chimed in after hearing the quick and dirty version from Lisa. "Check it. Before we even see the problem, He has already provided us with a way out."

Hearing that, I excused myself. "I'm gonna take a walk. You comin', Jake?"

"Nah, I'm good. I'ma talk to Lee for a minute."

Assuming he wanted to get a different perspective from my brother, I made my way out of the ballroom for some air. The D.C. Convention Center was humongous and the Black Caucus had put together a week's worth of events. None of which I planned to attend after this one. This reception was for the media, and people from all over the country were in attendance, but mostly it seemed there were people who belonged here.

I was a schoolteacher and had no desire to network with these people. Unless someone here was going to get me a raise for being overworked and underappreciated, there wasn't much for me other than the drinks and the free concert. I made my way to the bar and pulled out the free-drink tickets that Lisa had given me and ordered a double shot of Hennessy and Coke to wash it down.

I stepped outside the bar and made my way across the expansive carpeted hallway. The whole side of the building was glass and it was a beautiful night. I walked over to a window and stared down to the street below. A flow of cars passed underneath and just across the street there was a well-lit park with a historical look to it.

The difference between the loud music inside the ballroom and the peace of the lobby sent my mind swirling. All of a sudden I had time to think. I found myself looking down into that park wishing that I was down there with someone I cared about. With Alicia.

I missed her. No one knew how much. Sure, I'd talked to Jacob, Lisa, my mom, and even my barber, but not a soul truly knew how much it hurt me that we weren't together. I had spent the last couple of months thinking about how I'd done nearly everything possible to ruin our relationship. I'd fucked other women and possibly gotten one pregnant. I'd allowed the dirt I'd done in the streets to follow me home, which broke rule numero uno of the player's code.

Looking back on it all, I wished that I had simply jerked my dick off because, truthfully, all the pussy I'd gotten just didn't seem worth it now. Women never understood that at the time men just didn't know that. It's like we have to see it to believe it. But now that I'd punched that ticket, I was out in the cold.

I couldn't count the number of times since the wedding when I'd tossed and turned all night. The sick feeling I'd get just thinking that I'd seen her driving by. I missed her, and needed her, like I needed air to breathe.

"Excuse me," the voice said from behind me.

I turned around and saw a sister standing there in a black strapless gown. She looked to be in her early forties, but only because as she stepped forward, I saw a bit of gray splashed in her short cut. I tried to focus on her face as I realized she was speaking to me, but it was hard. She had the most wonderful set of hips and her dress was cut as low as tastefulness would allow.

"Yes," I responded.

"I know this is a weird request, but I was in the middle of a business call to my assistant, and just like that . . . the friggin' battery on my cell died out. I was wondering if you have one that I could use for one minute. I'd gladly pay you. I just don't have time to walk back in there to find a colleague. I've only a few minutes to relay some important information," she said with a slight smile.

I smiled back and reached to my hip to take my phone off the holster. "No problem, and the minutes are free right now, so don't worry about paying me." I laughed.

"Thanks so much . . ."

"Diego."

"I'm Jonetta. Jonetta Cleveland, but everyone calls me Jo," she said as she extended her hand and then took my cell phone.

"Okay, Jo." She didn't look like anyone's Joe. When she turned I noticed that she had a real nice donkey on her.

Not wanting to seem as though I didn't trust her with the phone, I headed back to the window and she drifted casually a few feet back. I could hear her going into all-business tone and she even seemed a little angered at the person on the other end of the line. In less than two minutes she was at my side, handing me my phone.

"Listen, Diego, I really appreciate this. If I hadn't made that call . . . you just have no idea," she said excitedly. Her demeanor seemed to calm. "The very least I can do, brother, is buy you a drink," she insisted. I noticed her accent.

"Where you from?"

"That thick, huh?" she said. "Long Island, and before that Boston. What about you?"

"I'm from here. Born and raised."

"A Washingtonian. Well, sir, how about that drink?"

I shook my now-empty cup and said, "That would be lovely."

We headed off to the ballroom and stood in line as we tried to make some small talk over the music. Vivian Green was already finished and a DJ was providing the music.

"Did you come alone?" Jo leaned in and asked.

"Actually, I came with a couple of friends."

She nodded and the look on her face showed that wasn't the answer she'd wanted.

"Why do you ask?"

"Well, since these lines were so long, I was going to suggest that we walk back over to the bar at my hotel. I'm at the Renaissance over on Ninth. I was there last night for a glass of wine before bed. It was really nice and cozy. I'm not all that big on these big party thingies. Only here now because they are honoring my boss."

"I understand. I'm not all that big on crowds or hobnobbing either. I just really needed to get out tonight."

"Tough week?" she asked.

"Tough month."

She laughed. "No, they didn't just put on my jam." Keith Sweat's "Make It Last Forever" came through the speakers and she began to sway back and forth.

I looked her up and down and tried to get a gauge on her. Was she offering me up or just trying to make a friend? Then I looked down and saw the rock on her finger. It had to be at least three carats. This woman was sophisticated and very much used to calling the shots, it seemed. I reasoned that if she wanted me, she would be more clear. Plus, I wasn't really sure if I found her all that attractive. She was a nice-looking woman, but she reminded me more of someone's aunt than a sistah I'd be trying to bang. She seemed sort of regal in her nature and that alone had me feeling compelled to give her more respect than I gave most women. The more I studied her, the less likely it seemed that she would be the type of woman who'd sleep with a man like myself. Someone whose swagger and actions screamed *no strings attached* at times and *emotionally unavailable* almost always.

"C'mon," I said, and led her to the dance floor.

She was a good dancer and it became easy to forget that there were a few years between us—like fifteen probably. After we finished, a cut by Charlie Wilson came on and we danced right through. When the song ended I told her that I'd go have that drink if she still wanted to, but I needed to find my friends. She smiled and told me to meet her in the lobby.

I found Jacob in much better spirits. He was drunk. Lee reluctantly agreed to give him a ride home. He needed to punch a clock, I was sure, but after a little coaxing, I was off.

It was in the fifties, cool for September in the nation's capital. As we walked Jo began to talk about her job. She worked as a senior editor for Johnson Publishing, doing work for *Essence* magazine. I was surprised when she told me that she'd been married for sixteen years and had a fourteen-year-old daughter.

"A bottle of white Zinfandel, please. Diego, what are you drinking?"

"I'm drinking Hennessy."

She looked at the waiter. "Bring the bottle, please, and put it on this card."

"The bottle? I won't be drinking that much."

"You sure?"

"Absolutely, and as a matter of fact, I think I'll drink some wine with you. I have to drive home."

She nodded and the waiter was off.

"So, Diego, tell me about yourself."

"Not much to tell. I'm a schoolteacher. I teach second grade."

"Here in D.C.?"

"No, out in Prince George's County."

"Isn't that pretty much the same?" She laughed.

"Believe it or not, nope. Every other school district around here gets paid better than PG County teachers."

"Well, why do you stay? Why not go to another county?"

"Because . . ." I paused and thought about my answer. "I love my kids. I went to school here, my mom taught here in the county, and it's rough for the kids. People think that because we're not in the District that we don't have the same problems as inner-city schools. In fact, oftentimes we got it worse."

"*Have* it worse." She laughed as she corrected me. "Well, I commend you. I think we need more black men—more men, period—to teach the kids."

I nodded in agreement.

We finished off the bottle of wine while I told her my stories about teaching. The triumphs and the horrors. She ordered a second bottle and I told her that she'd be drinking most of it herself. After making a bathroom run, I realized that I was drunk and she had to have been, too.

As I walked back to the table she was fiddling with her phone. "Battery is still dead," she hummed.

"Well, you didn't charge it."

"Sometimes, once it's off awhile, it'll come on by itself."

"So, do you need to make a call?" I offered my phone.

"No, I was going to call home, but it's okay really. My husband is probably sleeping by now anyway."

Her tone gave away a little something, some dissatisfaction maybe, but I didn't want to pry. "Well, maybe you should go up to your room and call. I can wait here for you."

"You're sweet, Diego," she said, taking my hand in hers. Staring deeply into my eyes, she asked, "How old are you?"

"Thirty."

She closed her eyes. "A baby, your whole life in front of you," she said. Then she went on, and out of nowhere came "Diego, never fall in love and never get married."

I was shocked and leaned back.

"You know, Diego, I don't think I love my husband anymore. And I'm not sure if he still loves me." I wasn't sure where this was going, but I began to get the feeling that the wine was bringing this out of her. "I don't know why I'm telling you this." She covered her mouth with her hands. "I'm sorry. I'm sorry."

"No, it's fine. If you want to talk about it, I'll listen." For the second time that night, it seemed as if I was going to find escape from my own jacked-up life by listening to someone else's miseries.

After I assured her that I wanted her to talk, she confided that she was scared that her marriage was falling apart. She said that she'd lost respect for her husband over the last year. He'd lost his job in the computer field, where he'd been pulling in six figures, and had yet to rebound. Her problem was that he hadn't accepted any offers for new positions because the salaries were too low, and on top of it all he was now saying that he wasn't even sure he wanted to stay in that field. At this point he was thinking about opening up a sandwich shop in Manhattan. The bills were piling up and their savings had been dwindling. It had been too long without him bringing anything in and Jo was growing tired of carrying the load.

They were beginning to fight about money all the time. An hour passed and her eyes showed her pain and disappointment as she confided in me. Though she was a nice-looking woman, something in her voice and manner beyond the physical spoke to me while we sat talking in that booth in the Presidents' Lounge. I realized that I had a purpose and a reason for meeting her. For the first time, a woman was telling me the reason behind the problem in her marriage, and for some reason, I felt compelled to help instead of trying to take advantage. I told her everything that I imagined her husband was going through. "Jo, you probably have no idea how hard it is for a man to work and feel unfulfilled."

I explained to her that she needed to understand her husband's reluctance to accept a job at which he felt underpaid and undervalued. "I'm living it every day. The only thing that keeps me showing up is the kids. And once I get to the point where they aren't enough to keep me from being miserable, then I'll have to leave, too."

I advised her to tell her husband that it was okay if he wanted to make a career change at forty, but just explain to him that she was tired and needed his help taking care of the finances before their savings disappeared completely. I then explained that a great way to do this and get what she wanted without attacking his manhood would be to simply make him believe that her biggest concern was to get behind him and support him. "I'm not trying to stereotype you, but it seems that black women don't really understand how much we need their support. Especially if it means making yourselves uncomfortable. That's not unconditional love. That's 'I'll love you as long as you don't make me uncomfortable,' and that's not right. Sounds like that man lost his way when he lost that high-paying job. You weren't hard to find when he was bringing home that cash." I smiled at her. "You were at the mall." I laughed. "Don't be hard to find. Help him find his way or just stick by him while he does."

When I finished speaking there were tears welling up in the corners of her eyes.

She loved my advice and began to say "thank you" over and over again. "You're right. In fact, no one's ever been more right, as far as I'm concerned." She waved to the waiter. "I want to pay this, please," she said, waving the small tray with the check when he came over.

"**You know, I've** never been unfaithful to my husband. Not once since we've been married."

I don't know why she said it at this point. We'd kissed in the elevator on the way up like two teenagers and now she was lying back on her bed with nothing but her bra on. She hadn't worn panties with the dress. I didn't reply because I didn't know what to say. *Congratulations,* I thought.

My shirt was now off and I slipped out of my pants to reveal my erection making a tent out of my underwear. "Mmm, wow," she said. Even in the dark, she could see that I was blessed. "Let me see it."

I moved toward her and pulled my underwear down. She reached for it and began to caress it. "I can't believe I'm doing this," she whispered. She was still really tipsy. I was drunk, but still strong. My body was used to performing while drunk and I moved closer and pulled her head slightly toward my dick. "Kiss it."

She looked at me in shock. For a moment I thought I'd gone too far. This woman was classy and professional, and here I was, about to treat her like a whore. I really didn't have another mode. Either I didn't know how to make sweet love to a woman or I'd convinced myself long ago that women didn't really want that. That shit was for the movies.

To my surprise, Jo opened her mouth and took me inside. Her mouth felt good the second she began to suck. When she began to use her tongue on the tip, a shiver went up my spine. I wanted to lie on my back. I said, "Hold up." Before I could climb on the bed, she stopped me.

"Do you have a condom?"

"Of course," I said calmly, and reached into my pants and grabbed my wallet. I pulled two Lifestyles out and climbed onto the bed. Jo guided me onto my back and dove right back to feasting on me. I could make out her face in the bit of light that crept in through the curtains. She had gotten sexier as the night'd gone on. Her skin was the color of light chocolate and her short hair felt like silk as I ran my hands across it. Her mouth fit my penis like a glove. Any bigger and I imagined she wouldn't have been able to fit it inside.

Now she was on her hands and knees. I thought about our evening and all that we'd shared up to this point. How it always led to this.

"You like that?"

"Oh yeah," I responded. She gripped it tight and flicked her tongue over the tip and then massaged the head with her wet lips. "Don't stop."

She didn't and I began to feel that tingle. I rode it out for a second or twenty. Feeling like I was going to shoot, I pushed her back. "Let me do you."

"What's wrong?"

I shook my head while I caught my breath. "Nothing, just not ready for you to make me cum yet." She smiled. "Take your bra off and get on your back."

Kissing her stomach, I could taste the sweetness of her skin. The subtle scent of her lotion mixed in with the slight moisture on her belly made me want to lick her more. I caressed her thighs and rubbed the insides of them while I kissed her. Her skin was well cared for, soft like a baby's. When I got a handful of her breast I was greeted with her thick, rock-hard nipples.

I slid my body down hers and she whispered, "You don't have to do that."

I ignored her and planted my lips on her midsection and slid right down into her pussy. "Ohhhh shit, uhh, uhhh," she panted out. Her body jerked and she arched her back. "Yessss, ahhh yesssss."

She was really appreciating my art and I began to pull out all my tricks. I took my index finger and began to trace circles along the base of her vagina all the while sucking gently on her clit. When she moaned even louder I stuck that finger inside of her and pressed against the bottom wall of her pussy to open her up. More sucking and then I slipped two more fingers inside of her. I was surprised at how tight she was. For some reason, I expected a woman over forty to have a looser booty. "Oh, Diego. It feeeels sooo good."

I pulled her lips slightly with my teeth, and when I had her clit in my grasp I increased the flickering of my tongue. "Oh, bayybeee," she screamed. "I about to . . . uhh . . . I . . . uhh, uhhh." She let out one grunt after another as her hands dug into my scalp. Her legs wrapped around my shoulders, locking my face in her lap, and she came all over my face.

She panted heavily as her body recoiled. Fine beads of sweat coated her. I reached for the condoms and slid one on. As I was about to enter her she tensed up. "Diego, I'm not sure . . ."

I knew where it was headed. She was about to let the guilt overwhelm her. She knew she was wrong and this was the last chance for her to catch herself. If in fact she wasn't lying about never having committed adultery, she was about to cross a line that she could never return from.

I pretended I didn't hear her and slammed all nine inches of meat into her. "Owwww, ohhh shit," she screamed. That was all she wrote. I banged her for thirty minutes straight. The liquor.

I'm good for ten or fifteen minutes on the first round usually, but the cognac had my senses dulled. "I never . . . I've . . . never been fucked like this," she said. I had her ass in the air as she rested with her face in the pillow. She came twice and never got dry.

She climbed on top of me and humped me like a woman in heat. She leaned over sucking my nipples while reaching back to massage my balls. She was so horny that I was enjoying the show she put on. "Get on your back again."

She obliged, and when I entered her she began rubbing her breast with one hand and her pussy with the other. When it seemed as if she was about to have another orgasm, my own excitement took me over the edge and I began to fuck her harder until I tensed up and filled the condom with my sperm.

Atlantic Star's "Am I Dreaming?" was now playing on Majic 102.3 as I lay in her bed. She was sleeping soundly next to me. It was surreal. She had pleased me and I had done the same for her, yet I was in her bed now wide-awake, thinking about Alicia and my life.

I left my information on a piece of paper and got dressed. It was almost 4 A.M. and I didn't want her to feel awkward when the morning came. Once I made it to my car, I thought about the things I'd said to Jo. Then I wondered if she would actually take my advice, or if all the good I'd set out to do had once again been undone by a fuck.

(((9)))

After-school Special

Jacob waited anxiously as the minutes ticked away at second period. He was halfway hoping Anna wouldn't show up for class. She was never late for his class; his students knew he didn't tolerate it. The circumstances were a little different today, though. It was Monday and the first day of school for students since she'd shown up at his door after the incident. At a quarter to ten he thought, *Maybe she isn't coming.* Then, as he dimmed the lights and prepared to put in a videotape on music from the Harlem Renaissance, the door to his room opened.

Jacob strained his eyes a bit to see who was coming through the door. He breathed deep and prayed that it wasn't Anna followed by members of the board of education, coming to haul his ass off. He didn't recognize the girl who entered and cautiously made her way toward his desk with a piece of paper in her hand. She was tall, maybe five-eight, and a redbone. He'd never seen her before, even in the hallways. She was gorgeous and had a quiet but commanding presence. He would have remembered her.

"Hello, Mr. Marsh?" She had a very low voice for a girl. She almost sounded hoarse.

"Hello," Jacob said with a nod.

"Um . . . my name is Elise Jackson. This is my first day here." Jacob nodded again as he looked at the paper. "I'm in your class. I was also told that you are the head of the marching band."

"That I do. You play?"

"The piano. I'm also a vocalist, mostly jazz, some R and B. I know that doesn't help in the marching band. But I also am a choreographer."

"A choreographer?"

"Yeah, I used to help my old instructors with our band. I just moved out here from Indianapolis."

"Nap-town. I've been out there a time or two, the Black Expo." Jacob brushed off the subject and then explained quickly the assignment as he reached into his file cabinet and grabbed a syllabus for her.

"Oh yeah, it's a huge event in Indy, growing every year." She smiled. "I'd like to get some more information on the band if I could."

"Okay, we'll talk a little more later. You can take that seat right there." Jacob pointed to the empty desk just in front of him.

"Okay, thanks."

Jacob watched her take a seat. She was wearing a loose pair of jeans that were fashionably ripped and a snug-fitting hooded sweatshirt with JUICY written across the chest. As she sat and crossed her legs like a real lady, Jacob tried to ignore how attractive she was. It was a task he'd grown used to. There were so many attractive and sexy young girls in the school. Silly as they were, there wasn't much difference physically between them and a grown woman. So, as usual, he took one last glance at this Mya look-alike and made the decision to never again pay any attention to her beauty.

As the tape concluded Jacob instructed the students to write a summary of the career of one of the musicians from the tape. He quickly scribbled five topics on the chalkboard on which they could write. Then he took his seat at his desk and logged onto the Internet to check his e-mails. After he clicked on his in-box he scanned over the subjects. Irritation set in immediately when he saw two e-mails with forwarded messages and then one advertising hot sluts yearning for rough treatment. Then he scrolled to the next one and saw an unfamiliar address: mocha2munch@yahoo.com. The subject read *Mocha Dreams*. Jacob peeked his head up and looked around the room before clicking the mouse.

Jacob,

I just wanted you to know that you have an admirer, me! I can't believe that I finally have the nerve to send this. I've thought about doing it for some time now and finally worked up the nerve. You should know that someone is thinking of you all the time. I am longing for the day when you and I can spend some time together getting to know one another better. You'll be really surprised when you find out who this is and I hope you'll be as happy as I am nervous. I think of you all the time, and at night before I go to sleep I can hear your voice, singing me to sleep.

Until the time is right,

Mocha Dreams

Jacob read the e-mail three times and bit his bottom lip. He began to think that he had really made a mistake letting Anna spend the night. He wasn't one hundred percent sure that she had written it, but if she hadn't, then it had come at the most inauspicious of times.

When the bell rang he breathed a sigh of relief as the kids scurried out the door, all except the new girl.

"Mr. Marsh?"

"Yes."

"When would be a good time for me to speak with you about joining the band?"

Jacob had a whirlwind of emotions going through his mind. He was trying hard not to make eye contact with Elise. Staring into her eyes for some reason reminded him of what he'd done with Anna.

He did his best to look interested solely in what was on his monitor. "I didn't know you were interested in joining the band. We don't do any singing. Perhaps you might want to join the chorus. Mrs. Caruso is right up the hall. She's the—"

"No, I'm not interested in that. I really wanted to be a part of the band. I had a chance to see you perform a couple years back in New Jersey at the Battle of the Bands, and I remember your performance. You guys were great. You came in second to Gatewood out of Houston. The only reason they won was because they had a more advanced step routine."

Just like that, she had his attention. "Is that so?"

She nodded. Then she said, "Last year, my high school beat them in a similar battle held in the New Orleans Superdome. I choreographed the whole routine, with a little help from my instructor."

She reached into her shoulder bag. "This is my reel. Check it out at your convenience. If you think I can help a good band get even better, let me know. I'm sure I can help you get your band to do everything that you see on that reel. All I'm looking for is the credit on my résumé."

Jacob took the DVD from her and placed it on his desk. "I'm impressed. I'll take a look at it."

"Okay, great. Let me know when you've seen it." She smiled again and Jacob noticed that she had beautiful eyes, but they had the sleepy look. "Thanks, see you tomorrow."

Jacob finished the day without seeing so much as a trace of Anna. As relieved as he was to have been able to avoid her, he couldn't help but worry about how she was doing. He began to wonder what he should do about the whole thing. Perhaps she had broken down and told her mother, or even worse, the police.

His fears got the best of him and he found himself in the teachers' lounge dialing the number he had on record for her home. He let the phone ring six times and was about to hang up when a groggy voice answered, "Hello."

"Hello, um . . . this is, um . . . Mr. Marsh, calling from—"

"Hey, Mr. Marsh," she said in a whisper. "This is me, Anna. What's up?"

"I was just calling because I didn't see you today . . . and—"

"That's sweet of you to call," she said, sounding too mature. "Yeah, I was really tired today. Haven't really been sleeping well the last few nights."

"So, are you okay? I mean, I know it's been rough, but is there anything I can do?"

"Funny you should ask. As a matter of fact, there is, but I'm really tired right now, so how about I call you later?"

"Well, you tell me when you'd like me to call you back . . ." He paused. The line was silent. "Hello . . . hello," he repeated. Anna was gone.

He returned to his classroom and gathered his belongings. He couldn't find his keys and began to search for them frantically. He'd left them on his desk. They'd been there all day and now they were gone. He panicked. Had Anna stolen them? No, she'd been home all day. He'd just spoken with her. He was losing his mind, he thought, behind all of the madness. He sat down and took a deep breath and tried to remember where he could have put them. Just then he looked on the floor by his feet and there they were. He laughed at himself for a moment.

Jacob was puzzled by his own paranoia. He was wondering what he'd gotten himself into. He was thinking that it was time to go to his principal, which would probably get him fired. Then he thought about calling the teachers' union to get a lawyer through the NEA, but it might turn into a full-scale scandal.

The more he thought about it, the more he realized he didn't know what to do. The fear of losing his job and his reputation sent him sinking into a deep depression. As his imagination began to run away with more dire possibilities, he felt a lump in his throat and his eyes began to water. He tried to close his eyes and regain his composure, but it was too much. He began to cry at his desk, softly.

"Excuse me, Mr. Marsh. You okay?"

He looked up and saw her staring at him. He felt like dying.

Lisa came through my door like the fire department bursting into a burning building. I looked up from my desk. "What?" I asked.

"You got drama." My look told her I needed her to continue. "Some black motherfucker is down in the principal's office cussing Ms. Knight out. He's screaming that you've been fucking his wife."

"Get the fuck outta here. You serious?" I stood up and looked out my window. I could see the parking lot and I looked for a strange car.

"Hell yeah, I'm serious. I think he's going to kick your ass. Maybe you should leave out the back."

Now I was nervous as hell. Shit was popping off. It had to be Kenard. I wasn't afraid of a fight. I didn't want to lose one at my job, though, and I was afraid of getting killed. I'd played out this whole scene a couple of times over the weekend and still couldn't calm myself down. "All right, all right. Okay."

Lisa was just standing there with a wide-eyed expression on her face. "Do you want me to call the police?"

I hadn't thought of that. "Yeah, um . . . but if he comes up here before they arrive, that won't do me any good . . ." I paused for a second, then I went to my backpack and started digging around. Lisa was shocked when I pulled out a tall can of pepper spray.

"What the hell? What are you doing carrying that shit?"

My breathing was getting labored as my adrenaline began to rush. "For shit like this."

"Are you serious? That shit is only good if the nigga wants to rape you. What if he has a gun? You gonna Mace his ass before he can get a shot off. You're fucking nuts. I love you, boo-boo, but I'm out." With that, she quickly headed for the door. No sooner had she stepped out of my classroom than she jumped back in. "Oh shit, here he comes."

Panicking, I said, "Cut the lights off. You go in the bathroom. Hurry up." I would never have forgiven myself if something happened to her.

She didn't put up a fuss. I quickly moved behind the door and got ready. I heard the footsteps outside the door and braced myself. Just then my door opened up. I jumped from behind the door, and Mace in hand, I yelled, "Freeze, nigga, or I'll burn your eyes out."

"Oh shit," the custodian yelled out, and put his hands up to cover his face. As I peered into the face of the seventy-year-old man, I heard Lisa in the bathroom dying of laughter.

I looked at her and was fuming mad. I came that close to emptying a can of Halt into the old man's face and getting myself fired for sure. "Aw, man. Mr. Waverly, I'm sorry to scare you like that. I thought you were someone else."

"Oh, okay," he huffed, looking confused.

I patted his shoulder. "Really, I'm so sorry."

He nodded and took a deep breath. "Mrs. Llamar waved me in. Is she in the bathroom?"

Lisa poked her head out. "Yeah, Mr. W. I just wanted to ask you when you guys were cleaning my carpet so I could move my furniture back against the walls. I didn't mean to rush you down here."

"Oh, okeydokey. We'll get it done this coming weekend."

"Thank you," she said. Then she added, "Ignore Mr. Christian. He's crazy."

"I see," the old man said, and headed out the door.

"I ought to kill your ass. You know I almost Maced his old ass."

She smiled and laughed. "You need help. You really do. Listen, I got to run. But let me ask you: Did you have fun the other night?"

"Oh yeah, it was cool."

"You disappeared. I heard you went out like the man whore that you are."

I laughed and thought about the night. I hadn't heard from Jo, and I figured she was back in New York by now being a devoted wife again. Lisa left and I went back to my desk to finish up work.

It was well past four o'clock and nearly every teacher had left the building, since the kids left at two. We were only required to stay until two forty-five. I usually tried to grade all of my papers from the previous week and have them ready to go home with the kids on Tuesday, so I was used to working a little later on Mondays.

Most Mondays I would meet Jacob for a bite to eat around five before he went to play with his band at a club on U Street. I'd tried calling him five times earlier in the day, but his phone had been turned off.

I put a CD in my computer and turned the volume in my speakers up. *"Tell me what kind of man would treat his woman so cold. Treat you like you're nothing when you're worth more than gold."* I sang the lyrics along with Joe, and as they sank in, I could hear someone singing them to my Alicia. It was so strange. Now that she was gone, and wasn't coming back, I could truly appreciate her. And deep down inside, I knew I didn't deserve her, but that didn't stop the longing or the pain I felt with her absence.

I imagined a conversation between her and me. "Baby, I still love you," I say.

She gleams at me with her eyes half-closed, letting me know that she doesn't believe me, and then says, "You don't know the meaning of love. You've never loved anyone. Not even yourself."

"What do you mean?"

"You have no self-love. If you did, you wouldn't behave the way you do. You wouldn't have thrown us away." With no response to her truth, I sit there looking dumb. "Diego, the only thing you've ever loved was your own dick. It's all you've got."

She'd be right. Even amid all the pain I'd gone through and caused, I still couldn't stop seeking out more women, more sex. I thought about the temporary escape from the pain I felt when I was with Erin, and the other night with Jonetta. Then I thought about all the women, *all* the time. Even before Alicia. In that moment of clarity, it dawned on me that perhaps on those occasions I'd been trying to escape. I just didn't realize at the time that the escape had been from myself.

(((10)))

A Song Worth Singing

Listening to Jacob sing made me proud. I knew one day my friend would make it big. He was too talented not to. He could play nearly every instrument in the band and could outsing most platinum artists who were on the radio.

He was singing a version of John Legend's "So High" and making it his own with his signature riffs. My back was against the exposed brick wall near the bar as I sipped on my third glass of Absolut and cranberry juice, appreciating my homey's gift. What I found amazing was that he could pour his whole soul into his performance even though he was going through some changes.

The spotlight was shining on his head as he stood on the edge of the small stage. Jacob almost imitated Legend's raspy voice, yet he blended in his own smooth falsetto. As he hit the high notes his voice reverberated off the walls and seemingly penetrated the souls of everyone in the room. He held the mic and the stand as he wound the song down. *"This is how love's supposed to be,"* he sang expertly.

Women were screaming at him and he stared into their eyes for a second or two at a time before closing his own tight and giving his sexiest soul-singer look. There was now pain all over his face as he pulled the microphone from the stand and dropped down to his knees. *"You got me up sooooooo higggghhhhh, my shoooooooezzzzz are scraaaaping the skyyyyyyyy,"* he crooned. It was over as the room erupted in applause.

"Thank you," he said. "We're going to take a short break and be right back for the next set."

He didn't even see me standing in the back. When he stepped off the stage he was greeted by a girl I thought I recognized. She had a studded bandanna on and two plats on each side. Jacob smiled at her and hugged her. A second later, he looked my direction and headed over.

"What's up? I didn't know you were coming out tonight."

I nodded. "Yeah, I tried calling your ass all day. I even texted you a couple times."

"Yeah, my battery was dead and I forgot my charger at home."

"You want a drink?" I offered.

"Not while I'm performing."

"A Coke or something?"

He nodded at someone who spoke to him. "Yeah, that'll be cool. With lemon in it."

A couple more people came by to give him pats on the back for his performance and a couple of women came by hoping that he would be interested, but he showed none. All they got was "Thanks for coming out."

"So who was that shorty with the bandanna?"

"That's Kendra. The one I was telling you about."

"Oh, okay. She sings with that other group, right?"

"Yeah, but tonight she came solo. We're actually going to do one together during the second set." Jacob told me that Kendra had shown up after school in his classroom. He'd explained that he had been really down about the whole situation going on with Anna. Of course he left out most of the truth.

He said that she'd walked in on him crying and that she had comforted him with hugs and kisses. She then offered to stay with him after the show. He'd been more than cool with it.

"She's a cutie. I gotta say I don't remember her looking anything like that the few times I've seen her," I said, trying not to sound insulting.

"Yeah, I dig her . . ."

I knew him and knew that there was a *but*. "But . . ."

He laughed. "I don't know. Maybe it's the Baltimore versus D.C. thing. You know they have a whole different vibe up in B-more. I may be used to a more . . . I guess I wanna say . . . *refined* sistah."

"So what is she, a ghetto broad?"

He laughed. "Let me go get ready to wrap this set up." Before he walked away, he asked, with what seemed like concern, "Hey, have you talked to your brother lately?"

"Not since the other night. Why?"

"No, I mean *talked* to him. Really had a conversation. He seemed a little off the other night. Maybe it was me and what I've been going through, but he seemed . . . I don't know. Just not quite himself."

"Speaking of that situation—" I began, but he cut me off and kept talking.

"She didn't come to school today and the kid, Dean, he's out of there. I think it's gonna blow over." Jacob was more hopeful than convinced, but he put up a good front.

I responded, "That's good."

A few moments later and he was back on the stage singing. By the time he finished with the first song, the room was packed again. "Listen up, everyone. There's someone here tonight who's a special friend of mine and she's also a special performer. I would be honored if she'd come up here and share the stage with me to bless you all with a song."

Jacob looked over and saw Kendra shaking her head no. Then he said, "A round of applause." When the room erupted he knew that she'd have no choice. She walked toward the stage, and after she climbed up she got her footing together and punched Jacob in the arm. He feigned serious pain and rubbed his arm.

Kendra not only looked cute with the rag on her head, she had a real ghetto booty. She looked as if she belonged up there with Jacob, though he was straitlaced and Kendra had more hood flair. "So what you want to sing? Your choice," Jacob said.

She took a deep breath and leaned in to whisper in his ear. He immediately smiled and then he turned to the keyboard player and gave him instruction. He and Kendra turned to face each other and the band began to play the music to one of my favorites, "You Don't Have to Cry." One couple stood up and began to dance.

Jacob began singing. As usual, the crowd was immediately sucked in to the syrupy sensuality that he gave up. The women and the men were hypnotized by him. Hearing him sing, no one would guess that the brother had a day job. He belonged on the stage and he commanded the attention of anyone who listened. Jacob had everyone hypnotized with his voice, so much so that it was a complete shock when Kendra broke in at the top of her lungs and stole the song and the show with her verse.

It was as if she was singing for her life or Jacob's. *"There's someone here now, who cares about your needs. We'll make it somehow, 'cause I'll share your grief."*

The girl was so good that even the women couldn't hate on her. Everyone stood as she shimmied her body and walked right up into Jacob's face as she delivered the lyrics. When she finished with the words she grabbed him by the neck and pressed her lips against his. I was shocked to see the two of them kissing onstage like two people in love.

I couldn't help but laugh. Then, as people began to clap, I turned to my left and saw a sistah come flying in my direction. She'd been shoved right into my arms. She pulled away and looked as if she was ready to lunge at the woman who'd pushed her.

"Bitch, I told you to get the hell out of my way," the girl who'd done the pushing yelled. "I'm out of here," she barked, and turned to head toward the exit.

Just then I got a chance to get a look at the girl who'd been shoved as one of her friends walked over to her. I recognized the friend as soon as she walked up. She'd been a bridesmaid at my wedding. We locked eyes momentarily and she turned away from me and focused on her friend, who was wiping the remnants of a spilled drink off of her sweater.

"You all right, girl?"

"Yeah, I don't know what was up with that crazy little bitch. She better be glad she rushed the fuck up outta here," the girl said in a voice that chilled me. "As soon as Jacob kissed that girl onstage the chick started going off, talking about 'let me by.' "

By the time she finished speaking, I placed my hand on her shoulder to confirm what I'd thought. She turned and my heart skipped a beat as nervousness, excitement, and fear all attacked me at once. All I could do was mumble her name. "Alicia."

11

One Way or Another

Anna came back to school after missing three days straight. On the fourth day, Jacob was prepared to confess all to his principal. He figured that Anna was probably sitting at home in her room, without eating or bathing, becoming more unstable with each passing moment. If that were the case, then it was just a matter of time before she let it all out anyway.

When she rolled up into his class on Thursday, his fears were eased by her relaxed attitude. There was nothing out of the ordinary from her. In fact, her appearance was even nicer than usual. Perhaps he was looking closer than he would have normally. For one, Jacob had never noticed the eyeliner she sported, but it looked nice on her and it appeared she had on a touch of mascara. She had even changed her hairstyle. It was braided into plats, very similar to Kendra's the other night, except Anna had a zigzag part down the middle of hers.

During class, Jacob tried not to make eye contact with her. It was hard because she was seated next to Elise, the new girl, and the two of them kept talking. They'd seemed to hit it off, which Jacob found odd. Anna hadn't been the best at making new friends, and up until that point, he hadn't seen Elise speaking much to anyone.

When class was over he heard Anna say, "Wait up, girl. I'll be right there. I need to ask Mr. Marsh something."

Already back at his desk trying to act disinterested, Jacob flipped through a catalog. "You look nice today, Mr. Marsh. Those shoes are fly as I don't know what."

"Thanks, Anna. You been okay?"

"Yeah, I'm good. Well rested. That's why I wanted to ask you if there was any work I needed to make up."

"No, don't worry about it. Just the paper due a week from Monday."

"Oh gawd. Almost forgot about that. I'll do my best. I haven't really been able to concentrate much lately, though, so I'm not sure how it'll turn out."

"Well, it's a quarter of your grade, so definitely do your best," Jacob returned.

Anna had a smirk on her face that Jacob couldn't really make out. "Yeah, right," she said as she started to walk off. After a couple steps she turned and said, "Oh, by the way, I saw you singing the other night. You were the bomb. You tore it down, but your girl-friend, man, she was the bomb. And the passion between you two onstage . . . mmmphh." She fanned her face.

Jacob's face showed shock. "What?"

"Yeah, you sounded really hot. You should make a CD or something. I would have stayed longer, but I almost had to go upside some chick's head. One of your fans was getting a little overheated with your performance and got on my nerves."

"Oh?" was all he could come up with.

Jacob had never mentioned where his band performed, but it wasn't like someone who was looking couldn't find out. Still, he never talked much about No Question at school for this very reason. He didn't want his colleagues or his students showing up at his performances.

"Anyway, I gotta run, Mr. Marsh," Anna said, and headed for the door, where Elise was standing. Jacob, tongue in cheek, made a face that showed his discomfort with what he'd heard. If Anna had turned around, she'd have realized what he was feeling, but she didn't. So instead, Jacob stared her down as she walked off. He noticed the low-rise jeans she was wearing and how they exposed her almond-colored hips. They were on the list of banned items in the dress code. As she swished her ass like a streetwalker Jacob realized that she was definitely fucking with him. It wasn't working. He had no desire to get involved with her, and even if he'd lusted after her enough to risk everything, which he didn't, she was too damned scary. A psychotic woman in the making.

When his eyes left her ass, they panned up to see that Elise's were glued to his. He'd gotten caught peeping and Elise smiled to let him know she'd seen him. Jacob turned away, trying to play the whole situation off. The two girls left giggling and Jacob sat there feeling violated.

He picked up his cell phone.

———

I couldn't figure out why it had taken me so long to figure out the solution. If Kenard dialed my phone, it would say the number was out of service. And there'd be no way for him to link his lady's night out to me.

This also meant having to give my number out all over again to everyone I wanted to have it, which was a pain, but worth it if I remained anonymous to Kenard. I would also be getting rid of a few pests in the process.

When the phone went off in my pocket I figured it could only be one of a few people. I'd only had the new number for a couple days.

"Whaddup?" I answered.

"Man, you ain't gonna believe this shit." Jacob's voice was a little shaky.

"What?"

"Diego, it's like you and I have reversed roles. I'm trying to figure out where all this drama is coming from in my life." Jacob sounded dejected.

"So what happened now?"

"The girl, Anna, finally came back to class today. She was acting completely normal. I studied her for the entire class and it was like nothing ever happened. I mean she certainly didn't act like someone who'd been raped."

"That's a good thing, right? Maybe she tried to pull the same shit that girl pulled with Kobe on your student teacher, and in all actuality gave that ass up willingly after all."

"Shit, I don't know, and at this point, that's not my major concern. On the real, this little broad is stalking me. Guess what she tells me?"

"What?"

"Her ass was at the show the other night. She saw me perform with Kendra onstage. The kiss and everything."

I was quiet as I thought about it for a moment. Then I responded, "You know, that might be a good thing. If she knows you're in a relationship, and the fact that Kendra made it look like you two are in a *heated* relationship, then maybe her little hot ass will leave you alone."

Thinking it over, he said, "Maybe you have a point."

"Of course, man. You can't let every little thing she does rattle you," I shot back. "You see, bruh . . . this is exactly why I teach the little ones. The high-school kids are crazy."

"Yeah, well, you keep them little germ-carryin' rug rats. I'll get through this."

"I hope so," I said, laughing. "Jacob, there is one thing you could always try."

"What's that?"

"Talk to the crazy bitch. Just have a heart-to-heart and explain to her where you're coming from. Don't tell her that you put Dean up to trying to get with her, just that you think she likes you in an inappropriate way."

"I don't know. That shit would be mad awkward."

"Well, maybe to keep shit from being awkward you could just give her the dick," I said, and burst out laughing.

"Nigga, you sick. You probably would," he shot back.

My door opened and one of my kids came into my room. "Didn't I tell your butt to knock before you come in here?"

"Yes, sir," the miniature Biggie Smalls look-alike shot back.

"Well go back out and knock." I put the phone back to my ear. I heard the kid begin to knock. I let him do that for a minute. "Jacob, I gotta run. We still on for tomorrow night, right?"

"Yeah," he said. Lee had a friend from church whose sister was getting married, some girl he sang with in the choir. She was having a small gathering for her sister and wanted to get Jacob to come by and sing a couple songs. The bride was a Maxwell fan and she was paying three bills for her sister to hear "Fortunate" and ". . . Til the Cops Come Knockin.'" I'd convinced him to do it for two hundred. No harm in capitalism. I was something like his agent.

"Cool. After that, we'll hit Ozio's or something." I waved little Biggie to come on in the room.

"All right, then."

After work I stopped off and got a haircut, went to the gym for a quick workout, and then headed home. I sat on the couch flipping channels for a while and watching ESPN. I would have done anything to have someone cook me a meal and serve it to me. I was so tired from all the worrying I'd been doing I didn't feel like getting up to cook. Plus the kids wore me out day in and day out.

I scrolled through my phone, preparing to pull up the number for a Chinese restaurant to order some shrimp lo mein. The first number I saw as I scrolled, however, was Alicia's. Home, work, cell, mother's home.

My mind went back to the other night. Seeing her at the club had thrown me for a serious loop. She'd been looking more gorgeous than I recalled, though the first thing I'd noticed was that she'd found the ten pounds that I'd lost in the last couple of months. Stress affected us all differently.

I replayed the scene from the moment I'd recognized her. "Alicia?"

She hadn't looked surprised to see me, yet she didn't answer. Her friend had begun to usher her away and I'd reached out to touch her shoulder.

"Alicia . . . can—"

She had responded with a backhand that caught me by surprise. "Diego, get your fucking hands off me."

Her anger had been apparent and I had no choice but to back away.

She'd stormed away, not looking back.

I still loved her, but I knew at that moment she was never coming back. My thoughts of Alicia were interrupted by my phone ringing. I reached for the cordless. "Hello."

"Hey, stranger," the voice on the other end said.

"Hey . . . who's this?"

"Daphne, damn. It's been that long, huh?"

"Oh, hey, what's goin' on?" Daphne owned a hair salon and used to do my hair when I wore twist. We had ended up going out a couple of times, but when it came down to getting her back to my place, she always had an excuse. She knew I wanted to hit that and I knew she wanted a relationship.

When it became obvious that neither of us was interested in giving the other exactly what they wanted, we fizzled out like a wet match.

"Not much with me. I had tried to catch you on your cell, but it was not in service. My girl told me she saw you out at the Black Caucus last week."

"Oh yeah, I did see Yvonne. I forgot she worked at your shop."

"So, what's good? I heard you didn't get married."

That struck a nerve. I wondered if she was being nosy or if she was trying to get back in the picture. "Nope, I didn't. But, Daphne, I have someone on the other line. I'ma need to call you back."

"Oh, okay . . . let me give you my—"

I hung up on her with the quickness.

I ordered my food and called Erin. I got her voice mail off the break. I was sure that she was on lockdown now that she had her man's attention. I scrolled down, looking at a few numbers and dialing a few. I got more answering machines and imagined that a few of the women I called were doing the same thing to me that I did half the time—screening their calls.

Then it was clear to me anyway that none of them would have sufficed. I was thinking about Alicia and she hated me. None of them would replace her anyway. The only one who even came close was Erin and she had a man. What I needed was some *strange,* meaning some new pussy.

At eleven, I was in my bed trying to blank my thoughts. I was tired of dealing with the emptiness that had been caused by her absence. Perhaps I could try a relationship and commit to someone. Someone who'd be here with me each night so I wouldn't have to stretch out in the bed alone. It wasn't like women hadn't tried to give me just that, but I'd go running as soon as they were ready to commit. When it came to staying power in relationships, I was majorly deficient.

If the right woman came across my path, things might be different. She'd have to be cute, smart, funny, and a nice body wouldn't hurt. I could see me getting along with another teacher, though we'd be broke. I would love it if we liked a lot of the same things, but above all that, she'd have to be a freak in the bedroom. Willing to try almost anything, almost.

Everything else would be a bonus. Maybe she would cook a good meal for me, and when I felt like I was feeling right now, she'd be coming out of the shower, body glistening from oils.

She'd pull the covers back and slide right under the sheets. I'd see those titties hanging and reach for them, grabbing a nipple and pulling on it. I would feel her vagina's moisture as she slid her body along mine. When she placed her lips on my chest and sucked my nipples, sending a chill up my spine, I'd moan out to her to let her know I loved her touch.

I wouldn't have to urge her to take me into her mouth. She'd be hungry for it, grabbing the base and making a ring around it with her thumb and her index finger as she began bobbing up and down on it.

My mind began to drift, and a few seconds later I had Vaseline on my hand, jerking up and down my rock-hard dick. My mind shifted into high gear to match my libido, and suddenly my imagination became the movie screen. Reels of kinky, freaked-out memories of bitches gone by were playing.

One wrong turn and I coulda been a porn star. Involuntarily, the faces and distinctive encounters came flooding my mind. Jeanine was my all-time favorite. Her thighs used to tremble when I made her orgasm and her pussy was incredibly good. I used to wait outside her house till three in the morning to see if she was cheating. I could see me on top of her for a while as my dick grew to full attention. Then there was Tonya; met her through a friend. The brown-skinned, double-jointed sistah was worth the ride over to Minnesota Avenue. She wasn't the cutest girl I'd ever had, but she'd put her legs behind her head like a circus act and take all the dick. Chi Chi was the first girl who sucked me off until I came in her mouth. I always remembered her lying in the bed with me, even though I had flu. The blow jobs were better than chicken soup for the soul.

Keema was the first girl I dominated. The girl was always angry when we hooked up; I used to have to cuss her out and tell her about herself before she'd let me fuck. She got wet when I told her how I was going to bang the shit out of her. I almost took that pussy from her, one freezing February night in a hotel room off Route 30 in Atlantic City. She loved it. The next morning she suggested I make her my wife. I actually thought about marrying her, because the ass was just that good.

Kim used to stop by on her lunch break or on her way home. We met in New Orleans at the Essence Fest. We knew each other twenty minutes before we were kissing on the dance floor, drunk from shots in Razoo's. I remembered playing in that long pretty hair. She worked so hard at giving me head and she so appreciated the fact that I'd fuck her long and hard, we were reckless. She always wanted me to cum inside of her. I knew she didn't want a baby, though. She was married.

Tionne, Pam, Shawn, Lupe . . . all in my hall of fame. I couldn't shake any of their images. I could hear all of their moans collectively as I stroked.

As the tingle began, I wanted to cum hard. So much that I'd fall right to sleep and wouldn't have to think about the emptiness.

I thought of Dana, a beautiful caramel sistah. She told me that she was Dominican, but the bitch was as black as me. When we met she'd been high on E pills, and she loved rolling off it when we fucked. She was slim, with a really small frame and a tight, hot pussy. She always talked about having threesomes and one night we let her sister watch us fuck. I thought about calling her now, but I didn't want to stop. I heard her asking, "Diego, why . . . are you . . . fuggginng . . . meeee . . . sssoooo . . . good, iyyeeee, iyeeee, ahhhh . . ." My mind had my body convinced that she was right there and that it was her pussy I was wrapping around me and not my hand.

Finally, as my balls tightened up and I felt the rush of sperm about to shoot, my movie went blank and I saw Alicia's face, her breasts, and her ass as I bent her over the steps. I saw the sweat on her back, and I began to cum. The first jet landed on my thighs, the second on my hands, and the rest poured out.

As I wiped myself off enough to pull my underwear up, Usher's song "U Got It Bad" came to mind and I admitted that very fact to myself.

12

The Love Experience

I woke up with a new attitude. The sun came bursting through my windows and I was ready for the day. Today was going to be the first day of the rest of my life. Thinking clichés like that didn't seem as corny as if I'd actually said them aloud. I jumped out of bed and hit the shower. As the hot water beat down on me I felt as though I was being renewed. Yeah, I'd done plenty wrong and I'd hurt people, but I wasn't going to let my whole life come to an end because of the stupid decisions I'd made.

As the aroma of the soap went up through my nostrils, I imagined me scrubbing away the old me. The me that had no self-control, the me that thought only of himself. I held out hope for myself and decided that I would make an effort to do, or at least say, something positive each day, something for myself *and* something that was a blessing to someone else.

Thinking these things and believing that I could make these changes, I felt something come over me right then and there. I climbed out of the shower and got dressed. It was Friday and I decided to dress down. I threw on my favorite black Izod shirt, a pair of Hugo Boss jeans, and my all-black Adidas Samoas.

I grabbed my wallet and a small stack of bills from my dresser. I was thrilled that it was payday and was going to call in a few of them during my lunch break. My house phone rang as I was leaving and I thought about going back to get it, but decided against it. They'd leave a message.

When I jumped in my car and started to back out, my cell rang. It was my brother, Lee. I adjusted my earpiece. "What's up, big brother?"

"Nothing much. I was just thinking about you this morning. I had you in my prayers. I have a feeling that things are going to start happening for you. I know you've been down about how . . . well, I assume you've been hurting over the whole thing with you and Alicia, but rest assured, things will work out."

"Thanks, man. I appreciate it. I must have really been on your mind for you to hit me first thing this morning."

"Absolutely."

"I heard the phone ring as I was leaving out the house, but I'm glad you called me, because—"

He cut me off. "Nah, this was my first time calling you. I got you on the first try."

"Oh?" I wondered, then, who'd called my house at seven-fifteen in the morning.

"Well, anyway. I just want you to stay focused and just look to the future."

"No doubt."

He was about to hang up when he caught himself. "Diego, man, by the way, whatever happened with the situation with the girl . . . was it Gina? The one that the little hellion said you had pregnant."

"Oh, well, that . . . It didn't pan out. Kristen was making up all of that to stir up shit. My bad, stir up stuff. I think it's her ex-boyfriend's kid." Truthfully, I didn't know what was up. I had tried reaching Gina a couple times at her job. She worked for Verizon. I called up to her job and they said she'd taken a leave of absence. I drove past her house, but her car was never there. I didn't bother knocking on the door. Didn't know who'd be up in that camp.

"That's good. Because that's nothing to take lightly."

"Oh, no doubt," I replied. "Look, though, I'm almost to work and I need to call and check my messages real quick. I think Comcast is about to cut my cable off."

He laughed. "All right, let me know if you need some help, little bro."

"Thanks, I'm good, though." Lee was a good brother. Ever since he'd gotten married, he'd changed quite a bit, but it was all good. I chalked it up to him growing up.

I hung up and dialed my answering machine at home as I turned the corner near my job and saw a couple children on their way. They were the ones parents rushed out of the house twenty minutes early, rain or shine, every day. I pressed in my code and the messages began to play. "You have four new messages." I pulled past the crossing guards and waved. First message, my mother calling. I'd already spoken with her, deleted it. Second message: "Good evening. My name is Vern Saban. I'm calling from Gateway Resorts in Hot Springs, Virginia. We got your—" A time-share . . . deleted it. I backed into an empty spot. Third message, a hang-up. Fourth message: "Diego, he knows everything . . . I don't know how he found out . . . For some reason, I think one of my friends . . ." It was Erin and she sounded panicked. I punched in the button: message dated 7:14 A.M. today.

"I don't believe this shit" was all I could mumble out before I heard a crash as the window next to my face was shattered and a brick landed in my lap. I quickly dusted off the shards of glass that were on my cheeks. Stunned, I looked over and there was Kenard, standing, fist balled up, ready to attack.

"Step on out this car, muthafucka. I'ma beat that ass," he yelled, and then banged his fist on the hood of my BMW. It sounded like he'd dented it. My ride was ten years old, but I still took pride in it. I knew I had to do something to keep him from trashing it.

As I contemplated my options he snapped me out of my thoughts, yelling, "I'ma beat that ass, you bitch nigga. You wanna fuck my girl, huh?"

Disbelief could hardly describe my state at that point. I was almost in shock. I thought to pull off, as my engine was still running. I wasn't sure if it was anger or self-preservation, but when I saw him step toward my window, leaning forward, with his fist in the air, I slammed my door open in an effort to climb out.

I couldn't have planned what happened next if I'd tried. As he lunged forward the corner of the door caught him in the forehead and eye and created a gash. His face became a bloody mess on contact. I climbed out of the car in a trancelike manner. I could see a few people in the background, but it felt more like I was watching the drama than participating in it.

"Ohhhh shiiiit," he yelled over and over, holding his eye. "Motherfucka, I can't see. I'ma kill you." He began to moan in agony.

At this point I wanted to get away from him, but he obviously took my swinging the door as an act of violence. When I moved in his direction, he obviously thought that I was preparing to attack him, so he charged me. All I saw was the blood that he had all over his face and hands and I definitely didn't want it on me or my clothes, so I sidestepped him and swung my foot, trying to keep him away. My foot happened to catch him in the kidney. He moaned like a wounded bear and fell to the ground. Again, if I had tried to do it on purpose, I wouldn't have been able to knock his ass down onto the big chunks of glass that he landed on. He began rolling around in agony; glass was stuck to his pants and sticking out of his leg.

The school guidance counselor, who'd seen the beginning of the attack, ran into the building to call the police. In the age since 9/11, the police come quickly for threats on school grounds. Kenard couldn't have picked a worse place to come for revenge.

Ten minutes later and he was being hauled to Hyattsville to lockup. Prince George's County Police had shown up five cars deep. One stayed behind to interview me and the counselor who'd called. I painted Kenard as some psycho jealous boyfriend who'd reacted on ridiculous suspicions.

I headed off to my class and was able to beat the children in. I wasn't there for more than ten minutes when my principal, Ms. Knight, showed up. "Mr. Christian, can I speak with you for a moment in the hall?"

The school secretary was with her and Ms. Knight ushered her into my room to cover the class for as long as our conversation would take. I cleared my throat once we were in the hall.

"Diego," she said, "I hope you understand how serious this is. Because I don't think you do."

"Well, I, um . . ."

Ms. Knight's face showed her tension. She was tight with a capital *T* behind this. At five-six, she wasn't the biggest woman, but when she became furious she seemed to stand at six-foot-five. "I have a television crew on the way up here and the *Gazette* is all over this. The phone has already started ringing with parents wanting to know if we had to evacuate the building."

"Evacuate?"

"Yes, evacuate. It's not every day you see ten police cars racing into the parking lot to start the day." She was exaggerating, but not by much. "So would you like to tell me the story behind this, because I'm sure I already know."

"Well, I'm not really sure what this guy's problem is—"

Shaking her head no, she cut me off. "Let me explain something to you. I'm heading down to make a couple of calls. I am within my legal bounds to have you removed from this school, if your presence is going to put my students in any type of harm's way. I'd appreciate it if you got your car, with the busted-out window, out of my parking lot, take the rest of today off, and I'll call you at home on Monday to let you know what's what."

"Am I being charged leave for this?"

Her eyes squinted. "I'll let you know." With her teeth gritted, she said, "You know you seriously injured that man. I got word that they had to take him to PG Hospital for head trauma. So the police haven't even gotten a chance to question him. Why don't you focus on the drama you've caused our school today instead of your leave. Grab your things and have a nice day."

———

When I reached the parking lot, I saw the custodian sweeping up the last of the glass. "I swept your car out, too, Mr. Christian."

"Thanks, Mr. Waverly," I said as I placed my briefcase in the backseat.

I looked down on the pavement and saw the blood on the ground and it turned my stomach a little.

"Mr. Christian?" Mr. Waverly said as I climbed into my car.

"Yes, sir?"

He moved slowly in front of my window and placed his hands on my roof. He leaned in a bit, and in his gruff voice he said, "Son, I hope you don't mine me sayin' this to ya. You need to slow down and get control. All this craziness, it ain't good for you. It specially ain't good for someone around kids all the time. You got to set an example." He stepped back and spread his hands to present my car as Exhibit A. "This right here is the same things they see at home. Fighting and craziness. You better than this, and with a name like Christian, you need to act like it. Those kids look up to you."

I sat there silent as I listened to the old man speak. He was beginning to strike a nerve, but it was okay, I needed it. "It don't take a scientist—hell, it don't even take a science teacher—to figure this out. You been messin' with that man's woman. Now you, a nice-looking young man, you need to go out and get your own woman, one that ain't got no boyfriend, no husband, and slow down. If I was you, I'd get one that ain't got no babies, but that's neither here nor there, son. If you keep this up, you won't make it to . . . how old is you? . . . 'bout thirty, I suppose."

I nodded. He went on: "Well, you won't see thirty-five if you keep this up. Mark my words."

"I'll keep that in mind. Thanks, Mr. Waverly."

"Do or don't, choice is all yours, but I seen a lot come and a lot go. I'll say this for sure 'cause I seen it proved true: 'In his day of fury, a jealous man will show no compassion.' The Bible says that. Think about it."

I nodded again and put my car into gear. As I pulled out of the lot I saw a cameraman and a reporter packing up in front of the school. As I drove out the entrance one of them pointed in my direction.

"Four hundred dollars. That's how much that shit cost." I was complaining to Lee as we sat in Ruby Tuesday's eating lunch. I'd just hung up the phone with my boy Nick from over at Safe-Lite Auto Glass.

"Man, you need to count your blessings. It could have been worse. It could have easily been you in that hospital. God is trying to tell you something."

"Yeah, that I need a better-paying job. Hell, I'm broke again till payday."

As we drove to pick up my car I took notice that Lee hadn't taken off his sunglasses the entire time. "What's the deal with those dark-ass glasses?"

"Bruh, could you calm down with all the foul language?"

"My bad. I just noticed them things. You look like something out of the eighties." I laughed. Lee had never been the most fashion-conscious dude, but the shades and the sweater he was wearing were both a little wack.

"Thanks, man."

He let me off and I paid for my car with nearly the last of my dough until the next payday. As I drove I tested the window. It worked perfectly. I was really lucky to have gotten it fixed so quickly. I hit the Beltway and headed home. I thought about Kenard and wondered what kind of shape he was in. I decided to call Erin for the fifth time. I'd been pissed with her all day because she hadn't returned any of my calls.

This time she answered. "Yes."

"Didn't you get my calls?"

"Yes."

"Well, why didn't you call me back?"

"Because I've been at the hospital and then to get a bail bondsman for Kenard." Her tone was very sharp and biting.

"Why does it sound like you have an attitude with me?"

"No reason . . . Except maybe you tried to kill him. What was all that about?"

"Kill *him*? Are you crazy? He came to my job—"

"To *talk*, Diego. He just wanted to know if it was true."

"Talk, my ass. He threw a brick through my window. People saw him. I can't believe you bought that shit."

"Well, all I know is he needed nineteen stitches and he has a possible retinal tear. You really messed his eye up. He also was on dialysis until last year. I told you that, and still you kicked him in the kidneys?"

"How the hell was I supposed to remember that?"

"You're crazy. You need help."

"You're the one that's fucking crazy. This fool comes onto school property to attack me and you are defending him."

"Yeah, well, my son won't be coming back to your class or that school."

"C'mon now, Erin, aren't you going overboard?" No response. "Hello." No sound. "Hello?" I put my phone down. "I'll be damned," I mumbled.

I didn't care what I drank. I just wanted to get a buzz. All I knew at that moment was that I was glad that I'd convinced Jacob to do the bridal shower. The sistah who had put the party together for her sister obviously had money. Her home was laid out. She had at least six thousand square feet in the six-bedroom house. Original paintings and candles burning throughout the place gave it the original eclectic feel that you only seem to see in magazines or in movies. There was one room with nothing but huge throw pillows all over the floor and a smoked-glass coffee table in the center.

The bar was stocked with everything imaginable, but I kept going back for the punch. I was told that it had some blend of exotic rum that she'd brought back from Jamaica. All I knew was that the punch had fruit floating around in it to make it sweet, and I was fucked up after my third cup. In addition to that, I was getting warm as hell.

Jacob had enjoyed a plate of food and was planning on singing and then leaving. The bride was on her way and I was surprised to see how comfortable he was relaxing among the twelve women who'd been invited to the shower.

I was told that as many as ten more were on the way. As I sat back waiting for the hostess, Julia, to come back downstairs, I looked at the notepad she'd been carrying around. She was bringing me the remote for the stereo since Jacob was going to sing over the music from a Maxwell CD.

A few moments passed and five women walked into the basement and the girls were screaming and laughing in excitement to see one another. I scanned the room and took notice of the variety of sisters. There was also one Indian chick in there. There were some big ones, some small ones, and some just in between. When one of the sisters pulled off her jacket and revealed the bustier she was wearing, I thought to myself, *There's one in every crowd.*

Just then, Julia walked down the steps. "All right, ladies and gentlemen, Madelyn is about to pull up . . . so let's get this party started." Then she came over to me and Jacob. "I want you two to wait in the back room until I start the music. When Jacob walks out singing, she is going to freak out. Now, you two are welcome to stay for the toy party and the dancers."

"Excuse me," I slurred out. "Why would we want to see some—"

"Oh, I forgot to tell you, we have both male and female dancers. They're doing a show for Madelyn."

"Oh, wow." Jacob looked surprised. "Never heard of such. Sounds great, but I have an engagement for later."

She turned to me. "Well, Diego, you're welcome to stay."

I didn't have shit to do and Jacob and I had driven separately. "I may do that as long as you keep the rum punch flowing."

"For certain." She smiled. Julia was cute and fit the mold of a church girl. Nothing flashy and just a clean-looking sistah.

When the music started Jacob walked out the room. The lights had been dimmed and Madelyn was seated in the middle of the floor, blindfolded. Jacob drifted out slowly and burst smoothly into song—"*Whoooouuuuuu ooooooohhhhhh. Never seen a sun shine like this. Never seen the moon glow like this . . .*"—as he moved toward her. His voice sounded eerily like Maxwell. There was a resemblance, but when he wanted to imitate the soulful crooner with his moves, it was a wrap. I thought the girl was going to faint, go into a fit, have an orgasm, or all three at once right then and there. She began screaming.

I wondered why she didn't yank the blindfold off to see who was serenading her, then I realized that she couldn't. Her hands were cuffed and tied to that chair. She, too, was wearing a bustier top, but hers was leather, and I noticed how firm her shoulders and arms were. She was cut up. I also took notice of her skirt. It was a short black leather one with a slit up the thigh.

Tilting the cup to my head, I finished my fifth cup of punch. I was grinning as Jacob worked her with the song, then my mouth dropped open when I noticed that all the women were sitting around in either corset bustiers or camisoles. I tried to remember what Lee had told me about this group. I had figured that it was a church group, but it was starting to look more like a wrecking crew of freaks and dominatrixes.

Jacob finished the first song and the women erupted in applause;

a couple of them began to throw money. Without hesitation, I jumped up and ran over to the floor. The more I picked up, the more they threw. It was mostly singles, but a few fives and tens showed up in the batch.

"Bravo, bravo," Julia shouted. "Now, ladies, before I take off the blindfold to allow Maddy to see this beautiful, sexy piece of man candy, I'm going to ask that he give her one sweet kiss. After all, this is her last night as a single woman."

Jacob smiled in embarrassment and shook his head no. He was such a square sometimes that I walked over and pushed him to the side. A couple of the women's mouths dropped open as I straddled the bride-to-be's lap and proceeded to kiss her gently on her forehead, then her neck and ears. When I noticed no resistance, I placed my mouth to hers and kissed her gently; as her mouth began to open I tasted the wine on her breath and wondered if she was as high as I was.

Seconds later, I heard cheers and chants as our tongues danced for a short while and then I pulled away. I stood up and put my hands in the air as if to say *I am the champ*, then everyone clapped. I pushed Jacob back in front of her to make her think it was he who'd kissed her.

Julia unbound Maddy and a smile came across her face as the music to the second song began to play. Jacob sang it as good as he had the first. This time she stood up and she and Jacob began to dance. He held the cordless mic and she held his waist, grinding him like there was no tomorrow.

"Poppa gonna have to leave a message on the telephone, baby . . . There won't be . . . till the cops come knockin'."

When the song was over the ladies clapped feverishly for a strong thirty seconds. Jacob blushed. I walked over to him and whispered, "I already have the dough in the envelope. I'll hit you with it when we get upstairs."

"Yeah, how much did I get for this again?"

"Two hundred," I said.

"How much did you get?"

"Hey, man, did Tina ask Ike how much he got? Hell no. I'm insulted. As your manager—"

"Man, shut your drunk tail up. Look, I'm about to jet out. You can hold on to all of it until later. I know you're busted after paying for your window. So it's all good—hit me up next payday."

"You sure?"

"No doubt."

I was touched. Because of Jacob, I'd be able to eat for the next couple of weeks and keep my cable on. He knew that after getting stuck with the house Alicia and I had planned to live in, my funds were low. The house was almost completed and I couldn't finagle my way out of the contract, so my plan was to go to settlement and put a "for sale" sign up immediately, unless I hit the lottery between now and then.

I announced to the ladies that the entertainment was leaving. As Jacob turned to go one of the girls yelled out, "So are you going to give her a kiss or what?"

Maddy heard and replied, "He already did and it was the bomb . . . mmmm."

"No, that wasn't him. That was the other one who kissed you," she said, pointing at me.

I shrugged and said, "What can I say? He's a little shy." I caught a glare from her that spoke to me. I couldn't tell, though, if she was repulsed or if in fact she wanted another kiss.

An hour and a half later and I was still there sandwiched on the couch between a thick, brown-skinned sistah and a thin redbone. I had sat through the toy party and watched the women go crazy over technological advances in dildos, butt plugs, and bullets. A few of the women purchased things for the bride and she had a gift bag full of toys. I imagined her husband's surprise the day he found that stash. It might make him a little insecure to see that his lady possessed a twelve-inch toy called a Thrasher or a double-ended his-and-hers dildo.

Couldn't be me, I said under my breath. I even watched as the coed dancers put on an X-rated sex show. The voluptuous stripper had actually put on a clinic for giving brains. At one point I imagined myself standing up and yelling out, "What kind of fucking church people are you?"

At 1 A.M., the party was winding down; few of the women had begun to file out and the rest had begun to clean up. For the past thirty minutes I'd been trying to get my bearings to drive home. I finally stood up and began to bid the women farewell. I made it up the steps and thanked Julia again. I was surprised that I didn't get a speech about keeping the lid on their little secret society. But she acted as if this was the normal bridal shower. Maybe it was, and men just had no clue.

When I opened the door and the rush of October air hit me, it further sobered me up. I made my way down the walkway and was almost to my car when I heard footsteps. I turned around and there was Maddy.

"Can I come with you?"

I was shocked. "Are you serious?"

"I get married tomorrow at four P.M. I know my fiancé is having a crazy bachelor party tonight. I ain't dumb. I know what the fuck you niggas do at bachelor parties."

"So you wanna . . ."

She stepped closer to me and leaned in. "I wanna go with you. I want you to fuck me all night. It's my last time. Do you think you can handle that?"

Just then, Mr. Waverly's words crossed my mind. *You need to go out and get your own woman, one that ain't got no boyfriend, no husband . . . If you keep this up, you won't make it . . . You won't see thirty-five . . . Mark my words . . . "In his day of fury, a jealous man will show no compassion."*

"Baby girl. I don't think you really want to do that. That's not a good way to start a marriage. Not a good way at all."

I saw the disappointment on her face, so I added, "It's not that you aren't attractive, 'cause you're sexy as hell. I just been through a lot lately and I don't wanna—"

"Nigga, I ain't trying to be with you. I just want to spend a night. My last night, and tomorrow . . . I want you to forget me."

I couldn't do it. Not after all I'd been through. I had to make some changes and they had to start now.

The way her head kept banging up against the headboard I feared that she would wind up with a concussion. She had warned me that she liked it rough and she loved for a nigga to talk dirty to her, really dirty.

"Take that dick, bitch," I said, trying to oblige her.

"Fuck you."

"That's what I'm doin'. Stop trying to get away," I huffed as I yanked her by her hips back toward me. She was petite but strong. Her body was rock hard. I found out that she was a flight attendant as well as a fitness freak. She really was trying to go all night and was definitely in the shape to do so. It was almost five in the morning and we hadn't slept yet. I was wondering what the hell her man was going to think about her stretched-out twat when it came time to consummate the marriage later that evening.

"Oh shit," she yelled out. "Let me get on top again. I need to come again."

We flipped around and I rolled onto my back. Just like that, she was on her feet, bouncing up and down on me, causing a loud smacking sound to erupt between her ass and my thighs. "That's it," I moaned.

"Oh, you gonna cum? You ready to bust? C'mon, give me all dat nut, boy."

We worked a steady pace of our bodies colliding. It was all I could do to reach out to place a finger at her anus, sticking it in. "Nooooo, that's cheating." But it was too late. I jammed it way in there and her body went limp and she screamed out and shivered at the same time. "I'm cuummmminn' again. Ohhhhhweeeeee. Don't stop . . . don't stoooopppp."

I didn't stop because I was in the middle of chasing down my own orgasm, my third. "Uhhhhhgggghhh, yeaaahhhh," I moaned out as I filled the condom.

We were both panting and she collapsed onto my chest. We both dozed off and didn't wake up until a little after ten. When I looked at the clock I woke her. "Maddy, it's almost ten-fifteen."

"Madelyn," she said. I guess we were back on formal terms since the alcohol had worn off. "Damn. Okay. Can you call me a cab?"

"I can drop you off . . ."

"No thanks. No offense, brother, the sex was great . . . but not good enough to get busted on my wedding day." She smiled and asked for a washcloth and towel. I told her where to grab one and a toothbrush.

"Oh, I got you." I was lying naked still. I reached for the cordless and dialed the Silver Cab. When she stuck her head out of the bathroom, I said, "The cab will be here in fifteen minutes."

"Good," she said, glancing at her watch as she fumbled through her purse. Then she pulled out a condom and held it up. "Fuck me one more time?"

(((13)))

A Brand-new Groove

A month passed after the incident with Kenard in the parking lot and things were getting back to normal for me. Ms. Knight had gradually gotten off of my back about the whole thing. There hadn't been any real heat from her superiors, as she'd feared, and because of that, she'd seen no reason to try to rake me over the coals because of an article in the local paper. True to her threat, Erin had removed Dante from my class, the next Monday, and I was okay with it. If she chose to let him terrorize some other teacher in a new school, I figured it was her choice. I hadn't heard from her or Kenard. Even so, I was forced by Ms. Knight to get an order of protection against him. It kind of made me feel like a bitch, but to keep my job, I did what I was told.

It was a Thursday morning and I was thrilled that there was only one day left until the weekend. I looked out my classroom window at the pouring rain and was resigned to the fact that it would be one of those days. The rain tended to make the kids more docile, quieted them down like cough medicine. It was like some aliens had come and switched bodies with my little people. The quiet of my room was amazing as I looked around at them working quietly.

I began working on my lesson plan for an observation that I had coming up. I hated them. Here I had someone who hadn't been in a classroom in probably twenty years as a teacher, coming to critique me on my shit. People had no idea how kids had evolved in twenty years. Twenty years back I was in elementary school and I was a crazy kid, but I didn't do half the stuff that I saw these kids attempt on a regular basis. I thought the whole process was a joke, but I planned my ass off just the same.

I was halfway to the door when it opened up. It was Mrs. Whitmore, the second-grade teacher from across the hall. "Christian, can you come here for a second?" she said in a strained voice.

I walked over and looked at her face. Now, she was already one of those extremely pale white women, but at that moment her color was completely gone. She was no longer white—she was gray. "You okay?" I asked once I got close enough to her. I noticed her eyes had incredible bags underneath.

"No, I'm not. I need you to watch my kids. I need to go down to the nurse."

"Yeah, no problem. I'll leave my door open. You look a little rough. Are you feeling okay?"

"I feel hot . . . then cold, my head is pounding, and I'm more than a little dizzy."

"Well, do you need some help getting down there?" I asked, because she now had one hand on the wall. I backed up a little because I definitely didn't want what she had.

As we spoke a teacher's aide, who we called Grump, came

around the corner. "Yo, Grump. Mrs. Whitmore's not well. Can you escort her to the nurse's office. I'ma watch her kids till Ms. Knight can get a sub."

Grump, short for James Grumper, was a stocky fellow and could have easily thrown her on his shoulders if the need arose. "Yeah, of course. Here, check this out, front page of the *Metro*. It happened yesterday, right around the corner."

I took the newspaper from him and he headed up the hall. "Thanks, Christian," Mrs. Whitmore said sullenly as she followed him.

I stepped into my room and buzzed the office to let them know that Mrs. Whitmore was on the way and that I had her room covered.

I wound up walking back and forth across the hall for the next twenty minutes, until Ms. Knight walked through my door and over to the chalkboard where I had been teaching. She was carrying Mrs. Whitmore's belongings. "Mr. Christian," she said in a hushed tone. "Mrs. Whitmore made it to the office just in time. Once she got in there, she fainted. An ambulance had to come and get her. They had to revive her in the ambulance on the way to the hospital."

"Oh no," I said.

"Yeah, it's very serious. I have a sub coming in for the rest of the day. She'll be here by lunch. Can you take her kids down to lunch?"

"No problem," I said, nodding.

"Thanks," she said, and walked briskly up the hallway, heels clicking as she moved.

During lunch, I sat at my desk eating my turkey sandwich as I scanned the *Metro*. I looked at the article Grump had been speaking of. Someone had robbed the grocery store just up the street yesterday, in broad daylight, no less, and escaped on foot, it said.

"That's a bold mu'fucka," I mumbled. I read on. Authorities believed that the same person had robbed a Taco Bell, a 7-Eleven, and a CVS, all of which are in the immediate vicinity. No suspects, but it was possible that the assailant lived nearby. "I guess he worked his way up."

Then I began to wonder how much money he'd gotten away with. I could use some of that for sure. My money was getting funnier by the day and my change stayed strange. In other words, a nigga was broke messing around in the school system. But since I couldn't rap or play ball, this was my fate.

With each day I tried hard to forget that I might be losing my entire savings. I had long given up trying to forget about *her*.

"Excuse me." I looked up with a mouth full of food and saw an unfamiliar face. "I'm Lanelle Harris. I'm going to be covering across the hall. Mrs. Knight told me to come up and introduce myself to you. She said that you would show me where everything is."

I nodded as I chewed my food. "Oh, um . . . okay," I said as I wiped my mouth with a napkin. "I'm Diego—Diego Christian. If you go on in and put your things down, I'll be right over."

She smiled and I noticed her braces. "Sounds like a bet. Thanks."

"For sure."

I took the last bite of my sandwich and reached into my closet for some Listerine. I filled my mouth to gargle a bit and checked out my face. I made sure my clothes were fixed and then I stepped to my sink to spit it out. I was hoping that this girl was Miss and not Mrs. She was fine, or looked it from the distance I'd seen her, and when you worked a job like mine, you took your perks where you could.

I headed on over into her room, and when I entered, Grump was in there already. He'd obviously followed Lanelle up the hall after catching sight of her. I didn't know why. She looked to be out of his league, but I guess he figured that if she was subbing for ninety bucks a day, then the hundred and twenty per day he earned might be impressive.

Now here he was acting as if he knew what he was doing. "So, all you have to really do is get through the afternoon. I talked to Ms. Lancaster. She's the media specialist and she wants you to bring them down to the library once they come back from lunch, then—"

I cut him off. "Thanks, man, I got it." His face showed disgust. I extended my hand to Lanelle. As we shook I looked directly into her eyes. They were light brown, not quite hazel, but lovely nonetheless. She wore her hair in a long ponytail that hung down over her shoulders and rested on her breast. I paid special attention to her bronze lipstick. I loved it because it matched her skin color so closely.

She was about five-foot-three and her body was lean up top, but she had hips for days and a nice ass on her. Looking into her face, I found myself thinking that she had the kind of beauty that had probably hung around since grade school. That's saying a lot because every cute kid doesn't grow up to be an attractive adult. Lanelle though, she looked like she'd always been beautiful.

I proceeded to explain to her where everything was and gave her the list of the spelling words, because we gave a spelling test on Fridays. Mrs. Whitmore had gotten ill before it had been time to give it. I began to flip through her sub folder and didn't see her updated sub plans. She hardly ever missed a day, which, I figured, was the reason they were so poorly done. She never figured she'd need them. "When you give them the test, make sure they keep their eyes on their *own* papers."

"I'll do my best," Lanelle said with a straight face.

"I'm serious. These little jokers will cheat their tails off."

She laughed.

I looked over at Grump, who seemed like he wasn't planning to go anywhere. I recognized that he wasn't going to waste any time trying to put his bid in, so I said, "Mrs. Harris . . . is it Miss or Mrs.?"

"It's Miss."

"Okay, well, come on over here with me. I'm going to give you some of the things out of my sub folder and also put a few things together in case you come back on Monday."

"Okay, great. Mrs. Knight told me that she wanted to talk to me about that after school."

I nodded and we left Grump sitting there looking stupid. Once we were in my room, I quickly ensured that she had a handle on what she needed to do workwise, then I casually asked a few questions.

She was dressed in a black cashmere sweater, some gray pin-striped slacks, and I could have sworn I'd seen Alicia in the same boots before—Gucci. She had an expensive-looking watch, so it had me wondering. What the hell was she doing subbing? Of course I didn't comment on that, but I did ask her what made her want to sub.

"That's a good question. I actually want to run a school, a charter school. Me and three of my sorority sisters are in the process of choosing a location. We already have a grant in place. We are going to take about nine months to put everything together so that we can open in the fall. I actually have a business background, but I decided last month to do some substitute teaching. I wanted to get in touch with the kids of today. No better place than to meet them in their educational setting."

I was blown away and instantly I was no longer worried about her falling for Grump. Now I was worried about whether or not she'd be interested in a guy like myself. "That sounds really deep."

"What about you? What are your plans for the future?" she asked, as if my teaching job wasn't a career. I immediately thought to myself, *Bitch, ain't you got some nerve.*

I wasn't really sure, but it wasn't like the idea of doing something to make more money hadn't crossed my mind. But I didn't want to say that, so I told her, "Well, I'm in grad school. Getting my master's in child psychology. I want to become a school psychologist. There are not enough of *us* in that field to deal with *our* children. We need more than medication, ya know?" I offered. When I saw her eyebrows rise, I knew that I had her interested, so I figured just a little more wouldn't hurt. I'd just heard a cat in the barbershop say some impressive shit, so I decided that I could use it. "In addition, I'm putting together a consortium. Trying to buy a couple of apartment buildings in some depressed areas of the city."

"Now, that's a great idea. I own a couple myself. It's a lot of work at times, but worth it." She looked at her watch. "What time do we pick the kids up from lunch?"

I looked at the clock and said, "Shit. We gotta go."

She scurried out in front of me and I watched her hips sway back and forth in slow motion as she moved with the grace of Tyra on the runway. I wanted to fuck her for certain. I wondered if I would ever change. Why couldn't I look at a woman like this and see quality? Why couldn't I see that she was girlfriend or wife worthy?

I thought again about the words of the old man: *Get your own woman, one that ain't got no boyfriend, no husband, and slow down.* With that I took my eyes off of her ass and decided to respect her. I didn't know if she had a man, but I knew she didn't have a husband and that, at least, was a start.

This was the fifth e-mail and Jacob was tired of living his life on edge trying to figure out how far the girl was going to go. As far as it looked, Anna was fine now that Dean was gone. He even began to wonder if a rape had actually occurred. He sat at his desk reading another love letter. Each letter had gotten more bold. This one had been sent at two-thirty in the morning. He'd read it three times already.

Jacob,

I've been lying in this bed thinking about you for the last couple hours and I can't take it anymore. I can't wait until the time is right for me and you to be together. I'm just not sure that you can handle it yet. I know in time you'll be so happy with me. It's so hard watching you, knowing I can't have you yet. Believe me, though, when the time comes, we'll be together. I promise that I'll please you like you've never been pleased before. I'll swallow every drop of your love, make you shiver and moan. You might even cry like a baby. I'll give you every part of me. I'm tired of little boys. I need a real man. Jacob, I need you. I'm about to play with my pussy and cum while I imagine your handsome face between my thighs. And when I climb on top of you, I'll be the one hitting the high notes just for you.

> Until then,
> mocha2munch@yahoo.com

Now that the kids were gone, he replayed the entire day. As usual, Anna had sat in front of him and her constant glares had made him uncomfortable. But the letters were too much. This time it made him hard. Even imagining Anna's crazy ass at home typing them couldn't keep him from getting excited.

He hit the print button, grabbed the letter from the tray, and packed his things up to head for home. He had a date tonight. He was taking Kendra out to dinner and to the movies to see *The Gospel.* Things between the two of them hadn't gotten to the point where they'd be categorized as serious. The distance between their apartments kept them apart except on weekends, and because of it, they surprisingly hadn't had sex yet. Not that Jacob hadn't wanted to take it to that level with her, but a period here and a broken date there, and here they were, a couple on the verge. Tonight, though, Jacob had sex on the brain. He didn't want to admit it might have been the letters, but deep down inside he knew that it was.

Kendra dialed his house from her cell right around the time she was supposed to show up. Jacob figured she needed directions as usual when he saw her number on the caller ID. "You lost again," he said gregariously.

"Nah, nigga. Open the door."

He looked out of his window and saw her car. "Hold up. I just got out the shower. I don't have on any clothes."

"I'm not trying to hear it. It's cold out here." It was still wet from a rainstorm earlier that afternoon and a cold front had come in. "Let me in and then go put your clothes on."

"Okay." He sped down the steps in his towel and opened up the front door.

When he looked out at Kendra his jaw dropped. She stood there on his front porch. There was no trench coat. Instead, in the middle of November, in forty-five-degree, damp weather, this girl was clad only in a pink lace bra and matching lace boy-shorts.

Her nipples were rock hard from the cold, and as she stepped past him he struggled to regain his composure. He glanced around to see if any of his neighbors had seen her. Not a soul appeared to be paying attention, but as soon as he closed his door the headlights in a strange car, just across the lot, came on and the vehicle screeched out into the street.

"Oh, now that's better," Kendra said. She placed the shopping bag that she was carrying on the floor. "So are you just gonna stare, or are you gonna hug me?"

Jacob wasted no time giving her a hug. Then he found her lips. As their lips began to lock, their hands began to explore each other. Her skin was still cold from standing outside. His warmth comforted her as well as turned her on. She rubbed his chest, which was still moist from the shower. He didn't know it, but this was her first time with a man in almost three years, so her responses were even more heightened. She had been in a relationship with another female and hadn't considered being with anyone else during that time. After going through the same changes with her domineering mate as she had experienced with men, Kendra had decided it wasn't worth it. She was ready to try a "normal" relationship. She wanted a family and someone whom she could build a future with.

Jacob fit the bill. He was smart, talented, handsome, and they had so many of the same interests. It hadn't taken her too long to realize that he was the one for her. Now she was ready to give herself to him totally. Her hand reached his waist and yanked his towel. As it fell to the floor Kendra found herself with a handful of his manhood. Instinctively, she began to pull on it, trying to make it come to full attention.

"Uhhh," he moaned. Her hand warmed up quickly and he was ready to take her right there. He backed away to take her in. Her cinnamon-colored skin, her firm, perky breasts, and her doe-shaped eyes all made her look the part of some tempting seductress. She looked like something he'd seen on the Internet. Their eyes were locked on each other as she continued to stroke him.

"Nice," she said as she held him in her hand. He was at full attention now and she was pleased with what she saw and felt. He wasn't small, but he wasn't going to kill her either, and she was happy about that. The idea of being pounded by a Mandingo had never appealed to her. In truth, the whole idea of sex never really got her wound up. She was into Jacob, though, as a man and that was what provided the potential for her reaching unimaginable heights of ecstasy. "What do you want me to do?" she whispered.

"Huh?"

"Do you want me to suck it?"

Unaccustomed to being asked, Jacob was stunned. It was all he could do to avoid sounding goofy as he said, "Yeah, please do."

"Come here." Kendra led him up the steps, past his living room, and took a seat in one of his dining-room chairs. He made his way toward her and she reached for him. She kissed his belly twice and then swirled her tongue in his navel. Her next move sent a sensation from his head to his toes. Jacob looked down and saw her head completely covering his manhood and felt her tonsils tickling the tip of his penis.

She proceeded to give him the blow job of his life, slobbering heavily all over his shaft as she jerked him off. She kissed the tip and licked the underside until he felt like he was about to lose control.

Jacob closed his eyes and enjoyed the ride she was taking him on. Kendra sensed that he was about to cum and pulled her mouth away. She would gladly finish him off, but she wanted to feel him inside of her first.

She stood up and leaned up against the table. They began to kiss passionately as Jacob reached his fingertips into the cups of her bra. He pulled her nipples out and began to lick them. She moaned and sucked air through her clenched teeth.

He kissed her neck and unhooked her bra expertly. She didn't wait for him as she yanked her panties down to her ankles and stepped out of them. Then she turned her back to him and leaned her upper body onto his dining-room table. It was a move she'd done a hundred times, but usually before her girlfriend dove into her with a strap-on.

"Come on," she whispered. "Put it in."

"But I don't have—"

"C'mon, Jacob. Fuck me now," she insisted.

Hard dick, wet, inviting pussy a foot away, and Jacob eased up to her like a mummy in a trance and placed the head of his dick at her entrance. She was tight and he had to push past the opening.

"Awwww, ahhhhh, owwwwssssshhhhh," she murmured. "C'mon, push it in."

By the time she finished, he'd sliced into Kendra and slammed his dick all the way in, eliciting a grunt that made him wonder if he had the wrong hole. Then, instinctively, he began to move slower until he found a rhythm that brought the most response from her. She seemed to like his pounding her in short rapid strokes.

He looked down at her back and her round ass as he stroked her. "Fuck me. Fuck me," she cried out. He responded by hitting it even harder. He stroked and banged repeatedly with all his might until everything seemed to become a blur. He lost track of time and space and relished the fact that he had his dick inside of Elise's tight young pussy.

"Fuck me, Mr. Marsh," she begged. "You feel so good."

Hearing this girl, who he'd stared at day in and day out for the past month, drove him over the edge. No longer could he deny what he'd tried to hide even to himself. He wanted one of his students. Now, as he caused his dining-room table to rock, he could feel her finally. Kendra's body, but Elise's spirit. With that realization, he felt the rush and came deep inside of her.

"Ohmigod," he cried out, and stumbled backward out of her body as some of his semen dripped out of her onto his carpet.

Kendra's breathing was still labored and he waited for her to stand. When she turned around he looked into her face, astonished. He'd actually imagined it was Elise. Kendra cracked a naughty smile, happy that she'd pleased him. Not knowing the half of it.

Jacob stood there, still in shock. Neither of them said a word, but Kendra approached him and was reaching out to kiss him when they both jumped as they heard a crash. Jacob looked to his left and saw the rock that had just been hurled through his window.

"What the hell . . . ?" Kendra asked, panting in fear, her eyes glued to the rock and glass that lay on the carpet.

Jacob's heart was beating so hard it felt like it might burst through his chest. He looked at her, shaking his head. He was silent for a moment as his mind searched for an explanation.

"I need to tell you something," he said, with some hesitation in his voice. "First, let me call the police."

It was over. He was going to the principal to confess the first thing Monday and he was about to do a practice run on Kendra.

(((14)))

Don't Push Me

Jacob lost his nerve when Monday morning came. After explaining the situation to Kendra, he'd got the feeling that she was a little turned off. He'd called her the entire weekend, at least fifteen times. Every single time, her voice mail picked up. Finally, late Sunday evening, she called him back.

"Yo, Jacob, I got to tell you, I really enjoyed the time that we've spent and I really, really respect your talent, but, dude, you got some serious issues on your plate right now. I'ma have to step back a little and let you handle whatever it is that you got going on. I just got out of a drama-filled relationship and I can't really see getting back into another situation."

Jacob was more shocked at how he felt than at her statement. He felt abandoned. He really did feel like they had a connection through the music, but she was walking away so easily that his head was spinning.

"Well, if that's how you feel, then I have to respect that . . ." He wanted to sound unbothered, but his voice gave him away. "I mean . . ."

"Thanks, Jacob. Take care of yourself," she said as if they'd never shared a moment or as if the sex had never happened.

When Monday came, Jacob walked into the building and headed straight for the principal's office, where he promptly lost his nerve. All he could think about was the disapproving look he was sure to receive and the repercussions that he would have to face.

As he made his way toward his classroom he began to swallow repeatedly. He then noticed that it was hard for him to breathe. As he passed colleague after colleague he felt warmer with each step. The school and his job were suffocating him, he felt. "Good morning, Mr. Marsh," one teacher said. Jacob forced a smile and said good morning back.

It was all he could muster. Finally, when he reached his classroom door, he felt a sense of relief. He had thirty minutes during which he could panic in peace. He had a tiny refrigerator near his desk where he kept his lunch. Grabbing a bottle of water and unscrewing the top, he realized that his hands were trembling.

He needed something to calm himself down. He sat down at his desk and placed his hands over his face and realized that he couldn't take it much longer. There was too much pressure already, with the band and the upcoming competition that he was due to start practicing for in two weeks. Now, with being stalked on top of the possible exposure of his involvement in a student's rape and a cover-up to boot, he was close to the edge.

Just like that, it came to him. He jumped up from his desk and headed across the school to the phys-ed department and found Willie Hargrove. Jacob and Willie had been cool for almost five years. The two never hung out other than at work, for the obvious reasons: Willie was the junior-varsity football and girls' basketball coach and a sports extremist. He respected the fact that Jacob won competitions, but not the fact that it was for the band.

Jacob enjoyed Willie's "I don't give a fuck" attitude about everything in life that you're supposed to give a fuck about—sometimes. Other times, he found it plain-out ignorant. When Jacob walked in, he found Willie at his desk eating out of a McDonald's bag.

"Jaaaycob. What's up, dawg?" he belted out in a deep voice that matched his face. Some of the other teachers called him "bowling ball" behind his back. Willie was big, round, and black like one of the balls you get from the alley when you don't have your own.

"Nuttin' much. Just trying to maintain." Jacob knew exactly why he'd come down to see Willie and it was just a matter of time before things fell into place.

"Me, too, bruh." Willie put the last of the food from his bag into his mouth. He then turned on his CD player behind him. Russ Par was on the air acting a fool. "He cracks me up in the morning. I miss the chick—Olivia. They were funny as hell."

"Yeah, they were." Just as Jacob was about to try to cut to the chase, Willie cut him short.

"Listen, you know me, man. I got like twenty minutes before those little bastards get here and I gots to get my head right. Ya feel me?"

"Willie, you know something? I might join you today, with all the stress I been under." Jacob had long known that it was part of Willie's daily ritual to get himself a nice buzz. He was high off of something when school started nearly every morning, and was usually high when the day ended as well.

A look of someone who was pleasantly surprised appeared on Willie's mug. "Well, come on wit' it, then."

He stood up and headed to the showers on the other side of the locker room and Jacob followed the mammoth-size brother. When he reached the last locker he pulled a ring of keys from his pocket and opened the lock. He pulled a small backpack and looked around as if he was being watched by the FBI.

"Here we go," Willie said. He sat on a bench and pulled out a bottle of Seagram's gin and two Styrofoam cups, and began to pour. He handed Jacob a cup and said, "Listen, if this is too strong, I have some orange juice."

Wanting to get the full effect of the alcohol, Jacob replied, "Nope, I'm okay." Then he surprised Willie once again by taking the cup straight to the head and turning it up until he downed a full shot.

"My, man." The big fellow laughed deep and hard. "You better pace yourself if you want to make it to lunchtime."

"I got this," Jacob shot back. "Hit me again."

His second cup was filled a third of the way. Jacob took small sips. As he began to feel the effects Willie looked at his watch and then moved swiftly over to the showers. He turned on the shower and in a matter of moments steam began to rise. Willie walked back over to the bag and grabbed a film capsule from inside and popped the lid. He pulled out a joint and lifted it to Jacob. "Grade A, the sticky, my bruh."

Eyebrows raised, Jacob couldn't believe that his crazy ass was about to smoke reefer inside of the gym. "Man, are you serious?"

"Yeah, man. I smoke in the shower. The steam kills the smell and keeps it from getting in your clothes. Plus the smoke doesn't irritate your eyes, so they won't get red or puffy." Jacob stared in disbelief. Willie went on: "You ever smelled weed on me before?"

"Nah, I can't say that I have."

"Well, I get high every day, sometimes twice a day, right here. So what you wanna do? You know I wouldn't let you get in trouble."

Jacob wasn't really into smoking, but he recalled the stress he was under and thought what the hell. Maybe he'd get fired and the whole problem would disappear. The only problem was that his reputation would be ruined. He watched his drinking partner head to the shower, and against his own better judgment, he followed.

They stood in the rear of the shower, passing the weed back and forth. Three minutes and the joint was done. Jacob stepped out of the shower feeling buzzed, high, and ready to take on the world, or at least the students.

"Thanks, man, I really appreciate it," he said to Willie.

"Don't worry about it. Anytime," Willie said, voice a couple octaves lower. "Hold on, before you step." He held up a finger as he looked through his bag once more. He pulled out a can of spray. Willie rolled up on Jacob and sprayed his upper body with a body spray. It smelled like something a woman would wear.

"What's this?"

"Body spray, from Bath & Body Works. It smells good, huh?"

Jacob nodded. It did. Reminded him of pears and apples. "It's nice."

"Oh yeah, women love it on a man. You'll see."

Jacob thought Willie's comment over for a second. As much as people talked about his size, no one had ever said he was funky.

"Peace, I'm out," Jacob said, slurring his speech. Willie tossed him a pack of spearmint Life Savers, which he caught and popped open with the quickness before bopping out of the room.

As Jacob moved back toward his room he thought about how relaxed he felt. In fact, the more he walked, the less he thought, period. Everything was suddenly all good.

He breezed through first period, putting on a film and having the kids write. He had forgotten that he had scheduled a test, but not one student reminded him.

When second period came around he was still mellow from the liquor, but still sharp enough to recall the rock coming through his window. When Anna came through the door he gave her a look that displayed his anger until she'd taken a seat. Her face frowned up and she looked as if she wanted to say something to him.

Then Elise came in, and when he looked at her, he recalled everything that had happened over the weekend, especially the sexual encounter she'd invaded. She offered a smile without showing any teeth and Jacob had a hard time not taking it as sexy.

He remembered the test. "Elise, can you pass these out for me?"

Without a word, she got out of her seat and moved toward him. It was a cool morning and Jacob took notice of the fact that Elise had on a sweater that kept riding up on her belly button. He also noticed that she had a ring in her belly button. Then his eyes scanned over her entire body. She had on a tight pair of Seven jeans, and as she began to move up and down the aisles he likened her ass to a heart-shaped box of chocolates. "Damn," he said.

The students all looked up in surprise. It was at that moment that he realized that he had spoken out loud. "Excuse me, class. I poked myself." They went back to work and heads went down, all except Anna, who'd watch his eyes filled with lust as he'd spoken. She knew exactly what had caused the outburst. When Jacob's eyes met hers, it was his turn to get the nasty look.

Each time he looked up from his papers, Jacob caught Anna staring at him. She was blowing his high, so finally he waved to her and called her over to him.

She stood up and walked over to him. "Yes?"

In a hushed tone he said, "Is there a problem? Every time I look up, your eyes are on me."

"No, there's no problem."

Jacob scratched his cheek and thought about the rock. He wanted to say, *Bitch, why are you stalking me, then?* But he knew he couldn't call her out without some proof. So he just stared at her for a second. He looked into her eyes. It might have been the first time he'd ever looked her in the eyes.

He felt an energy coming from her that he couldn't really put his finger on. The way her face went so easily from any expression of joy into an anguished look told him that she was pained but resilient. Even so, she was pretty, though probably nowhere near as pretty as she would be when she finally blossomed into adulthood. With the girlish charm she possessed, Anna never seemed aware of her assets.

In spite of it all, she was acting out and Jacob felt that she was trying to reach him. Whether it was the weed, the liquor, or both, he was reading something from her finally that he hadn't been able to read before. She was definitely crying out for help. That had to be why she had thrown the rock, and why she had shown up at his door that night.

As far as the e-mails went, Jacob summed it up as one simple thing. In addition to all that he suspected he knew, she was also probably oversexed and definitely wicked.

Once she went back to her seat and finished the test, Jacob checked his e-mails. Like clockwork, another message from mocha2munch, but he waited to read it. When he dismissed the class he saw Anna whispering in Elise's ear, probably telling what she knew of his earlier gaze. But the one key thing that was different today was that Jacob didn't give a fuck.

A few minutes after class was dismissed, Elise walked back into the classroom and Jacob didn't notice her standing there. It was his planning period and he had planned to make a few phone calls. But before he could get to the calls, his eyes had been glued to his monitor reading his latest e-mails. He noticed another one from his admirer. It proved to be just as sexually charged as the previous one, and because of it, Jacob had made a tent out of his pants.

Jacob,
The time is almost here. I can tell that you're longing for what I'm going to give you so willingly. You need to stop looking for love in all the wrong places. I was trying to be patient until the perfect time, but I can tell you can't wait. You need me now. You need my warm body next to yours at night. You need to smell it before you go to sleep at night. You need my hot, tight pussy wrapped around your dick. I can't wait to feel you inside me. I want you to fuck me like you've never fucked anyone before. Then I want you to sing to me like you sang to that bitch.
I know she's fucking you, but I'll fuck you better. She can watch if

you want. If she does she'd probably go out of her mind watching the
way I swallow you up, and when you fuck me from behind it would be
over, that's my spot. I'm a screamer and a creamer.

Almost time,

mocha2munch@yahoo.com

By the time Jacob finished reading the e-mail, he needed to adjust
himself in his underwear. The messages had gotten progressively
more explicit each time. Elise watched as he reached into his pants
and grabbed his dick. He didn't play with it, only shifted it so it
wouldn't press against his zipper.

Showing a part of her personality Jacob had never seen before,
Elise cracked a joke. "Am I disturbing something here, Mr. Marsh?"

Jacob jumped and turned quickly. In a scramble he turned off
his monitor and said, "What are you doing in here sneaking up on
me like that . . . aren't you supposed to be in class?" He was rambling and embarrassed, wondering how much she'd seen. Then he
realized that she must have seen his hands in his pants or she
wouldn't have made the comment.

"I'm not sneaking up on you, Mr. Marsh. I need to speak to you.
I actually have an early departure today. I have a doctor's appointment. But I felt like I should come past here and talk to you before
I leave. It's kind of awkward but important. I really didn't have anyone to talk to, so I began talking to Anna about my life. I mean, I
really let her into my world, which I've always kept private, and in
return she opened up and shared some things with me. To keep it
real with you, Mr. Marsh . . . she's told me some things that sort of
have me confused and worried. *Some* of them are about you."

Jacob's face showed concern. "What sort of things?"

"Too many to rush through, and I really don't think this is the place. But listen, I work at a hair salon up in College Park. I get off tonight at around six or six-thirty. If you're free you could meet me at the Starbucks. It's in the same shopping center as the Home Depot."

"I know where it is."

"So how about seven?" Jacob didn't respond. "Here, call me if you can't make it. This is my cell." Elise handed him a card. It had her name on it and said *All Things Braids by Elise* on it.

"So you do hair, huh?"

"A girl has got to pay the bills somehow."

"*Bills?*" Jacob said sarcastically. He was thinking that the young girl had no idea what bills were.

"So I'll see you later." Jacob was silent and she asked, "Are you okay, Mr. Marsh?"

"Yeah . . ." He cleared his throat and continued. "I'm fine."

Her face showed a hint of suspicion. "Well, if I ain't know any better, I'da thought you was high or something. You seem a bit off today," she said, giggling, and headed for the door. When she reached it she turned back. "I'll let you get back to what you were doing."

Jacob's eyes went down to the card. He placed it in his pocket and then he thought about some of the possibilities of Anna and Elise's conversation. His stomach began to grumble and he put his hands over his face. Three minutes later, he was asleep, drooling out of the corner of his mouth onto his desk calendar.

15

Who Knows Where This Could Go?

The intercom buzzed. Mrs. Holiday, the school secretary, said, "Mr. Christian, can you take a phone call? It's an emergency—your brother." I was just finishing up my reading groups but hurried from the circle of children when I heard her.

"Kids, I'll be right back," I said in a rush. My brother seldom called my job, so to hear he had an emergency scared me. I immediately thought of my parents. They both lived alone, had been divorced for twenty years, and both suffered from high blood pressure.

I moved briskly up the hallway toward the teachers' lounge. "Hey, what's up?" I said, barely getting the phone to my mouth before I got the words out.

"Listen," Lee said. I could tell he was panicked. "If Nicole calls you or comes to your job . . ."

"Why would she come to my—"

"Diego, be quiet. I need you to listen. If she comes to your job before I get there, or calls you, I need you to tell her that I stayed at your place last night."

I didn't understand at all. "Lee, what's going on?"

"I don't have time to explain. But I need to come by to get your keys and I may need to crash at your place on the couch for a night or two."

"Yeah, okay."

"And another thing . . ." He paused. "Never mind. Just leave the keys in the office for me if you could. I'll be at your place when you get there after school."

"Okay."

I was about to head out of the lounge when the intercom buzzer went off. Again it was Mrs. Holiday. "Mr. Christian? Are you in the lounge?"

I hit the call button. "Yes, I was headed back to my room right now."

"Well, you have another call on eighty-five."

"Okay." I picked up the line and said, "Hello."

"Well, sir, I can say that it hasn't been easy tracking you down."

I was ready for Nicole's overbearing attitude. She had it twisted if she thought she was going to berate me the way she did my brother. "Listen, I'm in the middle of teaching and I have to get back to work. What do you need?"

"Excuse me. Do I have the right person? The man I met would surely have more manners than this."

I didn't recognize the voice. "Who is this?"

"This is Jonetta. Jonetta Cleveland. We met at the Black Caucus event."

I immediately felt embarrassed by the way I'd spoken to her. "Oh wow, I'm sorry. I thought you were my sister-in-law. I am really sorry about that."

"Oh, that's okay. I didn't mean to disturb you on your job. I tried you on your cell phone, but it was disconnected—nonworking or something."

I thought about my changing the number after the Kenard and Erin situation. "Yeah, I have a new one. But how's everything with you?"

I could hear her smiling through the line as she replied, "Oh, Diego, everything is absolutely fabulous. Stellar, in fact. I have some really great news."

"I'd love to hear it, but can I call you back on my lunch break?"

"Absolutely. Take my number. Be sure to call me back because I have something to propose to you."

Propose, I thought. I was hoping she hadn't left her husband when I heard that. "Will do."

Thirty minutes later I was leaving the school for my lunch break. As I pulled out of the lot I saw my brother's car stopped on the corner and there were two police cars behind him, lights flashing. I immediately pulled over and saw that he was no longer in the vehicle. When I looked closer and saw the guns drawn, I put my car in park and jumped out. "Officer," I yelled. "I'm a schoolteacher at that school right there. That's my brother."

I was greeted with "Put your hands up. Don't move. Don't move or I'll shoot."

In shock, I threw my hands in the air. "I teach right here at Ridgewood. I teach second grade."

"Shut your mouth," the officer said. "Slowly turn around and put your hands on the vehicle."

Two officers ran up beside me. In a matter of seconds, three more squad cars pulled up. "Lee, you all right over there?"

I felt a firm grip land on the back of my neck. Next, my head was forcefully slammed down to the hood of my car. "Shut your mouth." They began rummaging through my pockets and then my hands were placed in string restraints.

"What's going on, Officer?"

Things were quiet for a minute and then a fourth car pulled up. It was unmarked. The officers helped a man out of the backseat and then stood my brother up. They whispered something into the man's ear and he shook his head. Then I heard one of the officers ask, "Are you certain?"

The man shook his head no and said, "There's no way that's him. He's much too tall and not dark enough."

The officer whispered again and then turned to Lee and said, "State your name, sir, then your address and the make and model of your vehicle."

My brother seemed shaken and said, "My name is Lee Christian, I live at—"

The man interjected again. "No, that's not him. Sounds nothing like him." Five minutes later, after checking IDs and taking information, the police officers had the nerve to apologize before releasing us.

"Mr. Christian, the person we're attempting to apprehend is a very dangerous sociopath and we know he's armed. This person just robbed the Bank of Maryland across the street and we believe he's in, or was just in, the vicinity. We really apologize for the rigid behavior, but we have to be very aggressive in our efforts to catch him. He was seen fleeing in the direction of this neighborhood. We believe that he might be parking his car near here and fleeing the scene of the crimes on foot."

He then handed me a business card and continued: "If you see any suspicious vehicles parked in this neighborhood, please, don't hesitate to call."

I looked over at Lee, who was dusting his clothes off after being pinned on the ground. "I don't believe this crap," he mumbled. The two officers who remained looked over at him like he was crazy.

I nodded and tucked away the card. When they pulled off I walked over to Lee. His lip was swollen and bleeding and his eye looked as if he'd been hit with a bag of nickels. "Whoa," I said when I took a closer look. "Man, they beat the hell out of you. Did you resist arrest?"

He wiped his mouth. "Just let me get the keys."

"I think you need to go to the hospital. Get your face checked out."

"I'm fine. I just need some rest."

As I was about to hand him the keys I heard tires screeching to a halt and right behind me was his wife, Nicole. She jumped out of her car as if she was on a warpath. "Is this what you do, huh, Lee? Run out on your wife with the first problem?"

"The first problem? Are you kidding me?"

"What are you doing here? Trying to get your brother to cover your lies?"

"I . . . was . . . um, bringing him his keys back. That's all." I was surprised to hear the lie come off of his lips, though he didn't sound smooth at all.

"So, you need to bring your tail on home. Right now. We have some things to discuss."

"I'm not ready to come home."

When he said this, Nicole's face twisted so bad that I feared her head was about to spin around. "Who is the bitch?" she yelled. "Who?" She proceeded to march up to him.

"Listen," he said. "I'm not going through this in front of my brother. Come on, I'll go home."

"Ride with me," she ordered. "We'll come back later for your car." I couldn't believe the scene as it unfolded. He didn't even argue. He locked his car and climbed in with her. She didn't even so much as mention that he was bleeding and she didn't seem concerned.

When they pulled off I stood there in disbelief and hungry. Because my lunch break was nearly over, I turned around and headed back toward the school. As I headed through the doors, I was glad that no one had seen me or my brother pinned down like two criminals. Or so I thought.

"Yo, Diego, what's popping?" Grump was standing at the doors of the steps when I breezed in. He had a KFC bag in his hand. "Everything cool?"

"Yeah, everything's cool." If he'd seen me, then he'd have to bring it up. I walked by him and headed up the steps. As I cleared the first flight he yelled up, "You want some chicken? I got enough for Miss Thang, but she said she was having a salad. I can't stand them salad-eating bitches."

"You talking about Lanelle?"

"Who else? I know you wanna hit that, too."

"Nah, I'm chilling right now."

"Yeah, right." He laughed. "So you want some chicken?"

"Okay, cool."

"I'll have one of the kids run it up. I have to take out my platter."

"All right, whatever."

As I made my way back to my room I peeked into Mrs. Whitmore's classroom to see what Lanelle was up to. She had been asked to stay on as a long-term sub. I can't lie and say I wasn't happy about it. I was still laying back, not wanting to come off too eager to get all up in her face. Didn't want to seem like I did that all the time. Workplace romances can get really tricky if you don't navigate them. They are one situation where a brother has to be friends with a sistah. After the sex, if there's no continued romance, there has to be somewhere or something to retreat to. The friend zone is that somewhere. Otherwise things tend to get real funky.

She was at the board writing, trying to stay on top of the lessons that we'd been instructed to give. I watched her for a moment. I realized that I was witnessing a sight that very few men ever got a chance to appreciate. Watching a woman write on a chalkboard, arms extended, back arched, breasts jiggling, and oftentimes ass wiggling back and forth. When she looked out the corner of her eye and saw me, I didn't even move away. Instead, I just smiled and she smiled back. For a moment, I'd forgotten the ordeal with the police. Then my hunger pains brought it rushing right back.

When the sixth grader came through the door to my room with the box of KFC, I was all too happy. I had five minutes to eat it. I wolfed it down and got ready for recess. Then I dragged through the rest of the day, thinking about the police and how they'd beat my brother down. I understood that they were in the flow of duty, but the force had been excessive. I was going to call him and urge him to file a report. There might be some money in it, and the more I thought about it, the more traumatized I felt. When the final bell rang and the kids were dismissed, I walked them out of the building then ducked back in my room. I was about to dial Lee when I realized that I'd forgotten to return Jonetta's call.

I pulled up her number and hit the send button. She answered and sounded really happy to be hearing from me. "Diego, Diego, Diego, I've been waiting for your call."

"I've had quite a day."

"I believe you. Molding young minds is quite a challenge, I assume," she said.

"Among other things. But how's everything going and what is the news you wanted to share with me?"

"Well, both things are actually related." She cleared her throat. "You know, Diego, you saved my marriage."

I thought back to the night we met and how it ended. "No way."

"Yes, you did . . . and before I go any further, I want to thank you for all you said to me that night. I needed to hear everything you said. I don't know, you just really spoke to my heart and helped me come to some really good realizations about my attitudes . . . how detrimental they were to my marriage. I actually went home and found a way to talk to my husband, a way where we were able to receive one another. I humbled myself for the first time in a long time, and because of that he was able to express his fears and still feel like a man. Like you said, I offered him some support instead of tearing him down."

I listened to her and tried to remember any of what I'd said.

When I couldn't I just listened some more. "Well, I'm glad I could help you." I was. After all the home wrecking I'd done, it was good to be on the positive side of that.

"Well, that's not the only good news. Last month I took the position as editor in chief of *Girl Talk* magazine. You've heard of it?"

"Of course, that's the one where you bash the men like it's nobody's business." I laughed.

"No, Diego. Not at all. It's about empowerment and sharing. A lot like *Essence,* only we take the gloves off a little more and share some of the things that might not get talked about otherwise."

"I see. Well, congratulations are in order."

"Well, not just for me. For yourself as well."

I was puzzled. "Why is that?"

"Because, sir, you are going to write my brand-new advice column."

"You've got to be kidding."

"Why would I be? Let me tell you this. It's damn near impossible to get me to take anyone's advice that I'm not paying one-fifty an hour for, but you, my friend, obviously have a gift."

"At what?" I laughed.

She paused. "Anyone can give advice and be preachy, but, Diego, it takes something special to get the ladies to listen up. I know I'm not the first sistah you've moved or wooed with your ability to listen and then say exactly what needs to be said, now, am I?"

I paused for a second and I thought first of Alicia, then the others. Then it dawned on me, that's how I'd always gotten them to give me what I wanted. I listened first; they listened second. "I guess not," I replied.

"Good, then it's settled. Give me your info. I'll send you a contract, and some time in the next few days, you'll have to come to New York to go over the specifics. We gotta move fast. Shouldn't take but a day or two. Can you get the time off work at the school?"

I was taken totally off guard, but I answered, "I guess so."

"Great, so you're okay with this. I want your column to debut in the January 2006 issue. It's gonna be great. There's nothing quite like this in any other publication. You know what makes women tick and you also share the deepest secrets and fears that men have. The key is that you give it to them raw."

"So, let me ask: Do I get paid for this?"

"Of course. It pays a little something, maybe a grand a month, but it'll be great. You'll get paid for doing something you do for free and do well."

"Wow" was all I could say. A column in a national magazine and an extra grand per month on top of my teacher's salary was all good. I could live with that.

"So the only question is, what are we going to call the column?" she said, sounding really giddy.

I paused for a quick second, and as the whole idea of me doing this set in, it came to me just like that.

16

Sweet Thing

Girl Talk magazine sent me a confirmation e-mail that they were going to put me up in the Omni Berkshire Place in midtown. I had no idea where it was exactly, but it sounded really nice. When I at looked the pictures of the hotel on the Internet, I was impressed; when I saw what they charged for a room, I almost shit my pants. One night was almost four hundred dollars, which was close to half the monthly mortgage on my duplex.

I sat at my desk looking at the e-mail over and over. There was no denying that my chest was poking out. I was finally the *somebody* I'd longed to be. This huge magazine was actually giving me a column and paying for me to come to the Big Apple. It wasn't like I didn't feel rewarded teaching the little ones, or special because of my ability to reach them. But to be honest, I felt ordinary most of the time in that classroom, no matter how many kudos I received from my colleagues and parents.

My eyes kept going over the screen until finally I was convinced that I was indeed headed for New York City to sign a contract and iron out the particulars of my column. I didn't even realize that I was smiling at the screen like a maniac until I looked up to see Lanelle almost at my desk. "I hope that's not porn," she joked.

"Hey," I said. "Nope, not this time."

"Hey to you." She was wearing a grin that showcased her dimples. I noticed the deep bronze lipstick framing her smile. "Listen, I wanted to ask you a question about this huge test that we have to give in two weeks. I got a bulletin about a workshop that they are giving. I was wondering if you think I should enroll so that I'll know what I'm doing."

"Nah, don't waste your time. I'll walk you through it. It's just some more of the residuals of Bush's No Child Left Behind bullshit. Too much testing, not enough teaching."

"Oh, so I see you have an opinion on it."

"Hell yeah. You'll see. Once you're in here . . . in the trenches long enough, you'll get pissed at some of the policies the boards and the bureaucrats hand down. They want big-budget results on no-budget investments. Not a one of 'em could last two days with most of the kids. Being asked to do the shit they think is so easy."

"I hear you."

"But enough of that. I'm in a good mood. I'm headed to New York City. I got something really big brewing."

"Hmm, sounds nice. I love New York."

"Really, you should come along. I leave on Sunday, be back Monday."

Her face showed surprise either at my invitation or at my nerve for inviting her. But I was on a roll, so I figured what the heck. "If I should go, where would I be staying?"

"At the Omni Berkshire Place."

"And where would *you* be staying?"

"The same."

"The same hotel, or the same room?"

I laughed. "I could request a double—or a cot."

She frowned. "I don't think so. Nice try, but usually a guy asks me out on a date first before he tries to get me in a hotel room."

I paused for a moment and realized that she just might be interested. I hadn't even worked my way up to prying into her business, but her response made it obvious to me that she didn't have a man, or one that she was serious about.

Even though my life had been hectic enough lately without romance, there were quite a few things about her that made me want to at least get to know her better. She was smart, definitely attractive, and ambitious. Not to mention the walk. The more I saw it, the more I loved it. She was slightly bowlegged but still managed to walk gracefully in her heels.

I couldn't say for sure at this point, but she seemed to have some decent morals. I would have loved to show her around New York, though I didn't know one street from the next. Something about the whole notion of wandering around the greatest city in the world seemed romantic and I could have laughed at myself for even thinking about it in that kind of way, mainly because I'd always been romantically deficient.

One thing was for sure: I didn't have the funds to spring for another room, so I came with "Well, I'll tell you what, Ms. Harris. As soon I get back, how about we hang out and have a drink or get a bite to eat?"

"I *hang* out with my homegirls. Is that what you want to do, *hang* out?"

Though she'd made what I'm sure she considered a stand, my grin showed nothing but confidence, because if she cared enough to even try, I had her already. "Let me correct myself and be a little more clear. How about I take you out on a date?"

"Well, I normally don't go out with anyone I work with. However, since this is a temporary assignment for me, I'll give it some thought. When you come back from New York, I'll give you my answer."

Playing hard to get almost pissed me off. "Fair enough." I laughed at her. "You let me know."

Jacob sat nervously in the rear of the coffee shop. He looked down at his watch and saw that it was almost seven-fifteen. She was late and he took it as a sign that he should go. He grabbed the cup of cocoa from the table and took what would be his last sip. He stood up, put his Norfolk State baseball cap on, and prepared to head out the door. As if fate was intervening, up to the front door walked a fine sistah, dressed in a purple-and-black, skintight Puma workout suit. She also sported a light jogging jacket that barely covered a third of an award-winning ass, which caught Jacob's eye. He scanned her up and down quickly before he realized the woman he was looking at he already knew well.

As they were about to pass each other she smiled. "Jacob, what's happening?" It was Alicia.

"Hey, Alicia. How you doin'?"

"I'm good. Just about to head to the gym."

"Oh, I didn't know you worked out."

"Jacob, come on now. I'm fast approaching the big three-oh. If the years don't get me, gravity will. I gots to keep it tight."

Jacob nodded. *Some kickboxing lessons might be good as well,* he thought as he remembered her getting slapped on her wedding day. "I feel you."

"So what are you doing out this way?" she asked.

"Just stopped in for a quick drink of . . . and I had to meet someone, but . . ." At that very second he saw Elise heading toward the entrance. "But it was nice seeing you. I gotta run . . . tell everyone I said hello . . ." Then, almost midsentence, he bolted in Elise's direction.

"Oh . . . kay, Jacob. It was nice seeing you," Alicia said, and then watched intently as he ushered what looked to be an extremely young girl out the door before she could make it in.

"**Change in plans,** you have a car, right?"

Elise was thrown off by the way Jacob was acting. "Yeah, why?"

"Just follow me," he said as he headed for his car.

He pulled off and she began to follow him in her gold Pontiac. He headed down Route 1, wondering were he was going, then down Greenbelt Road. He pulled into the parking lot of a Bennigan's, but panicked when he saw what looked like a familiar family walking across the parking lot. He needed someplace discreet.

He looked back and Elise was on his tail as he'd instructed. He thought about the library in Old Greenbelt, but reasoned it was too public. Kids from his school might show up there. Five minutes later, he had found a secluded location. They needed to talk and he couldn't take any chances on being seen.

He hit the button on his garage-door opener and signaled for Elise to drive by him and pull her car inside. As she pulled past him she smiled and his heart skipped a beat.

What the hell am I doing? he asked himself as he parked in front of his garage. He sat in the car for a moment thinking about what could possibly come of the situation. Still, he wanted to hear what she had to say, especially if she had some information that could change his whole life.

He climbed out of his car and looked around before he slipped into the garage. Once the garage door went down, he opened Elise's door for her. "Thanks, such a gentleman," she said, trying to cut the tension that they both felt building.

"C'mon." Jacob led her in through the garage door then to the small rec room behind the garage. There was thick beige carpet and a butterscotch-colored couch and chair in the room. When Jacob offered Elise a seat on the couch, she sank into it and couldn't help but let out a telling "Ahhhhhhh."

"Comfy, right?" Jacob asked.

"Oh my gawwd, it feels so soft. I love it. Your place is really nice. Who painted?"

"I did. Actually, a friend of mine helped out, but I didn't hire anyone." Jacob's walls were all toffee-colored except for one wall, which was done in bronze suede paint. "It was time-consuming, but I like it."

"Yeah, it's really nice. I did something similar in my place. I didn't have anyone to help, though." She smiled yet sounded as if he should have pitied her.

"Your place?"

"Yeah, Mr. Marsh, I have my own place. That's one of the things that I wanted to talk to you about. I just didn't have anyone else that I could come to."

Jacob took a seat at the opposite end of the couch and looked into Elise's eyes. "Listen, I want to say something . . ." He paused.

"It's okay, Mr. Marsh . . ."

"What's okay?" He had no idea what she was talking about.

An understanding look appeared on her face. "Mr. Marsh, I know you want me. It's okay. It's normal."

"Say what?" Jacob's heart began to beat faster. Had it been that obvious? Even if it had become obvious, he would have never re-acted or told a soul. But now here this young lady was in his house, laying it all out on the table.

"I may be young, but I've seen a lot in my years. You're a man. I'm a woman. I can feel it and I'm not offended by it and I don't think you're a pervert. Without even talking to you, I've felt a cer-tain energy between us. Maybe you just wanna fuck me. Then again, maybe you wish you could get to know me better. Maybe you lie awake some nights wishing that I was older or that we'd met under different circumstances."

Jacob's silence affirmed everything she said and he just shook his head and looked down. She reached for his hands. "Mr. Marsh, it's okay. Seriously. But that's not what I came to talk about. I'm not try-ing to complicate your life. Actually, I'm here to help you if I can."

He looked back up. His voice was now shaken. "Help me?"

"Yeah, but you got to let me take it from the top."

Jacob nodded and Elise leaned back. Then she asked, "Do you have anything to drink?"

"Yeah, I've got Sprite, apple juice, and maybe some iced tea."

"Can I help myself?" she asked as she stood up.

Puzzled as to why she wanted to get it herself, he still said, "Sure."

A few minutes later, she walked back down the steps with two wineglasses and a half bottle of Joel Gott Zinfandel. "I took a sip upstairs. It was delicious, so I hope you don't mind. We're both uptight and could use a sip. Wouldn't you agree?"

Jacob was ready to laugh at himself now. "Sure, why not? I have a minor in my home; one of my students, no less. Of course I want to give her some Jesus juice like Michael Jackson. Next, I'll break out the porno."

She laughed. "That's funny as hell. But don't sleep. I might like that."

Jacob couldn't believe that he was actually laughing with this girl. There was something very womanly and mature about the way she carried herself. She didn't seem like a little girl trying to play grown. Instead, her demeanor seemed natural, as if she'd navigated herself in many an adult situation before. He accepted the glass of wine that she'd poured for him. He wondered if she'd like it. It wasn't your everyday bottle of wine.

"Nice," she said, taking another sip.

"So, Elise. Let's get down to it. Tell me what's on your mind. From the beginning, as you say." She was now fiddling with the remotes and in a matter of seconds she had his DirecTV on and tuned to the smooth R&B music channel. She took her seat and this time she kicked off her Indian tapestry boots. Jacob thought they were really cute on her. With her two braids, she had the whole Native American thing working overtime.

Anthony Hamilton was playing on the television. As she sipped

Elise began to sway her head back and forth to the beat. "All right, Mr. Marsh," she said as she killed the first glass and reached for the bottle. "You remember I told you I was from Indy?"

"Yeah."

"Well, I was in Indy, but that's not where I'm from originally. I lived in Baltimore most of my life—until I was thirteen actually. That's when my mom died of HIV. She was an intravenous drug user for years, but she did manage to get clean for the last four years of her life. She was good to me. She had a problem, but she did her best. I never knew my dad. When my mother passed, her sister sent for me. She lived in Indianapolis. At that point I had no choice but to go. I had begged her to let me stay with my best friend, Tiffany. Tiffany's mom had okayed it, but my aunt insisted I come. When I got to Indy, I realized real quick why she wanted me out there so badly."

Jacob was listening, already captivated by her tale. "Why was that?"

"She had three kids, all girls, and she needed a babysitter. From the day I got there, she tried to make me feel like she was doing me a favor, but one thing for sure, for all the things my mother did wrong, she didn't raise no fool. I became a cook, a cleaner, and I practically raised those kids for three years. The one good thing that came out of it, I became the best hair braider in Indy. By the time I turned sixteen, I was making five hundred on a slow week."

"Wow."

"Yeah, but how much of that do you think I got to keep? My aunt began hitting me up for money left and right. It got to the point that I would only do braids when she wasn't home so that she couldn't keep track of how much money I had."

"So how did you wind up here?"

"Tiffany. She brought me back."

"So you guys stayed in touch while you were gone."

"Actually, we didn't. Her mom got my aunt's number and called me one day." Elise's eyes began to tear up. "She called me to tell me that she had been doing really well and that they'd moved from Baltimore down to PG County once her job transferred her to a new store. She managed a Victoria's Secret store." Jacob was silent as he watched tears begin to roll down her cheeks. "She had bought Tiffany a car for her sixteenth birthday. A month later, Tiffany was in an accident on the parkway. She died, driving back from Baltimore, after going to visit her boyfriend. She fell asleep."

She took a minute to calm herself and her breathing back down. "I came out here for her funeral. I ended up staying with her mom for three weeks after that. It was like I was grieving my mom and Tiffany at the same time. We cried for two weeks straight, honestly, not a day went by. Her mother felt like I was the only one who could have possibly understood what she was going through. Then one day we stopped crying. We got in her car and drove to Indianapolis and packed all my belongings up. I told my aunt that I wanted out. I wanted a better life than I was going to get there taking care of her kids. Tiffany's mom—her name is Olivia—told me about a salon that she went to and that I should try to get a job there. The rest is history."

She then explained how Olivia helped her get an apartment. When Jacob asked why she didn't move in with Olivia, she explained that they both agreed that they needed their own space, and since Elise was making even more money doing braids here than in Indy, she could afford it. She was even mastering the art of sewing in weaves. It wouldn't be long before she was making a grand per week.

This was where the problem with Anna had come in. She explained how a simple friendly conversation had led Anna to claim her as her best friend. "Mr. Marsh, I think something is wrong with the girl. She shows up at my house unannounced and she falls asleep on my couch and just expects it to be okay that she spends the night. I was trying to be nice at first, but she's starting to get on my nerves. Anytime I even start to tell her about herself, she goes into a near rant. She claims that the whole world is against her."

"So what kinds of things has she said that disturbed you?"

"You mean about you?"

"Well . . . yes."

"She says that you hate her. At first she said you were like a father to her—no, she said a big brother. But after the rape, she must have disgusted you."

"She told you about that?"

"Yeah. She said that the guy she gave a ride home forced his way on her. That's how I found out that she was gay."

"What?" Jacob's eyebrows went up in the air.

"Yeah, she told me that she told your student teacher that she was gay. He was trying to make a move on her, but when she told him he went ballistic and forced himself on her."

Jacob was floored. Anna *gay*. It didn't make any sense, at least not to his theory of her being madly in love with him. "That doesn't make sense."

"Well, that's what she told me. She said that before I got here, she lost all her friends because someone had let the cat out of the bag . . . about her liking girls. She goes on and on about how I was sent here to help her and about how much she needs me. I think she's a little bitter with you. She said after the situation with the guy . . . Dean . . . she said you changed and that you two aren't really close anymore."

We were never close, Jacob thought as he shook his head.

"The thing that concerns me is that she thinks you had something to do with him raping her. Everything with her is a conspiracy."

With that, Jacob's heart sank. His worst fears were founded. He was definitely going down. "So . . . um . . . did she say that she was going to go to the school administrators about this?"

"Oh no. She said she wouldn't ever want this to get out. She feels ashamed about the whole thing. She can't wait for the school year to get out. She wants to go away to school on a scholarship and get far away from here as possible. She wants to go to school somewhere in Florida."

"Bethune Cookman, I know she mentioned it."

"Yep, that's it."

"So what else were you concerned about?"

"Well, it seems like she has sort of tried to move in. She said that she admires me so much. And I won't lie: I enjoy her company at times, but I get tired. School and working thirty hours a week isn't easy."

"I can imagine."

"The other night I came home from work. All I wanted to do was go to bed, especially since I had to get up at six in the morning and go right back to work. It was Friday night." Jacob nodded, listening. "Well, here she comes knocking on the door. I don't know why I just didn't tell her I was tired . . . Instead, I took my clothes off, wet my hair in the shower, and wrapped a towel around my body. I went to the door and opened it with the chain still on. She wanted to know why I had the chain on. I told her that I had company and that I'd talk to her the next day."

"Okay."

"I wish. This bitch . . ." she blurted out. Then she caught herself. "Excuse me for cursing, Mr. Marsh, but when I think about it I get upset."

"It's okay."

"Mr. Marsh, her ass starts crying and eventually banging on my door. She knocks off and on for at least forty-five minutes. The next morning I head out the door for work and she's in the parking lot, asleep in her car. She never even woke up."

Jacob found the whole thing unsettling. Anna's behavior was definitely unstable. "So what happened after that?"

"I didn't see her until Monday at school and she acted like nothing ever happened."

There was silence until Jacob stood and asked, "So what are you thinking? How does this all turn out?"

"I don't know. That's why I came to you. I don't have anyone to speak to. I didn't want to put her business out there. But I don't really want to deal with her. I was wondering if you can get me transferred out of your class."

Jacob swallowed hard. That was the last thing he wanted. "Yeah, sure."

"Okay. I only told you this because I wanted to . . . just let you know that she had me a little nervous."

"I appreciate it."

"I'd better be going," she said, standing now, facing Jacob. She was staring into his eyes and he back into hers. He thought about all she'd been through in her young life. All the courage that she'd shown. Her independence was incredible. "I'd appreciate it if you don't share this with anyone. Especially my living arrangements. I just want to graduate and then get my own salon as soon as I finish business school."

"No problem," he said as he closed his eyes for a second, imagining what it would be like to kiss her lips.

"Good night," she said.

A minute later and he watched her pull her car out. He shut his garage and entered the house. He turned off the lights and headed upstairs for a shower.

After watching Elise leave Jacob's, she stood at his door fighting with herself. She wanted so badly to knock and to be let in. She was tired of watching. She was ready to give him her sweetness. In her mind, the idea was planted as firm as a hundred-year-old oak. There was no way he wouldn't love it.

(((17)))

Ain't Too Proud to Beg

My column was a hit. It had gotten great response for the first month, with hundreds of letters coming in. For the February edition the response was even stronger as the bags of mail came in with over two thousand letters. We weren't taking any e-mails or faxes.

"Gotta separate the pretenders from the people who really want your help. Anyone will bang out an e-mail and hit send, but someone who takes the time to write or type a letter and mail it in this day and age is serious," Jonetta had said. She'd come up with the idea of calling me Dr. C., instead of using my real name, and I loved it. Reminded me a bit of Dr. Phil.

The magazine, *Girl Talk,* had gone through a total overhaul. A multimillion-dollar face-lift and advertising blitz had it placed everywhere you saw *Essence, Vibe,* and *Ebony.* The articles were given more of an edge. The topics were racier, more compelling; there was some exclusive celebrity gossip and interviews, and on top of that, my column was being pushed as a real sounding board for women. I was billed as the next big thing. After the editors read the responses I'd given to a few of the letters, I was given two full pages. The key was that my advice was real, not watered down. I was given the green light to trash any letters that didn't warrant real attention and instructed to give it to them raw.

Dear Dr. C.,

Recently I met a man who was everything that I have been looking for. He always lets me know that I'm on his mind with phone calls and the flowers he sends to my job. We have so much in common and yet our differences only serve to intrigue me more. Whenever we're together he always makes me feel so sexy and his passion for me is unbelievable. I haven't had a man make love to me like this since I was in high school. I want to be with him all the time and lately I have been thinking about trying to make a true commitment with this man.

The only problem is that I am married, for eleven years now, and most people, including my husband, think that I am happily so. Do you think I should give it all up to be with my lover? He has been in a relationship for the past two years and says that the situation with her is no longer fulfilling him either.

Not Feeling an Ounce of Guilt in Greensboro, NC.

Dear Not Guilty,

The first thing I have to ask is . . . are you kidding me? Have you always been this foolish or have you recently started using *drugs? Here's a simple fact. Any man who doesn't respect the fact that you are married is a D.O.G. and couldn't possibly respect the institution of marriage. Furthermore, if you believe that you can take the stolen moments of fucking—that's what it is when you are both with someone else—and turn it into a meaningful relationship, then by all means shoot your best shot. What it sounds like is that you are extremely selfish and obviously good at being sneaky. That is one thing that you and your lover obviously have in common. Perhaps you two deserve each other and I'm sure you could provide each other many years of misery in the future.*

Just remember that when you lie down with dogs, you're bound to get fleas. Do your spouse a favor and either get some counseling or leave him.

Yours truly,

Dr. C.

It was so easy for me to deliver such biting responses. It was everything I'd wanted to say to the women I'd dated for so long, but now I had a soapbox to stand on and a nationwide audience to listen.

"Wow, you certainly have some strong opinions on infidelity and those who commit it. Actually, it's kind of refreshing to hear a brother say these things," Lanelle said as she scanned over the column. "A little brash, though, you think?"

We were seated in the lobby of Ruth's Chris Steakhouse in Bethesda. It was our fourth date. Two movies followed by dinner, a Wizards vs. Sixers game on Martin Luther King's birthday, and now here we were doing the unthinkable, going out yet again with no clear indication that we'd be getting our freak on. Getting to someone at a slow pace was a new thing for me. And don't get me wrong; I had never been the type to hound a woman for sex. It wasn't classy. Normally, I just played the game as it came to me. I usually took what sisters offered when they were ready. But most of the time they were ready really quick.

A little conversation and some time with a brother's representative would do wonders. I'd show women whoever they were looking for and that was the definition of game as far as I was concerned. It wasn't the man with the most money, or even the best-looking cat. It was the chameleon-like ability to transform to survive in whatever surroundings a brother was put in. Women were like snowflakes. Each one incredibly different, yet all pretty much shared the same properties. Big balls of emotion wrapped in pretty packages. Each one deliciously desirable in her own way.

I'd been the sensitive brother, the intellectual, the aggressive, the confident, and even the need-a-mother-type brother, when the situation called for that. If we men listened long enough, women always told or showed what they needed, and usually it wasn't you. So the best thing, I'd found, was to get something out of the deal before they discovered who you were.

The waitress took our orders, and as soon as she walked away I realized that I needed to figure Lanelle out. I had only so long before I went into the land of no return. The "we went out but it never got serious" zone. I had to attack.

I stared across the table at her. She had on a red V-neck cashmere dress. It hugged her frame in such a lovely manner that I had wanted to reach across the table and ravish her. I was hoping she'd get up to go to the restroom so I could steal the view that her fur coat had hidden from me on the way in. I wanted to see that walk in that dress. I doubted she wore any panties underneath, and no hose would hold that thing in place. Though she was always dressed to a T at work, her after-hours attire was so on point as to elicit excitement from me.

"So, Lanelle, I got to tell you that I've really enjoyed getting to know you and spending time with you."

She smiled. "Well, I hope so. I've enjoyed spending time with you as well."

I nodded and smiled. "I was wondering something." She leaned back as if to say, *Spit it out, then, brother.* "I was wondering what you thought about us?"

"What about us?"

"I don't know. I've just been really thinking lately about you. About us; taking things to another level."

The waitress came back with our bread and water. Lanelle squeezed the lemon in hers, then mine, before she spoke. "What level might that be? Sexually, emotionally . . . what?"

"Daaaammn," I said coolly. "I just meant more like seeing more of each other. You haven't been to my place and I would love to see you more on a relaxed-type level. Where we both kick our shoes off, watch a DVD. Maybe I'd cook you a meal or something."

She smiled and chuckled. "I guess that sounds all right." Then she asked me, "So, Diego, let me ask you this . . ."

"Shoot."

"Are you seeing anyone right now?"

Seeing? That was a tricky question. Ask a man that and he knows what a sistah means, but she should be more specific. I had fucked a couple of women in the past couple of months. After the situation with Erin had fallen apart, things had gotten a little lean. I'd gotten weak and invited Daphne, the hairstylist, over. She had finally gotten what she wanted, and I had to admit, she wasn't that bad, but she was nothing that I would write home about.

Against my better judgment, which was an oxymoron, because I didn't have much better judgment, especially when it came to getting my dick wet, I had hooked up with Maddy again. She'd been married all of two months before she called for a tune-up. Without the alcohol, she hadn't been worth the trouble either.

I was beginning to think that it was the empty sex that was turning me off. I was starting to feel the void again. The big hole that Alicia had left in my heart when she left for good, was aching. I didn't really see how I could be wrong in thinking that the answer wasn't sitting right across the table from me.

"I'm not seeing anyone right now . . ." I knew that if I left it there, she'd have an opening to question me further, so I kept it moving. ". . . I do think that the time has come for me to change that."

"Oh yeah. And you have someone in mind?"

"I guess that someone isn't listening?"

"Oh, I'm listening, but let me let you in on a little something . . ." She folded her napkin and put it on her lap. As the waitress came back to our table, she said, "My bullshit sensor is very strong, sir."

I didn't know where this was coming from. "So what is that supposed to mean?"

"Nothing at all. But be mindful . . . sometimes we're not as slick as we *think* we are. People talk, and it might be good if you knew that your reputation precedes you," she said, and then thanked the waitress.

I had a puzzled look.

"Diego," she said. "I'm new at the school and I don't plan on staying—meaning, I'm not there to make a bunch of friends. But people talk and you've been the topic of more than a few conversations—and deservedly so, I presume."

"So what did you hear?"

She was silent for a second, and when it became apparent that I wasn't going to move forward, she said, "Enough. I've heard enough."

I left it there and we ate dinner. She kept the conversation flowing as I tried to imagine what the women in the school had said about me. There was plenty that they could have said with all the ammunition that I'd given them over the years. It was odd that I'd never once thought much about what I'd done in a negative light—screwing a parent here and there, a few colleagues, a couple of the student teachers, the school secretary, the computer-lab specialist, and even the daughter of one of the administrators. In fact, I'd worn those conquests as a badge of honor.

Now that I was face-to-face with a woman I deemed incredible, I wanted her to respect me. To look at me as a real man, a catch. Instead, I was imagining the things that were running through her mind. When the check came I realized that she wasn't doing anything but enjoying my company. I wasn't what she was looking for. Who was I kidding?

As I took the check and acknowledged to myself that it was the last time that I'd be treating her to dinner, I was hoping she'd offer to pay. I would have let her. "You need some help with that?" she asked.

Oh, the nerve of this bitch, I thought. *Help.* "Nah, I'm fine."

"You sure?"

"Of course." *Some help. Pay this whole damned ninety-dollar check, but don't help a nigga,* I thought.

As if things could get no worse, my eyes began to play tricks on me—at least I hoped they were. Upon closer inspection, I saw Gina, Kristen's friend and my possible baby's mama, walk into the same exact section that Lanelle and I were seated in. She was with an older woman, who could have been her mother. I took a deep breath and tried to fight off the instant headache that was on the way.

"You good?" I said, and got out of my seat and quickly stood behind Lanelle. This put my back to Gina as I offered to help Lanelle with her chair and jacket.

"Yes, I'm fine. You okay?"

"For sure." When she stood up, I finally got a glimpse of her rear and it was magnificent in the dress. Having my way with it could have done wonders to bring me out of the funk I was slipping into.

As we walked away from the table I looked over at the gloves that I'd left there on purpose. When we passed Gina's table, Lanelle's eyes were on the door. I looked the other way purposely and made it out of the restaurant without Gina so much as looking in our direction. Though I'd all but given up on my chances with Lanelle after our dinner conversation, the last thing I wanted was to confirm any opinions of my being a dog in her eyes. Creating a scene right there wouldn't have helped me at all. If nothing else, I'd leave her wondering *What if?*

Once we were out front, I gave our parking ticket to the valet and then I patted my jacket pockets. "I think I left my gloves at the table . . . yeah . . . I must have."

"You want me to run back and grab them while you wait on the car?" She was just too helpful.

"Nah, I'm good. Give me a second. Be right back." I sped back into the restaurant and walked right up to Gina's table. As I stood there my chest began pounding and my nerves went into overdrive.

Gina looked up and her eyes grew wide. "Diego."

I looked down at her stomach and saw the bulge. "I've been trying to contact you. What's up?"

"Oh, nothing. I'm just out for my mom's birthday."

She knew that wasn't what I meant. "That's nice. But can I have a quick word with you?"

She seemed really nervous and her mother picked up on it. "Darling, is this a friend of yours?"

"Hold up, Ma. Let me just talk to him for a minute," Gina said, and stood up. I looked at her face. She was gaining weight and she had her hair in a short bob. I saw that she had bags under her eyes that I'd never noticed, but she was still attractive. Getting that glow that women get when they're with child. She was definitely knocked up.

She stepped away from the table. "I've been past your crib and tried to find out where you working now. What's up with this situation?"

"This really ain't the time . . ."

"Well, I need some answers. You crashed a nigga's wedding and ruined my life, in case you forgot."

"Listen, it's not like you didn't have a part—"

"Hold up—"

"Hold up shit. Diego, you got nerve. I'm the one having a

damned baby by myself. As for your wedding, I guess you learned you shouldn't shit where you sleep."

"What's that supposed to mean?"

"That means, you don't need to be screwing over anyone who can put their hands on you. Kristen is a nut job and you found out the hard way."

"Oh, so now she's a nut job. But you thought she was perfect when you followed her into my wedding." I shook my head in disgust.

"Diego, I'm trying to enjoy my mother's birthday. Please don't embarrass yourself out here."

"Embarrass *myself*! Now that's a joke coming from a wedding crasher. In case you didn't know, people don't do that shit in real life. I ought to smack your ass right now for this. You have no idea how many people you hurt."

Her arms were folded, letting me know she had no fear of my becoming violent. I moved on: "So where can I reach you? We need to talk." My voice was far more forceful than the volume I projected.

She walked back to the table and grabbed her cell phone. "What's your number? I'll call you tomorrow." I could tell by her tone that it was altogether possible I'd never hear from her.

I snatched her phone from her hands and dialed my number and hit send. She didn't want to make any more of a scene than she had already, but I could see the anger in her eyes. When I saw the number come up on my screen, I said, "I'll call you. Make sure you answer."

I handed her back her phone and stormed off. I made it to the front door and then turned back around and walked right back in. I'd forgotten my gloves.

The entire ride home I was quiet. Thinking about Gina and contemplating my future. We were on the Beltway when Lanelle asked, "You okay? You don't seem like yourself."

"Oh yeah, I'm fine."

"You seem like you just been *off* since we left the restaurant. Was it something I said?"

Honestly, it wasn't, but the concern in her voice beckoned for me to make a play on her sympathy. Though I was truly wallowing in the uncertainty of my future because of Gina, I was fighting the emptiness I knew I'd feel once I dropped her off. I just didn't want to be alone.

"Lanelle, I got to tell you that I'm a little disappointed that you aren't willing to even take me seriously. I'm not saying anything about jumping into a relationship. It's just that it's hard out here to meet a quality woman."

"Humph," she replied. "Is that so?"

"Absolutely. I mean, I can only imagine the things you've heard about me in that school, and I got to be honest. I'm not proud of everything that I've done."

"You mean every *one?*"

A quick sigh let her know that I was worn out and not up for defending my past. "No, I said what I meant. When I came to this job, I was a young man, single. A lot of women who've come through the school have thrown themselves at me. And I have to be honest. A few of them I've chased down, but let me ask you this . . ."

I had her full attention and she was hanging on my every word. I could tell I'd struck a nerve. I think she'd been thrown by the honesty. I looked over at her as we drove. "How many men have you dated where you've had the benefit of knowing their past . . . knowing the things that they're capable of doing before getting involved with them?"

Her mind seemed to be racing for a moment and then she answered, "Not many . . . I guess . . . maybe . . . none."

"Well, you still gave them a chance, and do you regret dealing with them?"

"Some of them . . . *Regret* is a strong word. But I've tried to take something positive, some lesson, from each relationship."

"Well, why is it that you think that a man who dedicates his life to teaching our children has no redeeming qualities simply because as a single man, he fucked women who *wanted* to fuck him."

"Diego, it's not that. Not at all."

"Then what is it?"

She stared into my eyes and let me know that my persistence might wear down her resistance. "Maybe I don't want to be just another one of your many conquests."

"I'm not trying to make you one. Listen, I'm not trying to convince you or change your heart, but I do want you to understand that I'll do whatever it takes to make you believe in me."

The ride was quiet again for the next few miles. I thought about the things I'd said to her. I wondered why I'd poured it on so thick. Was I really this into her, or was the challenge making me feel more desire for her? Deep inside, I knew it was the latter. Chasing Lanelle allowed me to forget that feeling. Allowed me to focus on something other than myself.

As we neared her exit she turned the radio down a little and said, "I'm not ready to go home yet." I said nothing. "Take me with you. Take me to your place."

"Are you sure?"

"I'm sure. But can you behave yourself?"

"Absolutely."

She nodded and turned the radio back up. "All right, then. You have any movies we can watch?"

"Oh yeah, I just picked up *Crash*. I heard it was really good."

"Okay."

We sat on the couch and ate Slice 'n Bake cookies and talked for a while before we got into the movie. Though the performances in the movie were gripping, especially Terrence Howard's, I began to fight the sleep that started tugging at my body.

Lanelle's head was now on my chest and I felt like it was now or never. I looked down at her body. She was covered from the waist down with a blanket, but her ass still made a nice imprint in the throw. "Hey," I whispered. "You sleep?"

"No," she replied, but I could tell that she had dozed off.

"Let's go upstairs. I'll give you a T-shirt." She didn't respond. "Lanelle, you hear me?"

"Yeah, okay."

It took a minute, but we made it up the stairs. I reached into my drawer and grabbed a T-shirt for her. I was shocked when she un-hooked her collar right there and stepped out of her dress. She folded it neatly in front of her and placed it on the chair in the corner of my room. When she turned her back to me, even in the darkness, I could make out her magnificent, thong-covered ass. Instantly, I had a hard-on.

She then pulled the shirt over her head and almost in the same motion she reached under and took her bra off. She tossed it on top of her dress and walked toward me. "I've enjoyed you and I'm glad I came here with you."

"I'm glad, too," I barely got out before she placed her arms on my shoulders. She leaned in and placed her lips gently on mine. My temperature began to rise, but then just as easily she pulled them away and moved toward the bed.

"Good night," she said, and climbed in.

There was something in the way she did this that let me know the kiss she'd given was all that I should expect. I used the bathroom and climbed in with her. I did manage to scoot up close enough to spoon her. My aching penis was pressed against her ass. She knew it, I knew it, but the unspoken agreement was that this was a test of wills. Could I be different, or would I try to fuck her and blow the opportunity?

As I lay there holding her, India.Arie playing softly in the background, it dawned on me. For the first time in a long time, I didn't feel alone. Though I was horny, I wasn't alone. I didn't know what the future held, but I was sure there had to be some middle ground between the two feelings. I closed my eyes and drifted off to sleep believing that somehow, someway, I was going to find it.

Taking Candy from a Baby

Dear Dr. C.,

There is something I just don't understand. My sister ain't worth a damn. She obviously could care less about her husband and yet he adores her. My best friend, Maria, got engaged last Christmas Eve and is getting married to a wonderful man in three weeks. I'm not hating on her, but she doesn't have anything to offer a man that I don't, and again I'm not hating, but in the looks department she can't hold a candle to me. The worst of it all is my friend Candace and her perfect relationship. She's a lawyer, he's a lawyer. I'll admit, the bitch has it going on, but so do I. Why can't I find a decent man? Is there some secret that women, even my closest friends, just won't share about finding the perfect relationship?

I'm not picky; I just want a man who is going to respect me from day one. Be consistent and not be afraid to commit. It *would be nice if he was good-looking, but that's not my determining factor. Just be healthy, straight, with a job, and preferably no kids.*

    Give it to me straight.

                        Baffled in Bladensburg

Dear Baffled,

The answers to your questions are simple. It's not impossible for you to find a decent man, but it is hard. Believe it or not, what you seek is an endangered species, the qualified and decent brother. Understand the plight of the world. Who would ever have thought that "decent" would be a standard too hard for many men to measure up to? As far as the secret that those women aren't sharing, it's easy. Either they aren't telling you the truth or you aren't listening to what they're saying. Let me say this loud and clear: "THERE IS NO PERFECT RELATIONSHIP!" Everyone that is in a relationship settles for sure. That's why they call it settling down.

    Your man is out there. He just might not be decent. Keep looking.

                        Yours truly,

                        Dr. C.

Jacob was onstage performing in front of a packed crowd. The Avenue was one of D.C.'s hottest new clubs and No Question had been billed as the main attraction by the promoter. After waiting outside in lines to get into the club, people were standing in front of the stage swaying back and forth as the band played a few original songs from an album they were working on as they warmed the crowd for the second set.

I was at the bar with Lanelle sipping on Amaretto sours when No Question came out and started the second set. For a while we listened and watched Jacob perform. As usual, he gave a great performance and Lanelle seemed to really enjoy the live music. We'd been seeing each other regularly for three weeks and it seemed like we were on the verge of getting at least semiserious. At first I thought that it would be hard seeing her at work every day and then being with her after work so much, but it was actually a really nice change of pace. Between my enjoyment of her company, work, and writing the column, my black book had begun to collect some dust, which didn't really bother me at all. I had never been with a woman who carried herself the way that Lanelle did. She was all business at work, yet able to let her hair down like an around-the-way girl when we were at home.

The only thing that I wasn't pleased with was our sex life. To this point we hadn't had one. She'd made it clear that she had a three-month rule and it had become painfully obvious that she was sticking to it.

"Diego, I don't have to spend the night if it's too hard on you," she'd said. The only thing that was *too* hard had been my dick. But the company had been almost therapeutic. The dreams of Alicia had begun to fade. Whenever I woke up in the middle of the night, I would look over and see Lanelle's angelic face right there.

As the band went into a rendition of R. Kelly's "Step in the Name of Love," Lanelle and I moved out to the floor to get our step on. Jacob's voice was much richer than even the Pied Piper of R&B, so when he hit the riffs, he moved the whole room. The band sounded so good that it almost made you high. I watched Lanelle's bright smile as she twirled around in front of me. We laughed at ourselves as we danced like two people in love. I moved back, slid my foot in front of me, and hit a quick shuffle as if I was one of the original Chicago steppers. I snapped my fingers as I bopped to the beat and never lost a beat as Lanelle and I grooved like we were the only two people on the dance floor.

"Step, step, side to side, round and round, take it now, separate, bring it back . . ." Jacob was singing at the top of his lungs. *"If they ask you why we did it, tell 'em we did it for loooooveeeee, ohhh yeahh."*

At one point Lanelle turned her back to me and gave me a rock and then several grinds. She'd felt me pressed against her on more than a few occasions, but for some reason, she seemed really turned on as we danced. I began singing in her ear while we danced, my song turned into a whisper and then a kiss on the neck. This led to even more grinding. It wasn't long before I was ready to head home. I was hoping, in my heart of hearts, that this would be the night when I closed the deal.

After the performance, Lanelle, Jacob, and I were talking near the stage when the promoter came over to tell Jacob the VIP lounge was open for him and his guest. "You guys want to go in?" he asked. He wasn't big on the VIP scene. Jacob struck me as the type who might even avoid celebrity status. He enjoyed being real and being around real folks.

Reading the look on Lanelle's face, I decided that it might be cool to at least investigate. She looked slightly intrigued. "Yeah, we can hit that joint for a minute."

"Hold up for a second," Jacob said as he looked off to his left. He headed over toward a girl who was standing near the soundman. I watched him talk to her for a minute. Then he waved for us to come over. He escorted the young lady and us into the VIP. We moved up a few steps and there were some of the other members of the group along with a few people from the radio station. Some were standing, some lounging on the couches. Jacob led us to an L-shaped couch in the far corner. He spoke to one of the guys sitting down and he jumped up and moved. Lanelle and I huddled closely enough for me to smell her perfume and become aroused by her warmth.

Finally Jacob turned to the young woman he'd escorted into the lounge with us. He nodded in response to something she said and then she smiled. She took a seat on the couch and crossed her legs. She was wearing a pair of tight jeans and a peach-colored leather jacket that fit more like a tight shirt. With her hair in a ponytail, accenting her features, she reminded me of a young Lisa Bonet from the old *Cosby Show*.

Jacob didn't bother introducing her, but started in on a conversation. "So, did you like the show?" he asked Lanelle.

"Oh yeah, you guys did your thing up there. As good as any group I hear on the radio. Diego said you were talented, but I was still surprised," Lanelle responded.

"Thanks, I'm glad you enjoyed it."

"Yeah, man, you all sound better each time I hear you. And that's coming from someone who hears you every single week, damned near."

Then the girl chimed in. "I can't believe you tore it down like that, Mr. Marsh. Unbelievable."

Did she say "Mr. Marsh"? "What did she call you?" I leaned in and asked.

"Oh, this is Elise," Jacob said. She's a senior at Johnson—one of my students. She is also a superb singer. She's going to do background vocals on our CD and I'm looking into helping her put a demo together."

I tried to keep my mouth from dropping. I couldn't believe he'd brought one of his kids to the club. On top of it, he was talking about working with her.

"Oh, that's really nice. How long have you been singing?" Lanelle said.

"For like five years. I can't wait to get up onstage in front of people in a venue like this."

"I'm sure you'll get the chance before you know it," Lanelle shot back, waving her hand to let Elise know that it was a feat easily within her grasp.

"Mmm, I love that bracelet you have on, girl. It is beautiful," Elise said when she noticed the diamond tennis bracelet Lanelle was wearing. "Let me get a look at it." Lanelle held her wrist out and Elise simply shook her head. "Gorgeous," she said without a hint of hateration. "One of these days, one of these days."

Jacob and I stood there like two men listening to their wives talk. I watched in amazement as the two women started into a conversation. I nudged him on the arm, and when I had his attention I nodded toward the door. I stepped and he followed me.

We cleared the door and walked into the stairwell. "Yo, what the fuck is you doin', man? You fucking this girl?"

"Hell no. I just told you what's up. She has some serious talent.

It's no different than any other student I've taken an interest in. How many kids have I gotten scholarships for? You didn't ask me if I was fucking any of them."

"Yeah, well, I never saw you hanging out in the effing club with one of them either. I hope you know what the fuck you doing." I paused for a second and then said, "She is finer than a motherfucker, though."

"Alicia Keys?"

"A cross between Alicia Keys, Mya, and Beyoncé," I said.

"I don't really see Beyoncé."

"Her young ass is bootylicious." Then I did my hands in a motion to show her shapely rear end.

"True dat," he said, nodding.

"But, Jacob, I thought you told me that you were afraid her ass was stalking you," I barked. "Didn't she throw a fucking rock through your window with her crazy ass?"

"No, you got it wrong. That's not the same girl. That's Anna, and I didn't say for sure she did it."

"Yeah, well, whatever. That doesn't explain this shit. What in the world is going through your mind? How old is she?" He started to answer, but I kept on. "It doesn't even matter. If she's a student. That shit is against the law."

"Look, she's only seventeen. Just like the Rick James song, but she has a chance to really make it. And to be honest, I need her."

"*Need* her?"

"Yeah. She is keeping tabs on the girl Anna for me. They talk and it's really given me peace of mind to find out some things about her."

"About who?"

"Anna."

"Such as?"

Just then a bouncer, who wasn't all that big but had his chest poked out, walked up and said, "I'm gonna need you fellas to clear the stairs."

"We'll be just a minute," I said in a dismissive tone. "This is Jacob Marsh, the singer who performed here tonight. We had to step out of VIP so we could hear each other."

The bouncer looked us up and down. "I'll give you a couple minutes, okay?"

"Yeah, cool," I said, without even looking him in the eye, then I got back to Jacob. "You said you've found out something about the girl Anna."

"Yeah, like for one, she's a dyke."

"What?"

"Right," he said emphatically. "Which means . . ." He waited on me to figure it out. When I didn't he continued. "Which means she doesn't have a crush on me. She just sees me as some type of father figure."

I shook my head. "But what about the e-mails you told me about?"

"Could have been anyone. I don't know."

"They still coming?"

"Not as frequent, but yeah, they come from time to time. They're probably from someone who looked me up at classmates.com. Maybe it's one of my exes or a former student. I don't know."

"What about the rock through the window?"

"I'm still confused about that."

"Well, you sure seem relaxed. A lot more than you were a few months back."

"Well, things are a lot calmer," he said.

"Jacob, I don't know about this. It could be trouble, plus it doesn't look good. What if someone sees you out with her?"

"She'll be out of school in three months anyway."

"Well, listen. I'm going to go in here and get Lanelle and hopefully your singing got her worked up enough for me to tap that tonight. Fucking with her, a nigga has gotten backed up."

Jacob laughed. I was serious. "All right, Diego. I'll catch up with you in the morning. You and Lee still going to meet me at the gym, right?"

"Yeah, but call me. Give me at least an hour's notice. I might be tired—ya feel me?"

Another grin and we headed back in. I interrupted Lanelle, who was still talking to Elise, and let her know that it was time for us to head out. As we made our way out the front door Lanelle saw someone she knew and screamed out her name. "Janet. Jannnetttttt."

Janet turned and a smile slid across her face, and the two ran to hug each other. I walked up on her. "Diego, this is my cousin Janet. Janet Divine. You've heard of her show, the *Love Divine* on 95." Janet's show came on every night at eight. She and her DJ played the best in old-school and new-school slow jams and allowed callers to dial in and talk about their love lives.

"Oh yeah. I love that show. I listen all the time . . ."

"When you doing your thing, huh?" She laughed. "I ain't mad atcha," she said.

We both laughed. "I was about to say, while I work on my column."

Lanelle covered her mouth as if she could barely contain her excitement. "Janet. You've heard of *Girl Talk* magazine. Well, Jacob is Dr. C. He's the advice columnist in there. He gives some really good advice. Stuff we sistahs should know, but don't because we spend too much time trying to figure it out on our own. Now we have a brother to ask who gets paid to tell the truth." She laughed.

Janet joined her in laughter and added, "I know that's right." She paused and then said, "You know, Diego, I'd love to have you on the show as a guest one night. How about it?"

I jumped at the offer. "I'd love to. Name the time and I'll be there."

"All right. Here's my card, and my producer's number is right below it. You call her tomorrow afternoon and we'll give you a date. Is one night next week good for you?"

I couldn't believe it. I'd imagined that it would take months to put something like this together. "Yeah, that'll be great. Thanks for even asking."

"No problem. Lanelle, I'll talk to you soon. You know Gi Gi's baby shower is coming up in, what . . . ?"

"Saturday after next."

"Well, I'll see you then."

"For sure."

We headed home and I was on cloud nine. I'd always wanted to be on the radio. Who hadn't? Now, thanks to Lanelle hooking me up, I was headed for some really good exposure. I couldn't wait to call Jo and tell her. I looked at my watch and thought about dialing her cell, but at midnight on a Friday, it was a tad late.

Back at my house, I took a shower, and as the water was beating down on my head I thought about how things were coming together for me. I'd cleaned up the drama from my life and good things were happening. I was really enjoying the whole Dr. C. thing. People were responding even more incredibly than I'd imagined or hoped. The readers were buying into the whole concept of having a man who was finally telling the truth.

I'd gotten at least fifteen letters from people saying that they'd been reading the magazine in a checkout line and decided to buy it when they stumbled across my column. Jonetta and the people at *Girl Talk* had gotten these letters as well, so it was obvious that they were seeing my value to the magazine.

I walked out of the bathroom butt naked, body glistening from the water. When I looked at Lanelle, who was sitting on the edge of the bed in just her panties and bra, my mind began to drift. It was time. She had to know it.

She reached out for my waist. "You're still wet."

"That I am." My voice was an octave lower than usual. I pulled her up to me and our lips met. She let out a sigh.

"You're cold," she said as she tried to pull away.

"Well, warm me up." I reached for her again. This time I locked my arms around her. My right hand palmed her ass and I squeezed it as if I owned it.

"Diego, I'm not even gonna front on you."

"What?"

"I want you."

"Well, I'm here. You can have me." My lips went down to her neck and then between her breasts.

"Mmmmm," she moaned. Then she huffed out, "Wait. Wait a second."

"What's wrong, baby?"

"It's just a bad time."

"Come on, Lanelle. How long you want me to wait?" My voice gave away my frustration, though I hid the disgust.

"It's not that. I don't want you to wait anymore, but, baby . . . I'm on . . . I'm on my period."

Like a hot-air balloon being shot with a harpoon, the wind left my body, taking my good feeling. A brother needed some ass. I wanted Lanelle, but if she had left at that moment, I would have dug out every number in my black book. I realized that we weren't at the level where I could ask her to give me some head for good measure and at least let me get one off. So instead, I climbed into bed and did my best to drift off to sleep.

Before I was totally out, she whispered, "Diego . . ."

"Yeah."

"Are you okay?"

"Fine."

"I promise you. As soon as I go off my period, I'll make it up to you."

I smiled at the thought, but was still a little miffed. "All right, It's okay, though," I said, then I threw a little extra on. "It'll happen when it's meant to."

"Exactly."

———

After drinking nearly a whole bottle of Moët in the VIP, Jacob couldn't find his keys. He couldn't find them because Elise had taken them out of his pocket. He had been celebrating the great news he'd just gotten. No Question had just been offered a contract. A producer had been in the audience and had come into the lounge to speak to the band's manager. After he heard the offer and shared it with the band members, they all agreed that it was the chance of a lifetime.

"I can't believe this," Jacob said, stumbling and nearly falling down the steps as he tried to exit the club. "I'm finally about to make it."

"You're not going to make it anywhere if you don't take it easy. You are drunk, Mr. Marsh. Matter of fact, you're pissy drunk."

"Nooooooooo," he said. "Um not." He was trying his best to get his walk together as he headed up the sidewalk toward the direction he assumed his car was in.

When they stopped in front of Elise's car, she opened the door for him. Jacob climbed in. They had pulled off before he thought to say, "Wait. My car. I drove here . . . I think."

"Yeah, you did. We'll come back and get your car tomorrow. I didn't want you driving home drunk."

"But—"

"Don't worry. If you want, your friend Diego can bring you down to pick up your car. The promoter asked the club owner about it and he said that your car will be fine where it's parked."

"Okay. So do you remember how to get to my house?"

"I believe so. If I get stuck I'll ask."

Elise turned on the CD player. As she looked over at Jacob she began to sing Mariah Carey's "We Belong Together." Jacob drifted off to sleep and never stirred as she cruised down New York Avenue, into Maryland, and onto the BW Parkway. Instead of waking him, she made a stop at a 7-Eleven and then she drove him straight to her apartment.

Jacob awoke, disoriented. "Where are we?"

"Come on," she said, helping him out of the car. She handed him a container of coffee she'd bought at the 7-Eleven. "Careful with that. It's hot."

Jacob followed her up the steps to her door and walked in behind her. He was still tipsy but not too much to realize that he was in the apartment of one of his students. She turned on the kitchen light and it was just bright enough for him to make his way to the couch. "Put that on a coaster. I stopped off and got it for you," she shouted. She walked back into the bedroom and came out a moment later with two aspirin in her hand.

She handed him a small Dixie cup of water and the two pills. "Take these before you sip the coffee," she said.

Then she grabbed a lighter and went to the huge candle in the corner of the room. She lit three candles in all, and in a matter of moments the room had a mixture of smells, cinnamon being the strongest. Then she hit the remote and her stereo came on.

Jacob sat back and looked at a picture on the table. "Is that you?" he asked.

"No, that's my mom when she was a kid. She was only fourteen in that picture, believe it or not."

"She looks older than that here. Or I should say she looks more mature, not old at all. She was beautiful."

"Yeah, thanks. Well, she grew up fast. Had to. A lot like I did. In that picture, she was wearing her work uniform. I think she was working for the city of Baltimore back then."

Jacob sipped his coffee and involuntarily began to bob his head to the music playing in the background. He couldn't help but sing to any song he knew the words to and he began to sing. "What in the world do you know about Rose Royce, young lady?"

"I know a little something."

"Is that so?"

"Yeah, you could say I have an old soul."

He nodded. "Well, show me what you know."

Elise smiled. "You sure you ready for that?"

Jacob got a little uncomfortable with the comment. Until the flirting had gotten blatant, he'd almost forgotten that he was in the company of one of his students. Over the past couple of months, they'd become something like friends. He'd actually shared huge parts of his life with Elise and she opened up to him about her life. She had her secret—an underage teen, living on her own. And he had his—the cover-up of a sexual assault on a student. They had trusted each other and it had led to this. Elise in the middle of the floor singing for him. Him enjoying it so much he couldn't keep the semidrunken smile off his face.

She was pointing directly at Jacob and mocked the singer as her voice fell and she almost cried out, *"Goin' down, goin' down, ohhhhhh bayyyyy, don't wanna live, if I can't giiiiivvvve, my love to you."*

Elise was like a snake charmer, her smooth, yet raspy voice, reeling him in. *"Sooorrrrry, sorry, sorry soorrry, what did I do wrong, please forgive me, and come on hooommmme."*

With that, he stood up and walked toward her. Her eyes were like those of a deer trapped in an oncoming car's headlights. She was about to get smashed. There were only a few seconds for him to think about what he was about to do.

The next song began to play—"Love Don't Live Here Anymore." He recognized that he had a vacancy in his heart, just like the words of the song said. Kendra, the only woman he'd connected with in the past couple of years, was gone. All he had was his work and his music. He loved his music like nothing else, and his job fulfilled him as well, but he needed more and he'd finally begun to admit it to himself. He needed to feel the way he'd been feeling since he'd first laid eyes on Elise. Excited, filled with passion and desire.

He paused when he reached her. Then he looked down in shame. She put her hands on his face and she called him by his first name aloud for the first time. "Jacob," she whispered. "Look at me."

When he looked up at her there were tears in his eyes. "I'm sorry. I'm sorry that I feel this way . . . about you."

"It's okay. You don't have to apologize. I know," she whispered. "I know how you feel. I've felt it. I've felt you."

"How, though . . . ?" he asked. "How did you know?"

"It doesn't matter. I don't think you're a pervert. I'm not a little girl. I'm a woman. Look around. I take care of myself. I don't need a little boy. I need a man. Please believe me. If it's not you . . . then it will be someone just like you. You're a good person. Strong and right. Any other person in your position would have tried me a while back. It's taken us all this time and *I've* had to take my time with you." She smiled. "I had to be sure that I could trust you and that you were the type of person I wanted to share my heart with. This means so much to me . . . you being here."

Jacob breathed deep. He shook his head and asked, "Is this real?"

"It's real. Don't be afraid. I'll take care of you no matter what."

They were silent for a few seconds and then Elise leaned in and touched her lips to his. At that moment, Jacob was hooked. He couldn't turn back if he wanted to.

"Come with me," she said, and walked to the bedroom.

Jacob entered and his eyes were drawn to her bed. It was a platform bed with a long shelf across the head. There were at least twenty candles all different sizes and heights, lined up on a long silver holder. Only two were lit. The bed was covered in shiny sheets that looked like silk. "Nice," Jacob mumbled.

She walked over to her walk-in closet, fumbled around for a second, and came back out. She was now standing in front of him completely naked. "Take those off," she whispered in his ear.

He complied and began to undress. By the time he finished, she'd put out the candles in the front room and was back in the bedroom. She moved to the dresser behind Jacob, pushed a couple of buttons. Her iPod was now playing through a set of speakers.

Jacob swallowed and tried to keep his composure as she brushed her body up against his. She looked into his eyes and this time he met her with a kiss. They held their lips together for a few moments until he felt her hand wrapped around his shaft. She began to pull gently on it with one hand as she tickled the tip of it with her thumb. Jacob was ill at ease and he didn't spring to attention the way he would have anticipated.

"Sorry, I'm a little nervous."

"No need to be. Lay down on your stomach."

Jacob complied and she rested her body on his for a minute, absorbing his warmth. Her next move caught him by surprise as she began to massage him gently. First his back and then his shoulders. He could feel the knots loosening up as her hands proved to be expert beyond her years. "Damn," he moaned out. "That feels so good."

She just kept going. Down the small of his back until she had his buttocks firmly in her grip. He'd never realized that he could collect so much tension there, but he had or there was no way her touch would have melted him like it did.

Next, she went down the backs of his thighs and all the way to his feet. Jacob was in heaven as Elise worked his body and took the tension away. It had been so long since he'd been massaged like that. She went on for twenty minutes, until he was on the brink of falling asleep.

"Turn over," she said as she guided him onto his back. Elise took in his body. She hid away her fears. She hoped that she could please him. She'd had a couple partners in Indianapolis, one who'd hit and run, and another who she wished had done the same. After that, she'd decided to take her time. Jacob was the next to be chosen.

Having watched many an hour of porn, she was confident that she could do something to make him feel good. She was now straddling him, her hands on his chest; they stared into each other's eyes. Jacob couldn't believe that this beautiful young girl wanted him. She could have had any man, he thought. At least in due time. He thought back to his days in high school. Although he'd had his share of attractive girlfriends, he'd never even dreamed of capturing a girl who was arguably the prettiest in the school. Now he had her. She was naked on top of him. Her creamy skin, full, perky, young breasts, and thick, light brown nipples were all within his grasp.

As Jaheim played through the speakers, she began to gyrate on top of him. His penis was in between their bodies and was getting wet from her juices and at the same time had grown to full attention. As Elise continued to grind, Jacob's mind was drifting slowly into outer space. Her lips were spread and dripping liquid all over him.

Suddenly she began to quiver and a tiny orgasm escaped her body from the grinding. She didn't lose her focus and slid down his body. Once again she held him in her hands. But this time she had to keep her grip tighter in order to control it. It kept wanting to press against his stomach.

"Mmmmmmph" was the sound that escaped her mouth as she took the head of it in her mouth without warning. Just like she'd witnessed in the movies, Elise sucked and slurped on his dick, making all manner of sounds that suggested that she was enjoying the taste.

Jacob lifted his head off the pillow and looked down at her head and her lips. *What am I doing?* he thought. Elise was incredible. "Oh shit."

She pulled her mouth away from the tip long enough to ask, "You like this?"

"Fuck yeah. I like it." His eyes were rolling in his head.

"Sllllllrrrrrrr," came from her mouth. "Mmmmm, mmm-mmph," she moaned as the head poked at her cheeks.

"Hold on . . . hold up . . . Elise . . ." Jacob panted. "Stooo . . . Stopppp." It was too late. The sensations took him first, then the convulsions that caused him to fold himself up from the bed as he began to cum.

Elise never stopped sucking and Jacob felt as if he might pass out as he squirted right into her mouth. She'd never had cum in her mouth, but she ignored it as it slid right down her throat. She did it to show him how much she felt for him. She belonged to him now. Elise had decided that.

She didn't stop sucking until he pushed her head back. "Hold up."

Elise rolled back and gave him a minute to catch his breath. She then slid her body up toward his. "I'm so hot right now . . . Jacob." She called him by his first name again.

A few more minutes would have been welcome, but he realized that he was with a young thing and he needed to step up his game. Before Elise realized what was happening, she was on her back and Jacob was between her thighs. He kissed every available inch of her body below her belly button. He used just the perfect combination of tongue and lips to cause her to squirm.

When his mouth found her opening, Elise felt as if she were dreaming. She'd seen women in movies going crazy from this, and now she knew why. His tongue was slicing through her and brushing her clit in a smooth, surgical rhythm. The waves of pleasure were pulsating through her body every other second, and every other second she struggled, trying to regain her composure. She wanted to bounce off her bed. She needed his tongue deeper inside. She needed him to fill her up. "Oh, Jaaaaccoob . . . I . . . I . . . fee . . . feeeeel it. It's coming."

Jacob was on his knees, both of his hands holding her ass in place as he licked and licked until she let out a scream that startled him. "Yeeeeeeooooow, shiiitt." Next, her body began to shake and jerk. Jacob didn't stop licking until he felt her nails digging into his shoulders.

When he pulled away she curled up into a ball. Now he had her on the run. He quickly strapped it up and helped her get back into position. When Jacob separated her thighs he felt a slight bit of resistance. "You okay?" he asked.

"Yes. I'm ready. Go ahead."

Jacob entered her slowly for the first time and was immediately sent into a state of pure pleasure. She was dripping wet but tight, as he imagined a virgin would be. "Oh, baby, you feeeeel so good."

She only panted back. Her eyes were closed and she gripped his forearms as he began to find a rhythm. If ever there was a case of one body calling out to another, it was happening between the two of them. Jacob had never felt so into making love to anyone. Elise up to this point had only been fucked. Jacob's taking his time had her feeling the earth moving. Each stroke sent tsunami waves through her body from head to toe.

"I love it. I do. Don't stop," she moaned. Each stroke was taking her deeper into uncharted waters. Jacob was losing himself and he didn't care either.

"Oh, Elise. Let me turn you over."

The young girl wanted to do whatever this man desired. She flipped over, and when he entered her from behind, she slammed back onto him. He gripped her hips and began to pound. Sweat had begun to form on both of their bodies and air was coming hard for Jacob as he felt the familiar call of another orgasm. He arched his back and held still as he announced his pleasure. "I feel it."

Elise felt him swelling inside of her and the idea of him emptying his sperm again had her on the brink of another gigantic nut herself. She clenched her teeth and concentrated on the feeling. "Fuck me. Fuck me. Come on."

Jacob lost control and let it all out. He pumped until his breathing became labored and his muscles went limp. He didn't even notice her cries of passion as she got off one more orgasm while he filled the condom inside of her.

Together, they collapsed on the bed.

Jacob inhaled deeply and stared up at the ceiling while he came down from the high. *Ohmigod, that young girl has the bomb pussy,* he thought to himself. *I think I'm in love.*

I haven't ever had no nigga eat my pussy like that . . . and the dick was off the hook, Elise said to herself as her vagina was still pulsating from the delightful pounding. *Anytime, anywhere . . . it's his.*

"So, Jacob . . ." He laughed when she said his name. "What? You still not used to me calling you that, huh?"

He chuckled again. "Nah, I guess not."

"Well, I got news for you . . . I been calling you that for the past couple of months."

"Huh?" Immediately he thought of the e-mails. "So it was you. You're mocha2munch?"

"Say what?" she asked.

"You've been sending me e-mails? About hooking up with me and how you feel about me . . . ?"

"Um, actually, no." She said it with a straight face as she lay on her side and stared right into his face.

"I'm not angry. I just want to know."

"I swear. I don't even have a computer. I've been meaning to get one. But your girl, Anna. She lives on the computer. She's always in chat rooms and singles sites. But how would she even know your e-mail address?"

That was true. Jacob wondered how she could have obtained his e-mail address. He brushed it off and his attention went back to Elise's body. "You're beautiful."

"So are you," she returned. "And talented. You have a great future ahead of you."

He grinned from ear to ear. It felt good to hear that. He believed in himself, but to hear someone else confirm his belief made all the difference in the world. "Thanks."

"No need to thank me. And you know it's just a matter of time before you wind up going solo."

"You think?"

"C'mon. I respect you wanting to help your band and stick with them, but you and I both know that it's your talent, your voice, that makes No Question special." Jacob was silent. He agreed, but he would never say so to anyone. "When you sing, it's like you're trying to survive. Like the music is all you have. It's the food that feeds your soul, the air you breathe. It's so beautiful and perfect."

Jacob felt an overwhelming emotion come over him. That was the most special thing he'd ever heard anyone say to him. "You know, Elise . . . that's how I feel when I sing. I love my music. It's the only time I feel truly safe. Like nothing can touch me when I'm up there performing."

"Nothing can," she said. "And when you're not onstage . . . maybe I can make you feel safe. Maybe I can protect you," she said softly.

She brushed his chest with her fingertips, and when she touched his nipples, his manhood began to stiffen again. Jacob saw the light from the candles flickering on the ceiling as she made slow love to him. The scent of sex filled the room and the ride once again seemed magical. It was going to be too easy to get hooked on the loving. Over and over, she rose and fell on his shaft, riding him until they both came one last time.

The last thing he saw was the clock showing 3 A.M. Elise's head rested on his chest and they slept in the afterglow like two old lovers.

(((19)))

My Mic Sounds Nice

Dear Dr. C.,

I attended a birthday party a couple of months ago, and through a mutual friend I was introduced to a guy who was there. To be nice, I gave him my number when he asked for it. Over the next month the brother asked me out at least ten times and each time I refused him. He really wasn't my type. First of all, I like 'em handsome, not Denzel handsome, but good enough to take out in public. This brother was fair at best. Second, he didn't even have an operational vehicle. He claimed to have just totaled his ride. Don't ask me why, but I finally gave in and let the guy take me out. To my surprise, I had a good time with him. His personality made up for what he lacked in looks and he was a true gentleman. He kept telling me how beautiful and smart I was all night. I went out with him a second time and had a great time again. Don't ask me why, but on the third date I decided to sleep with him.

The next week I hardly heard from him. I was completely shocked by this. Here this joker wasn't even what I considered in my league, yet I gave him a shot and he goes missing in action. I've called him several times, and to be blunt, he seems to be bullshitting. I don't know why, but I can't stop thinking about him, and for the life of me, I can't figure out what's going on with him.

What's the dilly yo?

Heated in Houston

Dear Hot Mama,

I'm not sure if you're ready for the truth. Let me start with the obvious. It seems as though you've been a victim of what is known as the ol' bait and switch. That's where a brother make you believe that he wants you more than anything in the world. He pulls out all the stops to get you on the hook like a fisherman catching a fish. Once he gets you, though, he switches up and throws your ass back in the water like a trout that's too small. Now, don't take it personal. Most likely it has nothing to do with you personally. Some men are just challenge junkies. The best thing to do in this case is to just move on and try your best to recognize these types early on. Most men who fall into this category are extremely persistent, almost competitive, as you described this guy to be.

> *The worst-case scenario could be that he found your sex was whack and wants no more of it. Sorry. This one is hard to determine because none of your exes are going to tell you the truth about that . . . just think about it and be honest with yourself.*
> *I'm pretty sure it's one or the other.*
>
> Yours truly,
> Dr. C.

A week after he'd met Janet at The Avenue, Diego's only problem was putting his microphone on right. Once he figured out how to attach it to his shirt, he'd been a real pro. Sitting in that chair in the studio, he felt like he was just where he should be.

"We're joined live tonight with the highly acclaimed, sometimes controversial advice columnist from *Girl Talk* magazine. This brutha is the latest and the greatest. I love his column. It's real and it's hot. I read it every month 'cause sometimes a sistah needs a man's opinion on some of those relationship and dating issues. Sometimes it's easier to get an organ from a brother than an honest answer. This guy, though, puhleeeze . . . he has got some answers for you folks, I tell you. As a matter of fact, he gets paid to tell the truth." She giggled. "The best part is, tonight, people, you can get 'im for free. It's my pleasure, folks, to have D.C.'s own Dr. C. How you doin' tonight, brutha?"

"Oh, I'm great. Thanks for having me on."

"The pleasure and honor is all mine. And for you ladies out there, you might want to come past the station when we finish up, 'cause he's a fine thing."

I laughed and played it off. Janet was such a pro. We got right into the show and she briefed me on everything we'd do while the music played. We took calls, decided which ones were good enough, and then recorded the whole thing, the question and my response.

"Trumaine, here. Hi, Janet."

"Hey, Trumaine. How old are you, sweetie?"

"I'm twenty-four."

"Okay, you've got it. Dr. C. is on the line," Janet said. "What's your question?"

"Hey, Dr. C."

"Hey, Trumaine."

"My question is this. I've been seeing this guy for about six months now and he doesn't seem to trust me. He's always accusing me of going out with other people. Granted, I do like to hang out from time to time, on the weekends. I like to dance. He doesn't. But the thing is this. If I'm out past midnight, he blows my phone up to the point where I'm embarrassed in front of my friends. To top it off, last week I was at his house and I found a piece of hair that wasn't mine. He said that he didn't know where it could have come from. What do you think? I mean, would he be jealous if he was interested in seeing other people?"

"Good question, Trumaine," Janet said.

"Yeah, it is. Trumaine, let me break this down for you. Your man has trust issues and they come from one of two things. Either he was hurt in the past, or he has a guilty conscience. Or both."

"Guilty conscience. So you think he's cheating?"

"I didn't say that. But a lot of times when you're stealing, you think everyone's a thief. Get it? Because of his own behavior or experiences, past or present, he believes everyone is capable of creeping. Now the issue is this. That hair didn't just come from thin air. We always know where that hair, that bobby pin, that rubber band . . . whatever. We always know where it came from. But there's no such thing as the perfect crime. So maybe you should step back from this relationship for a while. Let him address his issues while you enjoy dancing. You two might not be compatible in the long run anyway."

"Thanks so much."

"Thank you for calling."

"Wow," Janet said. "I just learned something, folks. So you always know where the evidence came from?"

I laughed. "Yeaaaahhh, but we'll never admit that. Ladies, you'll need a head attached to the strand of hair to make it stick, though." We both laughed.

"Next on the line we have Yvette. What's good, Mami?"

"Not much. I've been in a bit of a rough spot. I had a little girl a couple years ago, and since then I've been overweight. I don't really feel good about myself. My husband is constantly reminding me about how fat I am. He hardly ever wants to touch me, and when he does, it never feels like he's trying to please me. It's more like he's in a rush to finish."

Janet cut her off. "You sayin' the sex has changed? He used to be a caring lover? Attentive to your needs, but since the weight gain he's different."

"Yes, that's gone out the window. But recently, there's this guy at my job who has shown a lot of interest in me. He tells me I'm pretty and buys me lunch . . . I'm not really attracted to this guy, but he does make me feel good. I wish my husband could—"

"Let me interject, Yvette. You need to communicate with your man. Tell him how bad he makes you feel. When he makes you feel bad, what do you do?"

"I cry. And then I eat."

"I figured that. First thing you might need to do is get some counseling. Then go to your doctor and find out if there is anything physically wrong with you that is either (a), making you gain weight, or (b), going to prevent you from working out. Don't get me wrong. I'm not saying that there is anything wrong with you because you've put on a few pounds, but if you want to stay with *this* man, then you need to try to do this for him. Because there is nothing wrong with him because he prefers a thinner you, ya feel me? Now, if you try your hardest and cannot get a grip on your weight, then maybe he's too shallow for you, and at that point, it may be time to move on and find someone who will accept you for you, and not what size you wear, 'cause believe me, there are a lot of men who love a plus-sized sister. My buddy Emmitt for one."

Janet played a little John Legend, Jill Scott, then some Isley Brothers. We laughed and joked between the callers. "It's really interesting hearing a man's approach. I notice that you tend to say, 'Try this, if this don't work, then fuck it, leave,' " she said, and we both laughed. "That's a male's logic for you. But you got to remember one thing."

"What's that?"

"People are listening. You have a lot of people's attention now, and you're going to get more, so you have to be responsible for the things you say. They are going to take a lot of what you say or write as gospel. You're in print. You're on the radio. You *must* be an expert. That's how people think."

We finished up the show and Janet appeared shocked at how the lines stayed lit up. "You were a hit tonight. A great show. I'll have to get you back on."

"I'd love to come. I enjoyed it immensely."

———————

I was driving home when my phone rang. It was my brother, Lee. "Man, I heard you on the air. You sounded great. Almost like you knew what you were talking about."

"Thanks, man. It was so cool. I never told anyone, but I always wanted to be on the radio."

"I remember you saying that when you were a kid."

"Really?"

"Yeah, you loved music. You used to sit by the radio and wait for your favorite songs to come on, then you'd smash the record button once the DJ stopped talking. That was how you'd make your mix tapes." He laughed.

It kind of came back to me. "Yeah, I'd get pissed when they talked through my favorite songs."

"Those were the days," he said, his voice suddenly solemn. "But I just wanted to tell you I was proud of you."

"Thanks." I wanted to ask him how everything had turned out as far as he and Nicole was concerned, but he cut the conversation short when she began yelling in the background. "What's her problem?" I asked. I was beginning to hate her.

"Who knows? I'ma run . . . talk at you soon," he said, and then I heard a click.

At work the following day, I realized that my perspective was beginning to change. I'd cashed three checks from Girl Talk Inc. and now I finally realized what it felt like to have a little extra cash. I wanted more. I thought about the things that Janet Divine had said to me. I was an expert, so why shouldn't I be getting paid like one? It was indeed my time to make moves.

At first I'd been on a high just to have gotten the column; now I realized that I was making the magazine rich. I had a gift. Those responses were mine. They came from my mind, my heart, and as a result of my very costly life experiences. I'd fucked up so much that the right and wrong ways were so apparent to me. Now this didn't mean that I would always do right. I was starting to believe that I might not have been programmed for that, but I sure as hell could tell the next person what to do.

While promoting myself on the air, I was promoting *Girl Talk*, too. I spent the morning watching my students as much as I did teaching them. Something inside of me told me that I'd be moving on soon. And even though I believed it would be to greener pastures, there was a sadness in my heart. I loved the kids. I needed them. They needed me.

"Good morning," Lanelle said for the second time as she poked her head in my door and winked. She was looking incredibly sexy. She had on a short leather skirt and a fitted white dress shirt. When I walked over to her I looked right down her shirt and took notice of her black lace bra.

"Looking good, Ma." I paused and took a sniff. "Smelling good, too. I wonder how it taste."

"You can't even imagine," she said seductively. The kids hardly took notice of our flirting at the door. They were more interested in who was coloring the best.

"Wanna bet? I bet it taste like peaches," I said with a low laugh.

"Don't forget the cream."

"Damn, you making me hungry."

"And you making me horny."

"Well, why don't you come and let me have you for lunch, and I do mean *have* you."

"Nigga, you ain't built like that. You aren't ready for that kind of experience. I told you that you'd be getting it soon. Tonight's the night."

"Oh, you must have me wrong. I'll light you up like a Christmas tree right there on that desk. You just give me a half a chance."

"Yeah, whatever. Save that energy for tonight, 'cause if you disappoint . . . I will clown you." Lanelle smiled and headed to the music room to pick up her students.

I went back to my work. I watched the clock as it ticked toward lunch. I was planning to call Jonetta and tell her about the show last night and to ask for a raise. I had an hour to go, so I took a minute and looked at my e-mail.

Diego,
How you gonna be on the radio giving out some damned advice. You are about the saddest case I can imagine. Someone needs to give you some advice. You got the nerve to suggest someone get some counseling. Have you gotten any? You can't keep your dick in your pants and one of these days it's gonna catch up to you. One day, Diego. You'll get yours.

And whatever issues you have must be contagious because your boy, the broke-ass Maxwell wannabe, he's fucked up, too. He's fucking high-schoolers now. Both your days are numbered.

My hands were trembling after I read the message. I wanted to punch someone. I didn't appreciate the threats at all. And who in the hell was mocha2munch? I chalked it up to some retard's idea of a joke. But I did plan on calling Jacob later to find out if he had any clues. "Effing haters," I said aloud as I stood up to collect the students' work.

At eleven-thirty, I took the kids to the cafeteria, and on the way down I saw Lanelle heading my way with a mischievous look on her face. When we passed she stuck her hands in my pocket and then whispered, "Don't look until you drop the kids off."

My pace quickened and I hurried back toward the teachers' bathrooms after getting my class seated in the lunchroom. I barely made it into the men's room before I pulled out the contents of my pocket.

A smile came across my face when I held the black lace thong up to my face. I smelled it and my dick grew hard instantly. There was the unmistakable odor of womanhood. Casting aside any foolish ideas about what a clean vagina smells like, I love the smell of pussy. I loved eating pussy and I loved the way the moisture felt on my face once I'd made a woman cum.

I sped out of the bathroom like Superman leaving a phone booth. When I made it to the steps to head upstairs, I heard a banging sound. Thinking it was a student, I was annoyed that my trip was being delayed. I was going to find Lanelle and, at the least, was going to finger her insanely.

I looked over at the door and saw none other than Grump. He was waving frantically. I moved briskly to the door and he entered quickly. I looked at him strangely. He didn't seem himself. "Thanks, man. You want some chicken?" he asked.

The nigga always had some chicken. "Nah, I'm good. And don't send me any."

"Cool," he said as he pulled on the door and headed for the cafeteria.

I looked in my classroom first and saw that my lights were still off, and then I peeped in Lanelle's room and didn't see any sign of her. Perhaps all she'd planned was to arouse me and get me even more wound up for the evening than I was already.

As I walked back into my room preparing to get my lunch, I found her sitting on top of my desk. She startled me. "You were in here the whole time?"

She nodded. "In the dark . . . waiting for you." The room wasn't actually dark. But with the blinds closed, it was dim.

I moved toward her. "So what's up?" I asked.

"You're the one doing all the talking. We don't have much time. If you can hit it quick, I'll give you a pass this time."

Hearing her say that sent a rush through my body. I was now on her, kissing her neck, causing her to moan. My hands went up her thighs and found her mound. "Ahhhhh," she breathed out.

I dropped to my knees. "Keep your ears open." My room was the last one at the end of a hallway and you could hear anyone who approached, most of the time.

Time was of the essence, so I wasted little as I placed my face in between her legs. I had to slide her skirt up so that she could spread her legs. She did so willingly. The first taste was as sweet as I'd imagined, and even juicier. When I pulled my tongue a string of her juices and my saliva came with me. "Mmm, you're wet."

"Yeaahhhh," she said quietly. "That means keep goin'." She scooted her ass closer to the edge of the desk.

My tongue was finding its mark as she began to whimper. "Dammit," she cried out.

"Use your fingers. Spread it open for me so I can get that clit."

She obliged, and with the first direct swipe of my tongue across her exposed clit, she let out a "Damn, boy."

It took less than two minutes before she started knocking shit off my desk. First my tape dispenser, then a bunch of papers flew off. When her orgasm hit her, my paper clips and the tray I kept my folders on were next. "I'm cummmmin', I'm cummm . . . in' . . . ahhh . . . ahhhh . . . ohhhhh."

I didn't let her finish. Normally a very careful lover, I didn't have a condom and I was too horny to stop. In one motion my pants were at my ankles and the head of my dick began to slip inside her. "Goddamn, it feels good."

I kept pushing until I had most of it in. We had lost all track of time and space as we began to fuck like porn stars. Her rubbing her clit in fast motion and me pinching her nipples as I slid in and out of her. She pushed me out of her, slid off the desk, and turned around. "This is my fantasy. I always wanted to get bent over the teacher's desk and get fucked doggy style."

Lanelle was showing me a whole different side of her. I'd imagined that she was so prim and proper. She'd made me wait so long. Her freakiness now had me wondering if it had all been some front. That didn't stop me from waxing that ass from the back, though. I gave her long strokes and watched the white cream from her as it coated my dick. My orgasm began to approach with the familiar tickle. I felt my balls begin to tighten and I sped up and started to slam into her uncontrollably. She screamed out at the top of her lungs and scared the shit out of me.

Hoping that no one heard her, I kept going as I lost control. At the last second I pulled out and squirted nut all over her ass and the back of her skirt. I forced myself immediately down from the high. I pulled my underwear and pants up and reached for a Kleenex. "Here."

She wiped herself and I wiped her skirt. Once our body parts were covered, we looked at each other. I shook my head as if to say, *I don't know what that was all about, but I liked it,* and she shook hers simultaneously as if to say, *I bet you do this shit all the time.*

"Damn," I said as I buckled my pants. "This desk looks like a tornado hit it."

"Tornado Lanelle." She laughed. "Go ahead clean it up . . . and you can pay me later." Then we both laughed.

"Put it on my tab. That's just round one."

"Oh, you got some more?"

"I'm going to give you a new meaning for an *after-school special.*"

She blew me a kiss and turned to leave, and as soon she reached the door a police officer was coming through it with his gun drawn.

$(((20)))$

Under Fire

Dear Dr. C.,

Why are men such cowards? Every man I meet has the same situation. They're either married or in a relationship, but they all sing the same song and dance the same dance. They aren't happy. Well, if none of them are happy, why aren't they trying to give one of the other six sistahs in the legendary equation of the seven-to-one ratio a chance? Or do they have to try all seven at one time? If I hear another brother tell me that he's staying in a relationship because he doesn't want to start the drama with his child's mother, I am going to jump off the GW Bridge. If you want to be a player, then be the best kind and be up-front with women and give us the choice. That's all we ask. Please tell me, where are all the real men? The men who aren't afraid to stand up and be who they are.

Ready to Jump in Jersey City

Dear Jumpin' in Jersey,

I have to admit that your letter made me think deeply about this notion of men being cowardly. You're right. You see, most men operate out of fear. We're so afraid that if you all knew who we really were, you wouldn't be bothered with us at all. Here's the deal. We lie and we're greedy. We're also selfish and emotionally immature. Luckily for you all, some of us evolve at some point in our lives, but the sad reality is this: most of us don't. Men grow physically and intellectually into strong, handsome, logical beings. Except for the very rare being, though, all of us remain emotionally flawed.

Now, on the flip side, most women are too irrational, overly sensitive, spoiled, and have a tendency to nag. So my suggestion to you is this. Know what you can and can't deal with. From the sound of it, perhaps you need to first learn how to spot a liar; second, never date men with children; and third, quit dreaming if you are expecting men to all of a sudden start dealing in an up-front manner.

Oh… and from what I understand, all the real men are either dead, in jail, or gay.

Yours truly,
Dr. C.

When Lanelle burst into tears and started yelling that she was sorry the minute she saw the officer, I knew immediately that she was the last person I would ever want to commit a crime with. Before he could even tell her what he was in the school for, she'd begun confessing our misdeeds to the officer. "I'm so sorry, things just got out of control, he kissed me, and . . . It'll never happen again . . ."

The officer resembled a marine with his military-style haircut and he was imposing in size. As Lanelle began to ramble he simply looked at her as if she were a lunatic. "I don't know what you're talking about, miss. We're investigating the premises of the school to see if anyone fled into the building or forced entry. We had a robbery in the vicinity and our surveillance tracked the suspect to this block. Unfortunately, our dogs were unable to pick up a scent. We feared that the perp may have come into the building and tried to turn this into a possible hostage situation. We're simply securing the building. Making sure that each classroom is secure."

"Well, we're fine in here," I commented. "I'm Diego Christian. This is my classroom."

"Can I see some ID from the both of you, if you don't mind?"

"Absolutely. This is Ms. Harris. She teaches across the hall." The police officer looked at my desk and frowned up as he returned my driver's license.

He pointed at the desk and said, "You sure there was no struggle here?" He walked around my desk and looked around.

"No, sir, I was just cleaning it off. It collects dust."

He nodded a disapproving glance. I didn't give a damn. I looked at Lanelle and rolled my eyes. "Okay, then, sorry to disturb you . . . and whatever lessons you were preparing," he said sarcastically. Then he clicked his walkie-talkie. "Stockton, here. All clear on this wing." He turned and headed out of the classroom.

The second the door shut behind him, I began picking up some of the things from the floor near my desk. Lanelle was still standing there with a stupid look on her face. I contained my thoughts for as long as I could, which was about thirty seconds. "Are you nuts?" I asked her. "You trying to get me fired?"

She burst out laughing. "I swear, I thought someone called the police on us. I didn't know what the hell was going on."

We headed out of the classroom. "What if someone had come into the building? Would you have protected me?"

"Is this before or after I tapped it?"

She made an angry face. "You ain't right."

As soon as the students were gone I made it a point to dial Jo. I got her secretary and she put me right through. "Jonetta Cleveland."

"Hey, Jo, this is Deigo."

"Hey, man. You won't believe this. I was just about to call you."

"Really?"

"Yep. I heard you were great on the air last night."

"Where'd you hear that?"

"Well, that's why I was about to call you. Hold on for a second." I heard the music she had playing when she placed me on hold. It was the first time I'd listened to R&B music while on hold. She came back on the line and sounded a little more lively. "So, Diego, have you heard of WJDS, Smooth 99? They're a new radio station down there, I believe."

"Actually I have."

"Well, what do you think of them?"

"They play some pretty good music in the evenings. Why?"

"Well, the station manager, Andrea Jack, called me this morning. She was raving about your performance last night. She's interested in giving you your own show. The afternoon drive, three to seven."

I was speechless. "Are you kidding?"

"Nope. She wants to name your show after the column, but she's going to want to associate your real name with it. I don't really see where it'll be a problem, because you'll have to quit your teaching job to do this."

"Wow. I can't believe this."

"Believe it. She wants to sit down with you next week. You might need an agent. I have a couple of good ones you might want to talk to and sort of feel them out. But the show could be a huge break. The beginning of some major things."

"So is it definite?"

"Well, there's nothing definite in the industry. You'll find out, but she has the power to make that happen. And when you are dealing with the person with the power, then it's always a good thing. I think it's a go if you want it."

"If I want it? You got to be bullshitting. Of course I want it."

I could hear her sipping something. When she finished she said, "Diego, think about it. You will have to give up teaching, and it's not easy, becoming a public figure. People will place all kinds of demands on you. I'm not trying to discourage you. It'll be great for the column. I failed to mention, one of the things that I'll have to tie to her using the name *Ladies Listen Up*, which we've trademarked, is that you will have to write the column for as long as you use the name."

"Well, what if I become more valuable, are you guys going to pay me more money?"

She laughed. "That, my friend, is the name of the game. If you become more valuable, of course we will. But remember, where there's money, there's not always opportunity, and where there's opportunity, there's not always money. So never get fixated on the dollar signs. Suppose you'd turned down this column because it paid only a thousand dollars per month. Never mind that you got the chance to do Janet's show on your own. Without your column, that pays you only a thousand bucks a month, you're not on that show, you see?"

"I see. I see."

"So, you called me. What was that in reference to?"

"Oh . . . I just wanted to tell you about the show last night. But I guess I was too late."

"I'll listen to it tomorrow and give you more feedback. We had it taped and put on disc to use on promos. It'll arrive in the morning."

"Cool. You all think of everything."

"We try. Anything else?"

"Nope."

"Okay. I'll have my assistant call you tomorrow with the numbers of those agents and help you get ready for that next week."

"Sounds great." I couldn't wait to hang up the phone so I could scream.

"All right. Talk to you soon."

We hung up and I fell to my knees right there in my classroom and let out the type of scream that is usually reserved for lottery winners and newly crowned sports champions.

"You okay, son?" Mr. Waverly said as he stuck his head in the door.

"Yes, sir. I'm great."

"Okay, then. All that noise, people might think something's wrong."

"Nah. I'm sorry. I'm just excited. I just found out that I'll be re-tiring at the end of the year."

"Retiring. You too young to retire."

"Yeah, well, if everything goes well, then that's what I'll be doing. Retiring from teaching, that is."

"Well, okay, then, if that's what you wanna do. Hell, I'm looking forward to retiring from this job myself."

"How many years you got left?"

"Too damned many. I'm nearly sixty, but the pension is a joke. If I wasn't so damned old, I'd rob me a bank and get the heck out of here." He laughed. "You heard about that? Someone's been making some clean getaways. Knocking off every other joint around here."

"Yeah, I heard."

"Well, they need to quit while they're ahead. The police is on 'em now."

"I guess."

Mr. Waverly walked out of my room with my trash can. He tossed the trash and brought the can back. He was a good custo-dian. I was thinking about how unfair life was. Here he was going to have to work until he was seventy. But he was right about the pension. The government didn't give a damn about the teachers, custodians, or anybody who worked for the school system unless you were a policy maker. They needed a program called No Teacher Left Behind.

Jacob called in sick and Elise had played hooky. They had spent the entire day in southern Pennsylvania at a ski resort. Jacob had surprised her with a bag full of ski gear. He purchased a pink DKNY ski jacket and pants and left them in her living room. When she woke up to get ready for school, thinking Jacob had left, he was already dressed in his gear. Sitting in the corner with a huge grin.

"I called in. I took some *slick* leave. Now I want to show you a good time," he'd said.

She'd put up no fight. Elise didn't know what it felt like to have someone do nice things for her. Jacob was proving to be an angel. She'd been without family for so long, when he began to show her attention and caring, she easily fell deep in love.

Though it had been a frosty, early-February day, they'd gone tubing, tried snowboarding, and eaten a romantic dinner at a quaint steak house, and now they were headed home.

As they cruised down I-270 Elise thanked Jacob for the wonderful time. "I've always wanted to do something like that. Just take some time out to get away." She smiled. "You really are special."

"Thank you. I enjoyed it. I enjoy you," he said. Even saying the words still felt a bit taboo. She was twelve years his junior and he shouldn't have been looking at her in that way, but ever since he first laid eyes on her, there'd been an overwhelming attraction.

"What do you think is going to happen with this? I mean next year. Do you think that we'll still be like this?"

Jacob listened to each word. "Who knows? Maybe you'll still want to be bothered with an old man like me, and maybe you won't."

"Yeah, right. I'll always want to be with you. You are the best thing that's ever happened to me," she said in a tone that sounded sincere.

He looked over at her. She was beyond adorable. He could see the little girl in her that had never been nurtured, yet at the same time he could see the dazzling black woman she had the potential to become. He hoped that their relationship wouldn't do anything to stifle her growth. Most of all, he didn't ever want to hurt her.

When they reached the exit to his house he surprised her by getting off the highway instead of going to her place. "I've got a surprise. I was going to wait until next week to give it to you on Valentine's Day, but I want you to have it now."

She entered the house behind him and he told her to take a seat. When she did he said, "Now take off all your clothes."

"What?" she asked.

"Just do it."

She breathed out heavily, feigning some level of angst. "All right already."

"Be right back." Jacob ran up to his bedroom and came down and said, "Okay, you come on up."

Elise climbed the steps naked, ass and breasts jiggling slightly to Jacob's soul satisfaction. She entered the dimly lit room, placed her hands on her hips, and said, "What?"

He smiled at her attempt to come off as sassy. "Close your eyes and put your arms out."

She did as he'd told her and he went to his armoire and pulled out a bag. He slipped the silk kimono robe onto her. It was made of textured crimson fabric with a gold trim. Jacob had had it custom-made by a friend's wife. It was cut so that it hung right at midthigh. "Okay, take a look."

Elise had always longed for the day when she'd be showered with gifts, and to have a man like Jacob showing his love for her in this way was beyond her wildest dreams. The material felt so good on her skin she was instantly turned on. She eased toward the mirror and her face turned into a huge smile. "Oh, Jacob, it's so pretty and it feels wonderful."

He was grinning as he watched her caress the fabric. "Reach inside the pocket."

She located the small pocket and stuck her hand inside and pulled out a box. "What's this?"

"It's for you. Open it."

All manner of thoughts ran through her mind. Was this a proposal? If it was, then it was how she'd always imagined it would be. As she lifted out the box she immediately realized it was a little too big to contain a ring.

When she pulled the bow off and opened it, a rush came over her. She saw the small bit of light that was in the room reflected off the tennis bracelet she held in her hands. "Ohmigod," she whispered, and tried to catch her breath as her heart began to beat.

It was the most beautiful thing she'd ever seen. She remembered that Jacob had heard her compliment Lanelle on the one she'd worn. The only thing was that this one was bigger. Four carats, she imagined. But that didn't matter. The only thing that mattered to her was that the man who had given it to her was, in fact, the one.

She was young, but not naive. She knew that all manner of things could happen and come between them. The life she'd lived had been one of losses, and fights. Through it all, she'd never given up on her hopes and quest for happiness. Elise had decided that life was a journey and along the way she'd learn to pick her spots and enjoy the good things that came to her and try to grow from the bad.

But deep in her heart, she'd always believed that there would be one person who'd come into her life and make it better. She wouldn't have to work at pleasing him. She could be herself and still be loved and feel special. That person would make her feel safe. He would show her the way and make all the rough times seem worth it.

Though she could never have seen it coming, the day she walked into his classroom, Jacob was the one. He was her lover, her friend, and her protector. This man, even if he left tomorrow, had shown her what she was supposed to feel like. He was her teacher.

"I love it. Thank you," she said with tears in her eyes.

He reached out and hugged her. There was nothing else to say or do except call in for another day off.

(((21)))

A Brick Wall Has Got to Fall

Dear Dr. C.,

My husband is always complaining that I'm not submissive enough. My argument is that the whole submissive woman theory is outdated. If I start acting submissive after all these years, how is the mortgage going to get paid? Oh, did I mention that I make more money than he does? My argument is that if he truly wants a submissive wife, I shouldn't have to get up at six, take the kids to day care, commute forty-five minutes to work, and put in eight and a half hours. He has the nerve to say that I don't listen to him. The other day he complained that I don't cook in the kitchen or the bedroom enough anymore. Then he suggested that he wants us to sell our home and move to the South, where the cost of living is cheaper. He claims that once I give up my career, I will be able to value and respect him as a man.

I'm ready to tell him to move south…but without me. You tell me. Who's right?

Shaky Ground in Chi-town

Dear Shaky,

The issue of being a submissive wife is a serious one. It saddens me that so many women think the whole concept of being submissive is a farce. A woman should be so lucky as to find a man worthy of submitting to. Never mind who makes the most money. If your husband works hard and receives an honest day's pay for an honest day's work, stands on principles, is fair when dealing with his family, and most important, if he truly tries his best to be a success in the world, then he *is* worthy.

Now, your situation sounds a little different. It sounds like you're doing a little too much around that household for him to be making so many demands. Maybe he's tripping a bit, and *then* maybe you are insistent on living beyond your means. You've got to really look at the situation. He says that he is willing to relocate in order to allow you to give up working. If so, then he is doing exactly what a man who is worthy of a submissive wife should do…coming up with a solution.

This would, of course, open up another problem. Most women have no desire to even acquire an understanding of the concept. Find out what the term really means. You can ask your pastor, and see if you even have what it takes to be that kind of woman.

Yours truly,

Dr. C.

The slap came as quick as an alligator's jaws clamping shut and it stung like hell. I couldn't believe the words had come, or rather slipped, out of my mouth. "Get the hell off of me," she yelled at the top of her lungs. Another slap and I hopped back.

"I'm sorry." I was now on my knees on the bed, dick still hard, yet it was going down quickly.

"I have never ever in my life had a man call me another woman's name while he's making love to me. Diego, how could you do that?"

In warp speed, Lanelle was putting her clothes on. I had no answers. A brother had simply gotten caught up in the moment. "*Alicia*, it feels so good. Fuck you," she said, and jumped at me again. I flinched. "Go find that bitch. Go fuck that bitch, 'cause you won't be getting no more of this," she said as she left my bedroom and headed down the steps. I followed behind her, but not too closely. The next thing I knew, my front door was slamming shut with crazy force. She was mad.

I walked into my kitchen and poured a glass of cranberry juice. I sat down, ass naked, and began to think about what I'd done. I couldn't believe it. It wasn't like I was still sitting around thinking about Alicia. I stood up and reached into the cabinet so that I could add a little Grey Goose to my cranberry drink.

The wind howled a bit and shook my screen door. I thought for a second that she'd come back to finish me off. "Damn," I said aloud. At times like this, a brother needed a pet. A little dog that I could talk to and ask stupid ass questions like "Should I call her and apologize?"

The little dog could say, "You could try, but she ain't gonna want to hear that bullshit."

I put the bottle of vodka straight to my mouth and began to

chug it, a gulp at a time. After the equivalent of five shots had landed in my belly, I had to sit down on the couch and hold it together. My stomach started to hurt a little. Lanelle was a really nice girl. On top of that, I had just blown the best piece of ass I'd had in a long time. She was far better in bed than Alicia and I couldn't figure out why I'd slipped up.

I turned on the TV and began to flip channels as I tried to figure out my next move. It was eight o'clock on a Friday night. If I hadn't blown it, she would have been in my kitchen right at that moment making me a sandwich while I recuperated for the second round. Now I was ass out, owing myself a nut. I watched a few minutes of *Paid in Full* on BET before I lost complete focus. It hadn't taken thirty minutes before the thoughts started to drift back again.

I began to wonder where Alicia was, what she was doing, and who she was with. The emptiness would be coming next, but I decided to head it off. A hot shower and more liquor did the trick for a moment. I needed to get out.

I was buzzing and put on Trey Songz's CD while I got dressed. Once I finished, I took a look at myself in the mirror and began trying to motivate myself. "You're fucking, Dr. C. You don't need that bitch. You can go out and get anybody you want. You're a good-looking nigga, and look at that jacket you have on. You're a baller, my nigga." I was slipping, talking to myself. I made a note to get a dog.

And on the real, I was lying to myself. I definitely needed Lanelle, to some extent. She had grounded me, helped me actually curb some of my self-defeating behaviors, and she'd helped my career. Because of her, I'd gotten on Janet's radio show. After I followed Jonetta's advice and got an agent, my contract was on the way any day now. Though I wasn't technically a baller yet, the proverbial check was in the mail.

Speeding, for no reason, to a bar so I could get even more drunk made all the sense in the world to me. I picked up the phone hoping someone would join me. When I didn't get any responses I called Lisa to tell her what had happened.

"I told you not to fuck that bitch. Now you got to look at her funny face until Mrs. Whitmore comes back."

"Yeah. You right."

"Diego, your ass is retarded. How could you call her another woman's name. That's like the ultimate dis. What did she do, slap the shit out of you?"

"Yeah, how'd you know?"

"Because that's what a bitch does to a nigga who can't remember who's pussy he's in." She laughed at herself. "I got to go. Me and my man are about to roll up a tree."

"All right, cool."

"Gees up. Hoes down, my nigga." Then she hung the phone up.

I pulled into the parking garage and headed up the block for the bar. I had been calling Jacob, but he hadn't picked up the phone, and when I dialed my brother, Lee, all I'd gotten was a busy signal. He hadn't had a cell phone since the incident with the police near my job. The phones were in Nicole's name and she'd cut them off.

So here I was, solo, already drunk as a skunk just trying to keep my mind off my problems. I walked into Ozio's and made my way straight to the bar. I spoke to a few random folks who were nearby, simply because they were staring in my face, and once I was at the bar, I people-watched until I could get my drink order.

There was an attractive girl standing next to me who seemed to be by herself. "Excuse me, would you like a drink?" I asked.

"Sure."

She looked to be black, but she definitely had some Filipino or Japanese flavor working as well. The slanted eyes and the straight hair were the giveaway. "What you drinking?"

"Baileys, on ice."

"Cool." I ordered another double shot of vodka for myself and her drink.

"Thanks," she said. "What's your name?" she asked over the music.

"Diego. What's yours?"

"Rhiana."

"Diego, you look kind of familiar," she said as she accepted the drink.

"You don't." It was never a good thing when a woman thought you *looked* familiar. Most likely you did something to her, or one of her friends, that had made them try to forget about you. I figured I'd give her some time to think about it, so I said, "Rhiana, you're looking so beautiful tonight and I don't want you to think I'm trying to tie you up all night just 'cause I bought you a drink. I'm going to go take a look for someone I was supposed to meet here. I'll look for you in a little bit so I can keep that drink fresh."

"Oh . . . okay. Well . . . make sure you do that." She seemed a little thrown off that I hadn't gone in for the kill or tried to sweat her.

I stepped off and headed for the other side of the club. Then, as the DJ put on Young Jeezy's "Go Crazy," I saw her. A five-foot-six, copper-skinned beauty of a woman. Now, I knew that I might have been being shallow and that the alcohol might have been talking to me, but this girl had an aura about her. Before I said a word to her, something was telling me that she and I were meant to be . . . something. I moved toward her and we exchanged glances. When I was no more than ten feet away from her, I smiled and waited for a second. Then she smiled back and waved for me to come to her. Unless there was a glitch in the Matrix, it was clear to me that this chick was the *one*. She had crazy amounts of sex appeal. When I looked her up and down, I was certain that she was the one that could make me forget everything that I was going through. Now, face-to-face, I could see that she was truly a fine woman with a nice body and a mystique that separated her from the everyday girl.

She was actually smoking a cigar, which shocked me. I don't know why, because we were in a cigar bar. Something about the way she puffed it threw me off at first, made her look tough. Then at the same time she made the act look vogue.

She offered me one. "It's a Cuban. This is no habit for me," she said as she lit the stogie I'd accepted. "It's just a little conversation piece."

I nodded and responded, "Well then, let's converse." Ozio's was packed and we wasted no time getting another round of drinks and finding a booth in the back to sit and talk shit.

"I love your eyes," she commented. I might have heard that before but never really understood why. "They make you look so innocent, like a little boy."

I laughed into a smile when she said that.

"And those teeth, there's nothing like a man with a nice, sexy smile."

"Thanks, your smile is nice, too." I wasn't lying. I realized that my focus was more on her lips, though. She had big juicy lips like the chick Jill Jones from the UPN show *Girlfriends*. And truthfully, I had fantasized about a blowjob from Toni Childs on more than one occasion.

The girl continued to compliment me on all the things about me that she found oh so wonderful. By the time she finished, my head was big as a hot-air balloon. The last thing she said almost made me spit my drink out. She leaned in after taking the cherry from her martini into those big lips. "Now, as cute as you are, if you can fuck, then we're in business."

"Well, if you want, we can get out of here right now," I said.

"Slow down, brother. You don't even know my name." She laughed.

"Damn." I was stunned. "It hadn't dawned on me that we've been talking for almost thirty minutes and I didn't even ask you your name." I started laughing. I was so drunk, but it was my own secret. I was the type of person who could be highly intoxicated and no one would really know without a Breathalyzer. Other than some slightly slurred speech, I could hide it. The only thing it did was make me get more aggressive.

"My name's Paige."

"Well, Paige, my name's Diego. And wasn't it you who brought up the whole topic of sex?"

"Yeah, but I didn't say it was going to happen tonight. Did I?"

"No, you didn't, but let me say this. Correct me if I'm wrong, but

I've been hanging out in clubs and have been through the whole "meet-and-greet" process enough to know when there's chemistry there. We have that and it's strong. You're flirting with me. I'm flirting with you. I don't have anyone at home, and who knows what tomorrow brings, but tonight I wanna get with you. I've been through some shit and I'm just trying to chill."

She took a sip and eyed me hard, as if she were peering into my soul, trying to either deem me worthy or discount me. I went on. "You seem like an intelligent sister—"

"Seem?"

"Well, I'm just saying. From the conversation we've had . . . my bad . . . you are intelligent. I find that a turn-on. And we seem to have a few other things in common. So I'm not saying that we can't enjoy some of those things at another time, but right here, right now, give me one good reason why we can't go back to my place, where I can rub you from head to toe and make you feel like your body is being worshiped."

She looked at her watch. "Well, the first reason is because I told my husband I'd be home by ten and it's almost eleven."

"Husband?"

"And the second is . . . you're going to have to come better than that. I need to know a little more about you before I give you some of this. You see, this isn't something that I just do. A woman has to be *selective*."

"You're married?" She nodded yes and showed me her finger. I didn't notice a ring until she'd mentioned being married.

"But we can be friends and get to know one another . . . really well if you act right," she said and showed her smile. Again, my eyes were drawn to those big dick-sucking lips.

I couldn't believe it. Another married chick. I was trying to do right, but they kept coming across my path, married women who were chasing a little strange ding-a-ling. It was official. Women were just as bad, if not worse, than men.

"All right," I said, and we exchanged numbers. Of course she told me when to call which numbers and ran the whole drill, which I already knew. "You better head on in." I was sure I sounded dejected.

"Why don't you walk me to my truck? It's up the street in the garage," she said.

"Yeah, okay." I was ready to leave anyway. My mind was on getting some ass. I figured I'd get on my cell and call everybody and their mama to see if I could catch someone in the same horny state. If push came to shove, I'd stop off at the strip club and blow a little cash on one of my ex-girlfriends who shook it fast for a living.

As we headed toward the door Paige walked in front of me and I placed my hand on her hip, trying to steal a feel. The alcohol.

I was nearly at the door when I felt someone grab my arm. I turned and it was Rhiana. I paused momentarily. Paige didn't notice I'd stopped and kept walking. "You leaving?"

"Yeah," I said, trying to brush her off and keep it moving. "I'll catch up with you next time.

"Oh, okay," she said in a sinister voice. ". . . But I remembered where I knew you from." I started to walk again. "I was at your wedding. I know Alicia."

I looked back at her and was about to stop when Paige came back and tapped my shoulder, "C'mon, papi. What you doing?" she asked. Then she looked at Rhiana. The two traded glances and it was obvious that they'd had dealings of some sort. Rhiana rolled her eyes and walked off.

"I hate that Chinese bitch," Paige said. "She thinks she's all that."

We started off and headed out the door and up M Street. "Where do you know her from?"

"We used to work together a long time ago. Fuck her."

I'd thought about it briefly but didn't mention it to Paige. It wasn't that cold for a night in the middle of winter. I was thinking the upper forties. We still walked briskly to the garage where her ride was parked.

We took the elevator down to P2 and headed for a black Cadillac Escalade. She hit the alarm. "Climb in," she commanded.

She started the engine and "Burn" started banging through the stereo. She turned the volume down. "Where'd you park?"

"Actually, I'm at the other end of the block. The garage across from the bank."

"Okay."

We sat for a second as she let the truck warm up. "So, when can I see you?" she asked.

"When you ready?"

"What about tomorrow afternoon?" Over the next fifteen minutes, I learned all the times that she was free and why. Her man was busy. He was into the gym. He raced motorcycles. He hung out with his frat brothers way too much, and to top it off, he traveled for work. "When he's home, he has the nerve to tell me that I get on his nerves, that I want sex too much."

I smiled when she said that. It was an opening. I asked her what she liked as far as sex went and she told me. She liked it every way imaginable. Sometimes rough, sometimes soft. She liked to watch porno and then she made my night when she said, "I love to fuck in strange places."

I looked around and wondered for a quick minute if the bottom of a garage was strange enough. My question was answered quickly enough and I had to admit that I was surprised that she gave me head, but nevertheless thankful. She didn't give a damn if they had cameras in the garage. She opened the back doors to the truck and let me fuck her from behind while she laid her body flat on the storage area where the third row of seats would have been.

"So we still on for tomorrow?" she asked as we pulled up in front of the garage where I was parked.

"Hell yeah, just call me." I was still buzzing, but now both tired and relaxed enough to go home and get some rest.

"I will," she said, and leaned in for a kiss.

"I'll be waiting."

I barely remembered the drive home. I was half-asleep, to tell the truth, as I drove home with the window open. I felt bad and irresponsible for being a drunk driver. As I pulled into my development I thanked God for letting me make it. When I parked I sat in my car for a second. My head was spinning slightly and I didn't want to make it this close only to bust my head on the concrete in front of my door.

When I stepped out of the car and started up the walk, I had the shit scared out of me. "Diego," the familiar voice called. "I need you."

I turned around and saw my brother standing in front of me. He looked like he'd been attacked by Mike Tyson in his younger days. His eye was swollen shut, his lip was busted, and his face was scratched up. "Lee, what the hell happened to you?"

"Nicole, man." I was silent. I didn't understand. "She . . . been . . . beating the hell outta me."

He could have knocked me over with a feather. My brother, who used to give me the beat-down as a kid until he grew up and out of doing it, was sitting there telling me his five-foot-four wife was slapping him around. "What?" I asked in utter disbelief.

He repeated himself. I don't know if it was the liquor or the disbelief, but I started to laugh right in his face. He then looked down at the ground. "Man, you serious?"

He nodded. We headed into the house and he told me everything. From the beginning. How it had started with yelling, then her suicide threats. He'd been embarrassed at her behavior, and for that reason, he hadn't told anyone.

"And you met this bitch at Bible study, right?" I said. I shook my head in disgust. "Let me ask you this . . . did you ever think of fighting back?"

He was quiet for a minute, then he answered, "I always do."

"What you mean? Well, why you look like this?"

He shook his head. "Diego, man. She's good. She's like a black belt and she takes all these boxing lessons."

"You got to be kidding me. You mean to tell me that you can't beat her—" I didn't get the words off before my doorbell began to ring. It was one in the morning and I didn't play that.

I headed for the door. "Nah, that's her. Call the police," Lee told me.

I looked at him and all the respect that I could muster for him wasn't enough to keep me from saying, "Fuck that. I'll kick the bitch's ass if she try that karate shit."

"Who is it?" I yelled.

"Open the door. You know who it is. Tell Lee to bring his ass out here."

I swung the door open. "Lee is staying here tonight." I looked at her face and she looked fine. Not a scratch. She proceeded to open my screen door and make her way in. For some reason, my fraternal instincts kicked in and I yelled out, "Leave him the hell alone. Take your crazy ass home."

"Fuck you, nigga," she yelled, and tried to bull her way past me.

Like a scene out of a seventies blaxploitation film, I hauled my hand back like Ron O'Neal and delivered one of the hardest pimp slaps in modern history. It was like the alcohol and adrenaline had blended together to create some bolder and crazier me.

My hand cracked her across the side of her head and sounded off like a wet towel hitting an ass in the locker room. I was in shock as she fell to the ground, holding not her face but her ear.

"Yo, what's wrong with you?" my brother said as he ran toward me with his fists balled up. She was on the ground and she began to whimper. "That's my wife," he yelled.

Lee shoved me in the chest and I shoved him back. Nicole began to cry that her ear was ringing. "He busted my eardrum. Diego busted my eardrum."

"Man, you're crazy," he yelled in my face, and the spit was flying as he talked.

I couldn't believe his nerve. "Where was all this when she was kicking your ass?"

Hearing that, he swung and punched me right in the stomach. I felt the punch and it felt like my stomach was wrapped around his fist. I dropped to my knees and began to vomit. I was delirious as he picked her up. "Come on. Let's go, baby."

I picked myself up, still coughing, wanting desperately to get a punch off on Lee, but he'd made it out the door, carrying his wife. He was almost to his car and I yelled from my porch, "Y'all are sick puppies. You deserve each other."

"I'll get you, Diego," she yelled as she climbed into her car.

"Anytime, bitch. Anytime," I said, giving her the finger. "Lee, I'm gonna kick your ass when I see you, man."

He slammed his door and drove off, knowing that that was the first and the last time he could come to me with that bull crap. I slammed my door and went up to my room and fell across my bed. A few thoughts ran through my mind as I closed my eyes. After thinking about all the good and all the bad that was me, I realized that I was who I was. Perhaps it was time for me to accept the role that life had given me. Maybe I'd never change. Maybe I'd never find someone to take Alicia's place. Maybe true love simply wasn't meant for me. And maybe, just maybe, I'd been put here to take up the slack of husbands and boyfriends who didn't know how, or simply didn't care enough, to do their jobs.

I closed my eyes and reasoned with myself to get some peace. Aside from the emptiness it seemed I felt whenever I was alone for too long and destruction of my soul that creeping with the next man's wife brought, I thought to myself, *There are plenty of jobs that are worse.*

22

Just Like Cats

Dear Dr. C.,

I dated a man for two years and felt like we had a really strong relationship. Like any couple, we went through some things, but there was no denying the love that we shared. Then one day, all hell broke loose. I found out that he was cheating on me. The thing that really threw me for a loop was that all the things that he claimed to love most about me—my intellect, my ambition, and the way I carried myself as a woman—they obviously didn't mean that much in the end. The woman he left me for was a mess compared to me. I eventually met her after I found out that he'd moved in with her and was taking care of her two kids.

This was a year ago. Well, all of a sudden he wants to come back. He has been calling my job nonstop. I don't take his calls, even changed my extension. He has sent me e-mails and he has even gone to my mother to tell her how much of a fool he was. I have been seeing someone for a few months, but I honestly do miss my ex and what we had. What I want to know is: Should I give him another chance, and how do I know if he's real this time?

Still Loving Him in Los Angeles

Still in Love,

First off, I have to applaud you on being real with yourself. This is a tough one. Your situation is the epitome of damned if you do, damned if you don't. What if you take him back and he hurts you again? What if you deny him and yourself the chance to be with your true love?

You see, even your true love can take you through monumental changes on the way to becoming your ideal mate. Sometimes it takes a period of growth by trial and error. You have to look, with your eyes wide open, to determine if he is sincere. They say nothing good comes easy. If you decide to give him another try, which I would do if I were you, then move slowly. See what he is willing to do to get back in good. Make him earn it every step of the way, your trust included. If he proves worthy, then move forward. The only reason I suggest giving it a shot is that you still love him. Remember, though, it's not for him… it's for you. Remember that, but never mention it to him. And make the following agreement with yourself that you don't break under any circumstances. The second you find yourself unhappy… drop him like he's hot.

Yours truly,

Dr. C.

April 2006

The meeting had seemingly come from out of nowhere. A friend of a friend of a music exec had seen Jacob's performance with his group at Hammerjack's in Baltimore and the call had come two days later.

Talk of No Question recording an album had been going on for three months now and nothing had come of it. Jacob had begun to get frustrated. It wasn't so much that he feared that his time was passing him by, it was more that he didn't want to become just another member of a local band. He'd seen other artists blow up in the D.C. area and he knew that he was just as talented as any of them. One small record company out of Philly was interested in signing them as a band, but neither a contract nor any money had been offered.

Elise had also been in his ear during the couple of months he'd been seeing her. He'd been amazed that a girl so young could have such a practical outlook on life. "Jacob," she'd said. "Loyalty is a great thing and you should always strive to bring other people along when you find success. Unfortunately, you can't truly help anyone until you make it, not without sacrificing the very success you are striving for. You have a chance to be great. You can't give that up for your friends in the band. I wouldn't even want you to give it up for me."

As they sat in the bed she'd added, "People see you headed for stardom and they don't want you to hop on board that train without them. But a lot of times, they don't know what you did to get that ticket. They don't know your pain, the risk you've taken. All they know is their own fear and that they don't have that same ticket." She'd leaned in and kissed him on the forehead that night.

"You've got to punch that ticket, baby. Another train is leaving the station right behind you. They can prepare to board that one." Elise had become his biggest fan and his personal cheerleader.

A week later, Jacob recounted the entire conversation as he sat in Gladys Knight's Chicken & Waffles out in Largo. Sonny Kingsdale, an A&R guy from Warner Records, was ready to walk Jacob right into headquarters and get a deal done. "It's not a question of *can I get you signed*. It's just a matter of you being prepared to do what you have to do. I can't promise you anything about your band. I can't even tell you that they'll be able to play for you when you tour. Maybe, but maybe not. They do sound great behind you on the demo, but who knows? When it comes down to it, these things take on a life of their own. A year from now, they might not even be able to get a ticket to one of your shows. I've seen it happen before. I'm only telling you this because I'm a straight shooter. The last thing I want is an unhappy artist. You go solo. You blow up. You lose friends and sometimes even family."

Jacob felt pressured. "So how soon do I have to let you know?"

Sonny was a fast talker. It was how he got paid. He looked at his watch. "About forty-five minutes ago," he said in a matter-of-fact tone. "Listen, Jacob. It's a no-brainer. You sign with me and I walk you in. You get a deal and you have a career. If not, I walk away and your ship has sailed. Maybe you get another shot down the road. Maybe you don't. But you risk playing in these little hokey spots until you're forty-five. There's a million cats who can sing, but not a million record companies. I hate to be short, but I gotta run. I've got a flight to L.A. leaving at four and traffic's a bitch. What's it gonna be?"

Jacob thought about it. He thought about his band members

and all the things they'd talked about doing. How they'd believed in him and had helped him even get into a position to have someone offering him a shot.

Sonny went on about how Jacob was going to be the male version of Jill Scott. "You mean the next Maxwell, then, huh?"

"Exactly. That's putting it even more precise. You'll be huge, as far as neosoul artists go," he said.

Jacob signed the paper. He was officially in negotiations with Warner Records and could no longer shop for a deal or perform with No Question, not until his deal was done. Sonny hadn't left anything to chance. He didn't want anyone stealing away his new commodity.

"You won't regret this. Keep your nose clean and I'll talk to you next week to let you know when we'll be sending for you."

"Do you think I'll be able to finish out the school year?"

"Why would you want to?" Sonny laughed. "But sure. If you want. That's what, two months, right?"

"Yeah, about."

"Okay. We'll still get you out to Cali some time in the next couple weeks to get your deal done and we'll take it from there."

Jacob walked through the door of Elise's apartment. She was seated on the couch Indian style, watching *Hustle & Flow* on DVD. When she looked up she couldn't read his expression. "So how'd it go?"

When he explained how everything had gone down and that he'd signed the deal, Elise leaped up and screamed, doing a little dance on the floor. "I'm so happy for you. I'm so happy for you."

Then they hugged and she kissed him on the cheek. While she held him she whispered in his ear, "I'm so proud of you." He could barely contain his emotions. They were winning *together*. Then she added, "I hope this doesn't blow you, but I have some news as well."

Jacob didn't like the look on her face. "Oh yeah. What's that?"

She exhaled and said, "I'm leaving. I'm going back to Indianapolis."

Puzzled, he said, "You hated it there, though. Why?"

"My aunt is really sick and I need to go and help out. She really needs me. The kids need someone to look after them."

Jacob's heart sank. "So you're leaving as soon as the school year is over?"

"No, I'm leaving next week."

"What?" he yelled. "You can't leave . . . I—" He cut himself off. Then he went on: "Elise, what about your dreams? I'm going to do this music thing and I want you with me."

"You'll be fine. We'll be in touch."

"Be in touch?"

"It's not like you'll never hear from me again."

"You can't go, baby."

"Don't do this, Jacob. Don't try to make this hard."

"But, sweetheart, you inspire me and . . ." His voice began to crack. ". . . I need you." Jacob's heart was now throbbing. He couldn't bear the thought of her leaving. In an instant it felt as if his whole world was crashing down. Honestly, he felt like crying.

"I'm sorry, Jacob. But you're a *grown* man. Those kids need me, too. Their mother is sick and she was there for me when I needed someone." She sounded as if she didn't care about walking out on him. As if leaving was easy for her. Perhaps the whole thing had been in his head. Maybe the time they'd spent together had really been nothing.

Out of pain his tone became biting. "She used you as a house-keeper and a babysitter. You don't owe her." He moved closer to her and his desperation became clear as his normally smooth voice cracked. "She can hire someone to help. I'll pay for it. You don't owe her . . ."

"Well, I don't owe you either." Her expression turned ice-cold. She stood and shouted, "Man, I can't believe you're acting like this."

"I can't believe *you're* acting like this. What about all that stuff you just finished saying about following dreams and not letting any-one hold you back. You're acting like a gullible little girl right now."

"Yeah, a *little* girl, huh? Was I a little girl when you were digging all up in this?" She waved her hand dismissively and said, "Jacob, get the fuck out of my house."

"You—"

She cut him off and repeated herself three times in all, her voice growing louder with each demand. The last time she walked to the door, opened it, and yelled, "Now."

As Jacob moved slowly to the door he noticed a tear rolling down her cheek. He stopped and said, "Elise, I'm sorry."

"Jacob, just please go. Please."

He walked out the door and down the steps. He sat in his car for a minute before he started it. It should have been one of the most exciting days of his life; he was going to record an album. In-stead, he felt like his head was about to explode the same way his heart had. Before he realized it, he was crying. He drove off and tried to pull himself together as he faced the fact that he was in love with Elise.

Elise's hands were trembling as she dialed the number. "Hello" came the voice on the other end.

"I did it, okay," Elise said. "I ended it. Now please, just leave him alone."

"I'm warning you. If I see you with him again . . . any of his shows, I will go to the principal and the police. I will ruin him."

"Don't worry, you won't."

"I better not," she said as she watched Jacob pulling off.

"You made your point," Elise said, and hung up the phone. As the pain of losing what she'd built with Jacob began to consume her, she climbed up off the couch and struggled to make it to her bedroom. She didn't make it. Her knees got weak and it was all she could do to make it to the toilet, where she threw up, again.

Usually Paige didn't have much time when she rolled through. Half the time she came in the door and immediately devoured me. Fuck first, ask questions later. Since the night we'd met, our sexcapades had grown in frequency until I was sure that I was hitting it more than her husband. She was staying until the wee hours of the morning so often that I was wondering where her man was fitting into the equation and if he actually lived in the house.

I had gotten used to enjoying her company even when we weren't sexing each other up, but there was no mistaking what our relationship was about. We'd lie in the bed sometimes and talk afterward, and that was cool. Other times she'd simply admit that she only needed an attitude adjustment. On those occasions she'd come through the door, bend over the sofa, and take it hard and fast. Then she'd head home to her husband before her panties even had the time to dry.

This weekend we'd planned to really hang out some since her husband was off at a motorcycle convention of some sort down south. So with his absence, we'd spent the day out at Tyson's II, doing some shopping. Paige had been thoughtful enough to pick up a couple things for him while she shopped. When we finished we decided to get a bite to eat at Legal Sea Foods.

Over dinner we had a talk about my career. "Diego, I read your column the other day," she said as she sipped on a glass of Chardonnay. "It was pretty good. But I have to ask. Where do you come up with some of the bullshit answers you give?"

"Pardon me?"

"I mean, do you really believe the things you say? Like that women should be submissive. Or that men don't want to know that their women are cheating?"

"Everything I say is from the heart. Absolutely."

"Wow. So what kind of response are you getting? Do women like your answers?"

"Hell yeah. They write all the time with their praises. I get so many e-mails from sisters all over the county saying that they have been waiting for someone to come along to keep it real with them. Most people try to give politically correct answers, or say something simply for the sake of being controversial. That's bullshit. I say what's real. If you gave a nigga some truth serum and asked him some questions . . . that's what you get with me."

She nodded. "So, how much do they pay you for that?"

"They *pay* me." I laughed. I figured that she was trying to figure out my financial status. She'd seen me spend a thousand bucks at the mall and I figured it had her wondering. She knew that I taught school for a living, and the damage I'd done in Saks wouldn't add up in her mind.

"They must be paying you okay," she said. "You seem to stay fly all the time."

Actually, my stylish dress had been a new development. I had just recently been able to spend a few bucks on nice things. The first part of my advance from my deal for my radio show, *Ladies Listen Up*, had just come through. So Paige had come along at just the perfect time. With the money from the column and my school salary, I was able to blow a few dollars. Since she was the main woman I'd been sleeping with since I'd fallen out with Lanelle, she was the recipient of any generosity. I purchased her a Louis Vuitton bag and a couple pairs of shoes. She seemed really grateful.

WJDS had agreed to pay me $150,000 a year to host the show. My agent, Kenny Stein, whom I'd hired at the direction of Jonetta, had been incredible. He'd gotten me $50,000 up front, and after his commission, I had just cashed in a pretty nice check. We were going to begin rehearsing in a month and the show would launch at the end of June.

We finished up dinner and headed back to my place. Paige had brought an overnight bag and was prepared to spend the night. As we drove around the beltway she gave me head while we listened to the best of Barry White.

I didn't cum while I was driving as she'd assured me I would, but she more than made up for it once we got settled inside. I wondered why it was that I felt more free with married women. I was truly enjoying Paige. It wasn't just the sex either. When we were allowed the time, we could talk for hours on end. I would listen to her tell me stories about her childhood. She was from Camden, New Jersey, and she had the greatest stories about her childhood. Her father had been a member of the Harlem Globetrotters and she'd traveled the world with him.

An evening that had been all up suddenly went downhill when at around two in the morning her cell phone began to ring. Her husband was dialing her. From inside her home, no less, when he was supposed to be out of town. The fact that I'd picked her up, and that her car was parked in her garage, had me thinking that she was busted and in major trouble.

Though she was tired and worn out from our lovemaking, she remained calm. "Relax," she said.

She quickly dialed one of her friends. "Hey, girl. You got any company? Good. Did he call you? Well, if you see my house number or his cell, don't answer. I'll be to your house in fifteen minutes. I'll have him come and pick me up from over there . . ." She paused. "I don't even know. His ass must have come home early. No, I don't know why, but I'll call him when I get over there." Pause. "You know the drill. Pop a bottle of wine and put two glasses on the table. We were watching movies and fell asleep." Pause. "*Love Jones*, of course."

By the time she hung up the phone, I had my pants and shoes already on ready to walk out the door. So did she.

23

Out with the Old

Dear Dr. C.,

Last summer me and my girls went on a vacation to the Essence Festival in New Orleans. There were six of us, all of us married except two, and one of them is newly divorced. We talked and bonded during the trip and had a really great time. One thing in particular disturbed us. Through our conversation, we realized that by our last night there, we had all been hit on by a brother who was either married or in a "serious" relationship. It got us to thinking about our men. Were we cynical to think that given half a chance, our men wouldn't do the exact same thing?

During a round of drinks at dinner, one of the girls, I'll call her Katrina, suggested that we make a pact. The agreement was that we all take that last night and live out our fantasies with whomever we chose and that whatever happened in the

Big Easy would stay there. Of course we dismissed her as being crazy, but as the night wore on and the Hand Grenades and tequila shots continued to flow, a few of us decided to go through with it. I'm ashamed to admit that I was one of the girls who decided to do it. I don't know why. I'm not unhappy in my marriage and I love my husband. Yet and still, I actually lived out one of my fantasies and had a ménage-à-trois with two of the finest brothers I'd ever seen. The only problem is that I've been feeling really guilty about it for the last nine months and I'm considering being honest with my man.

It was the first time I'd cheated since we've been married, and only the third time since he and I started dating. The previous two times were both with my ex, who I'd dated the three previous years. So my question is: Do you think he would want me to be honest, or do you think he'd throw four years of marriage down the drain and leave me?

Hit by the Hand Grenades in Houston

Dear Hit,

Now, while it's true you went out like a real hooker, you have to understand one thing about men. We know that <u>you</u>, our wives and girlfriends, are capable of cheating. I mean, we've sexed other men's wives, so trust, it's no secret. It's just that we don't like to think about it ... ever. We're not built to stomach that type of thing. You didn't get caught, so unless you have a death wish, take that to your grave. As a woman, you're programmed to be able to do that.

> *Should the occasion arise in which religious reasons cause*
> *you to confess, I strongly suggest that you do so in a public place*
> *and have your things packed before you deliver the news.*
>
> *Yours truly,*
> *Dr. C.*

It had been three weeks since Jacob had seen or spoken to Elise and the pain showed on his face. He moped around the school and barely spoke to anyone. She had withdrawn from the school as she told him she would and he hadn't so much as heard a word from her.

He'd gotten another e-mail and wondered if Elise had, in fact, been mocha2munch. It had been a long while since he'd gotten one. More than two months, the last one right around the time he had started up with Elise.

> Jacob,
> Just checking on you and thinking about you. That's all.
> mocha2munch@yahoo.com

Most mornings, before the students arrived, Jacob thought about going back to the gym to get high with his partner Willie, but decided against it. Instead, he just did his best to suck up his pain and deal. He tried everything he could to forget about what had happened between him and Elise and made every effort to wipe the memories that he held from his mind.

He rearranged the desk in his class so that he wouldn't keep staring out at her empty desk. Next he scratched her name from his grade books. He did his best to ignore Anna, who seemed to be trying to act as if she didn't notice Elise's absence either.

In fact, he found it strange that Anna seemed to be in a better than usual mood and it was actually becoming irritating. Every time he made eye contact with her, she met him with smiles that he hadn't seen since the beginning of the school year.

As the final bell rang he gathered his things with little to no emotion. Just like getting up, leaving work to go home had become a chore. As the time was nearing when he'd officially be signed to Warner Records, there was nothing left for him to do other than to sit in his basement and listen to music. Since one of the stipulations of his contract banned him from performing live without the consent of the company, he'd lost his only release from the pressures of his day job.

As he headed up the hallway he recalled his announcement to the band that he was going to record his solo album. A serious grumble had erupted as they all sat in the front corner of the club. A couple of members had congratulated him. He could tell from their body language that the rest wanted to kick his ass. "This is some bull, Jacob. We started this together," Wally, the keyboard player, belted out.

"Yo, man, that's some snake shit," the drummer shouted. "But, it don't surprise me none . . . good luck, your ass is gonna need it." Then he walked out.

Mostly they had all just gotten really quiet. Jacob had realized for the first time that some of the people he'd thought would be happiest for him were not. He didn't really understand why they wouldn't be proud, but it bothered him nonetheless. The sadness from a chapter ending seemed more appropriate, but all the negative vibes seemed a bit much.

The only thing that was going right for him was that he'd been able to write three great songs in the middle of a night when he couldn't sleep. His deal hadn't even been cemented yet, but he had begun to compile material. When he did hit the studio, he wanted to be impressive. Of course all the songs were written to Elise, but no one had to know that.

He headed to his car and was preparing to head home to climb into bed so he could yank the covers up over his head. He didn't notice the car next to him. "Hey, Mr. Marsh."

He looked over and saw Anna parked next to him. "Anna, what are you doing over here in this parking lot?"

"I came to see you of course," she said, and giggled. "I came to repay you a favor."

"What favor?"

"The day. The day we had the talk. Some of what you said to me . . . well, it changed my life. I even was able to speak to my mother about some things."

"That's good. I think—"

"Yeah, it is. But I want to share a few things with you, *things* that I know about."

Jacob's face showed his nervousness. "Such as?"

"Such as . . . Elise is pregnant. And you're the father," she said with a straight face. She might as well have been telling him that there was a chance of rain.

Jacob felt the blood immediately leave his head. "What?" He wasn't sure if the words had left his mouth. "What did you say?"

"Elise, she told me everything before she left."

He didn't utter a word for a moment. Instead they both just sat there in their vehicles staring into each other's eyes. He wiped his hands over his face, and when he thought he had the energy to handle more bad news, he said, "So now what?"

"Nothing. I just wanted you to know and, I guess, ask you something."

"What's that?"

Anna put a Charm's blow pop into her mouth and gave it one suck before she asked, "Is she the reason why you've been looking so sad and sick? Are you in love with her?"

He didn't answer that question but had another. "So what is she going to do? Does she have a number, because I tried the one I have and it didn't work anymore."

"I'm not sure. The last we talked, she called me. But I just thought you should know what was going on, and don't worry . . . your secret is safe with me." With that, she pulled off.

When the call came through, I didn't know what to do. Gina and I had no real connection, yet her mother was on the line at Providence Hospital, telling me that she wanted me there.

"Mrs. Daniels, I don't know if I'm really up for that. You know that she and I—"

She cut me off in a stern but motherly tone. "Son, she needs you here. I don't care about the circumstances under which you made this baby. But you did do it *together*."

I had my doubts about this, and although I considered myself to be a respectful type of guy, I came out with "I'm not really sure if the kid is—"

"Diego," she said. "Let me say this before you go any further. I don't blame you for feeling like that. I've heard bits and pieces of the story and really it doesn't matter what led up to it. But one thing I know is this. I asked Gina, mother to daughter, if there's a chance that this child might belong to another man."

Her tone lowered and something in the delivery shook me up a tad as she went on. "She looked me right in the eye and told me that she was certain. And I *know* she wasn't lying to me. I've raised her the best I can and I know she's a good person. We all make mistakes. Hopefully, you won't make one today. So you can take a chance and come down and witness the birth a child that you believe *might* be yours, or you can sit home and do whatever you were doing and miss it. The worst thing to happen if you come is that you get a great story to tell. If you have any heart at all, I don't have to tell you the best thing that could happen."

There was something in the way she spoke to me. I found myself cruising toward the city. I picked up the phone and called Jacob. He sounded as if he was sick. "You all right?" I asked.

"Yeah," he said with his voice groggy.

"You won't believe what I'm about to do."

"What?"

"I'm on the way to the hospital to witness the birth of Gina's baby. She wanted me to come."

I heard him perk up. "Whoa. Time flies. You hadn't said anything about that lately."

"Jacob, you've been out of sorts lately. I haven't been able to catch you all that often, and when I do you seem to be so preoccupied that I just keep it real light with you. I figured that with your deal and all that, you'd just been busy."

He laughed. "You know, I was thinking the same thing about you. I'll admit, I've been kind of down, but I haven't really reached out like I could have. I knew that things were about to get hectic for you with your radio show."

"Well, since we're both about to blow up, we have to make an agreement."

"What's that?"

"We gotta keep it real with each other. I'm gonna always need my man having my back," I said.

"No doubt," he shot right back.

"So . . ." He was quiet and waited for me to finish. "Are you gonna come up to the hospital with a nigga or what?"

"All you had to do was ask," Jacob said. "All you had to do was ask."

I told him where I was headed and he jumped up and prepared to meet me there. During the rest of my ride, I thought about my life and everything that I'd been through lately. I wondered how it would change things if the baby turned out to be mine. By the time I made it up South Dakota Avenue, I'd thought of a hundred and one things and come up with a thousand questions. As I finally made my way into the hospital, I only had one answer. I was scared to death.

Gina's labor lasted another couple hours before she dilated enough to start pushing. During that time, I sat in the waiting room trading uncomfortable stares with a couple of her family members. Jacob was in the hallway with me when the nurse came out and said Gina's ready to see me.

I walked into the room and it wasn't at all like I expected. I took a deep breath and looked at my boy, who, oddly, looked like he was more nervous than I was. There were three nurses standing around and Gina's obstetrician was in the trenches. It felt awkward being the only male in the room. I wasn't sure where to stand. Gina's mom was at her side and her cousin was near a table by the window, funneling chips of ice into cups. Gina was panting and sweating profusely. Even when she wasn't making any noise I could tell that the contractions had her in a state of constant discomfort.

When I made eye contact with Gina, the first thing I thought was that she looked a mess. Her hair was in two big fat braids and her skin looked like she'd broken out with a heat rash. I didn't really know what to expect, but she cracked a smile and it was like all of a sudden I was glad I'd come. No matter what happened, I knew that she needed me there.

I asked, "You okay?"

She nodded and I walked toward her. Something told me to kiss her forehead, and as I leaned in she jerked up. She head butted me right in the lips as a contraction racked her body. "Ayyyyyyhhhhh-hhh," she let out.

"Mmmmmm," I let out as I tasted the blood in my mouth from the inside of my lips.

I didn't have time to absorb the pain as she grabbed my hand with the force of a bodybuilder.

After that, everything else was a blur. I heard orders to push, then push harder. Then there was a bunch of cursing, mostly *dammit*s and *shit*s. They all came from Gina. Forty minutes later the doctor delivered a six-pound, seven-ounce baby girl.

I was stunned at the whole spectacle of birth. I couldn't believe what my eyes had shown me, and I absolutely had a new and more profound respect for women. What really shocked me was when Gina whispered to me, "Come here, Diego."

I moved in close and she said, "Thanks for coming."

"You don't have to thank me. I'm glad I came. I'm glad you're fine and that the baby is, too."

"Speaking of the baby, I don't know what to name her. Do you know of any cute girl names?"

I was stuck. All the kids that I came in contact with, and I couldn't come up with one name. Then it hit me. When I looked at the baby, I felt like the sky had opened up, giving me a wake-up call. If she turned out to be my child, then I was going to be the best dad that I could. The kid would be my little slice of heaven, and so I said, "Let's call her Heaven."

Gina nodded and smiled in approval. "Heaven," she said aloud. "If I give her your last name, she'll be Heaven Christian." Then we both laughed.

"How about we make Heaven her middle name? Just name her after your mom."

"Do you even know my mom's name?"

"No."

"Well, you ought to know, it's Alicia."

We went with Heaven.

(((24)))

Right to Do Wrong

Dear Dr. C.,

I've been seeing a guy for two years now. I'm twenty-seven and this is the first real long-term relationship I've been in, but for the last six months, me and my man have been going through so many changes. I have to admit that it's mostly because of me. Some days I want the relationship, some days I don't. It's nothing that he's doing right or wrong. Sometimes I just can't seem to handle anything that comes my way. It seems as if I'm always going off on him or shutting down. At those times I don't want to even take his calls. This drives him crazy. He thinks I'm seeing someone behind his back and I understand why, but I'm not. When I slip into that dark place, I'm feeling so low that I simply can't deal with him or the world. A couple of my girlfriends tell me that they go through the same thing.

Then, other times, I love him so much and can't imagine my life without him. He says that when I'm on, I make him feel like a king and that no one has ever made him feel like this. I know that loving me is like a roller-coaster ride and that he is getting tired of the ride.

I don't want to lose him, but I don't know if I have the ability to straighten myself out. What do you suggest?

Dark Days in Detroit

Dear Darkness,

I have to ask you a simple question. Has it ever crossed your mind that you need counseling or even to see a clinical psychologist? It's true that a lot of women have those major mood swings, once a month, but it sounds like what you are dealing with is beyond that. Hear me loud and clear. There is nothing wrong with getting some professional help. If you had high blood pressure, you want some medicine or to have it treated, right? Well, if you are suffering from depression, or if you are bipolar, you need to be treated. Maybe you'll find out that you're simply immature and need to grow up, but you had better talk to someone because you are no good to yourself or anyone in the state you are. Remember, it's okay if you're not okay. We all have issues; some of them are too heavy to cope with alone.

If you are going to sit around and try to rationalize your be-havior and choose to do nothing to help yourself get better—

> *because you __are__ suffering from a condition, mental or emo-*
> *tional—then do all men and lesbians a favor, stay single.*
>
>

Yours truly,

Dr. C.
>

Life-changing was the word I'd use to describe the kind of month that April had been. I was, in fact, a father and had felt as if my life was now being transformed by a tiny little person. For the past month I'd spent time with Gina and the baby, unsure of what the results would be. But we didn't waste any time, and two weeks after she'd brought the baby home, we had the test performed.

Getting the results had hit home in a serious way and I felt as though I had to make some changes in my life. The first thing that I'd decided to do was get to know Gina. We didn't put any pressure on ourselves to try to all of a sudden become a couple. We both were content with just trying to build a friendship. I definitely had been attracted to her, at least before she got pregnant. She was sexy, and she was smart enough, but that was all I really knew.

In the meantime, I had Paige, who was taking care of all my other needs. She was more like a girlfriend, only she was married to someone else, which remained alarmingly comfortable for me. I couldn't help it, though; she always made me laugh and had begun to get to know me beyond the surface, and the sex was no holds barred, off the meter, hot. The catch was that we could only take it so far. She had a life and home and I still hadn't addressed my demons enough to stop doing what I knew was wrong.

Surprisingly, Paige was very supportive when I told her about the baby. It didn't affect what we were doing at all. "I'll babysit, but I'm not changing any Pampers" was her only rule.

There was one night when Paige and I were lying in bed and Gina called. She didn't really want to discuss anything to do with the baby, just to chat. I gave her a few moments of conversation before politely telling her that I was in the middle of something and would call her back.

Paige had rolled over and said to me, "You care about her, huh?"

"Gina?"

"Yeah. I can hear it in your voice. There's something there."

"I don't know about that. I think I might care about her feelings."

"Diego, there's nothing wrong with that. There's a bond between the two of you that will probably grow. I respect that."

I stared into her eyes and thought that other than her being a cheater, I really had respect for Paige as a woman. "Thanks. But I don't know if she and I would ever be more than friends and co-parents."

"That's fine, too. Just as long as you can be decent to one another. But you do seem to be getting attached to little Heaven." She smiled. "The daddy bug has bitten you hard."

"You think?"

"Brother, you light up when you talk about that little girl." I smiled at the mention of her. "See, I told you."

We kissed and then she climbed out of the bed stating she had to run. She put on her gym clothes. She'd been working out for the past few hours if anyone, meaning her husband, asked. This gave her the perfect excuse for her hair being a mess and for jumping in the shower as soon as she came through the door.

We had our little thing down to a science and it was working for me. It wasn't too heavy and it was just enough to keep me occupied.

The real shocker had been the conversation that I'd had with Jacob as we ate dinner at Fridays in Greenbelt. He confessed a bundle of confessions that had me reeling. After the cover-up of Anna's rape, I didn't think he could do any worse. But that had died down. Instead of playing it safe and being thankful, he gets involved with one of his students. I was a man and I could understand him lusting after a high-school senior, but he'd taken it to the limit.

"Pregnant?" I asked, stunned.

"Yeah, that's what I heard." He told me his sources and how he'd been trying to track Elise down for the last two months to no avail.

It didn't end there, though. When I asked him how he felt about it he responded with, "I love her. I want to be with her."

"Jacob. Man, you're almost thirty. She's almost eighteen," I said in a concerned voice.

"Well, it's a little late for me to be thinking about all that. Plus, I just turned twenty-nine, thank you."

I shook my head. "Well, what you gonna do?"

"As soon as the school year is over I'm going to Indianapolis to find her. I'm going to bring her back. Wherever I go, she's going with me."

"But she broke it off with you," I said, wondering if he had considered the possibility that she no longer wanted to be with him.

"She was upset and it just didn't seem right. I think her aunt really pressured her. I know she loves me, too, and I'm going to her."

"You don't think that anything will come out of it . . . you know, legally? You're not scared of this getting out?"

He paused, and after a second he said, "Hell yeah, but what can I do? What can I do?"

"You could leave well enough alone," I said, and took a sip of my Corona. "You can slip out of Dodge with no one the wiser about any of the shit you've done this whole year. That's what I would do. Go for the clean getaway."

He stared into my eyes and then laughed. Then he abruptly switched tones and said, "There's no such thing as a clean getaway. Remember that."

I would.

A week later, Jacob and I left the Land Rover dealership and headed down the Pike. We had both taken off on a Friday. We had sick days that we would never get a chance to use again. No looking back.

I had just purchased the vehicle of my dreams and was ecstatic about it. I'd gotten Jacob to ride with me. After leaving the dealership, we were going to go get haircuts, do some shopping, and hang out like we hadn't done in a while. I'd bought some clothes for the baby and Jacob some things for Elise. He was still bent on finding her.

My brother, Lee, and I had made up after the incident with his wife and he was supposed to meet up with us after he got off work. I was sure Nicole was still beating his ass, but I had decided that there was nothing I could do about it. She had actually talked about pressing charges against me for causing her to go deaf in her left ear, but Lee had told her that he would leave her if she did. After all, she had been the one trespassing. I was hoping that Lee would get the chance to talk some sense into Jacob, even though taking advice from a brother in Lee's predicament seemed a little crazy. Lee always managed to play the religion card and that would get Jacob's attention.

It was an extremely warm day and I was anxious to slide the roof back on my brand-new Range. Jacob, for his part, was obsessing with the stereo. He immediately tuned in to Natalie Case's show on 102.3. A second later both our heads were bobbing as Patrice Rushen's "You Remind Me" blared through the premium sound system. As far as I was concerned, I'd made it. My show was going to be a hit and I had convinced myself that I might as well enjoy the fruits of my labor. It was a Friday afternoon and we were going to hang out for a while until the sun went down, then we planned to paint the town red, even if we never climbed out of the truck.

Jacob had signed his deal and was preparing to head up to New York to do some work on his CD in less than a month. He was going to work in Electric Lady, the same studio Jimi Hendrix had made famous more than thirty years earlier. The school year was winding down. There was less than a month left and we had both turned in our resignations and were looking forward to moving on to new lives.

We ended up going to Takoma Station, where Jacob's old band was performing along with Eric Roberson. Jacob felt a little uneasy, since only one member of the old band was still speaking with him. Freddie, the backup singer, had not only been happy for Jacob, he'd been happy for himself. He was now the lead singer. He wasn't doing too bad either. He was no Jacob, but he was definitely holding his own.

I'd found a spot right across the street from the club, which had been the only way I would have parked my truck there. We went in and quickly ordered a plate of wings and a couple of drinks before the show started.

"Jacob, what's popping, bruh?" Freddie said the second he'd realized that we'd come through the door. "What's up, Diego?"

"Everything's good," Jacob said.

"I'm chillin', how about you?"

"Just try'na make shit happen."

"Indeed."

The show started and we sat at the bar drinking shots of Petrone, talking and listening to the band. The place was packed, plenty of women walking around trying to look cute, and brothers looking for women.

Lee never showed up, so instead of a bunch of talking, we really had a chance to listen to the performance and judge how badly the band was missing Jacob's voice.

The liquor had my boy acting really animated. "Damn, he murdered that note," Jacob said. Subsequently, he cringed every time Freddie didn't hit a note that was up to his standards. Before someone overheard him, I had to remind him that everyone wasn't blessed with his voice.

We barely left our seats the whole night. I asked him if he missed performing with his group. "Of course," he said as we walked out the door.

"But are you ready for the big time? No more small clubs like this."

He nodded. "I always planned on making it there. Everything was a stepping-stone to get where I planned to go."

"I hear that." I laughed as he pimped in front of me.

It was almost midnight and my phone rang as I'd thought it would. "What's up?"

"Where you at, boy?"

"On the way to the house."

"How far away?"

"I have to drop Jacob off first. So about twenty minutes."

"So, did you pick up the truck?" Paige knew that today was the day I'd planned to get it. I hadn't stopped talking about it for the last three weeks.

"Yeah, I got it."

"Mmmmmm, I can't wait to see it. Well, drop him off, then meet me at Jasper's over in Largo. I want you to fuck me in that new truck, in the parking lot. That's if you're down."

"Oh, I'm down."

"Well, hurry. I only have about an hour before I have to be in."

I pressed on the gas just a little harder.

Jacob entered his house and headed straight for his refrigerator to get some water and then he grabbed a couple of aspirin. He hadn't drunk in a while and his head was spinning from the tequila. He was also hot and decided to open the windows. He turned off all the lights and headed upstairs.

He was in his bedroom getting ready to take a shower when the doorbell rang. He was startled and went to the window to look out. Since he'd already lifted the window, he looked out and yelled, "Who is it?"

They didn't answer but instead hit the bell once again. "Stop fucking playing. Who is it?" he asked again.

After a brief silence Jacob heard the vaguely familiar voice say, "Mocha2munch."

Jacob made his way down the steps and headed for the door. He pulled it open, and standing there with a slick smile on her face, she said, "Surprise, surprise."

"Alicia?"

She stood in front of him in a white linen sundress. Her nipples were plainly visible through the material, and when he looked her up and down he saw that she was even more voluptuous than when he'd last taken a real look. Without asking, she walked right inside of his door. "You weren't going to leave me standing out there all night, were you?"

Jacob was confused and it showed on his face. "I'm not really understanding. You've been sending those e-mails?"

"I think you understand quite well," she said, pointing down to his underwear. His dick was semierect. Then she smiled. "It took a lot for me to actually knock on the door this time. I've come so close so many times, but I just got scared at the last minute."

"You've been to my house before?"

"Of course. I've been here with Diego a few times."

"No, I mean since you've been sending the e-mails . . . I'm confused. Where is all this coming from? You know that Diego is my best friend."

"To hell with him. Diego can kiss my ass. He doesn't love anyone except himself. After what he did to me, do you think I care? You know he doesn't deserve me. He never did."

"Well, Alicia. I understand why you would feel this way, but I can't do that to him." His mind was reeling. The whole time, deep down, he'd believed it was Anna who'd sent the e-mails, and then maybe even Elise. Not in a million years had he imagined that it was Alicia. "If it makes you feel any better, he was really sorry about what happened between you two. In fact, I think he still loves you."

"Jacob, I couldn't care less. I don't want to talk about him. I want you to sing to me, the way you did at my wedding and the way you do at your shows. Did you know I come to all your shows?"

"I've never seen you at one."

"I always stay in the back and out of sight. Especially when Diego is there."

Something about her didn't seem right. She wasn't the Alicia that Jacob remembered. "So, Alicia, I think we should just forget this whole thing happened and . . ."

"What?" She raised her voice and asked, "Are you kidding? I put it all on the line and finally tell you how I feel, and this is what I get?"

"Alicia, I can't get involved with you. Diego is my—"

At the top of her lungs she yelled, "Fuck him. He ruined my life."

Jacob was shocked. He feared that she was having a breakdown. "It's okay. I understand that you're angry with him."

"No, I'm not angry. I hate him. But he's going to get his."

"Don't be like that. He has suffered . . ." Jacob leaned in and touched her arm.

Alicia jerked away and said, "Jacob, are you going to fuck me or not? I want you. I need you and you need me, too."

Jacob shook his head no. "Alicia, that's not true."

"Oh yeah? Then why are you fucking your students?" Jacob was stunned and his face showed it. "That's right. I know all about you and the little girl I saw you with at Starbucks. All about it."

Jacob was silent.

"Jacob, you don't need a little girl. You need a woman." With that, she reached behind her neck and pulled the string that held up her dress. She then stepped out of her dress and stood before him naked, except for the small bit of material that composed her panties. "Please, Jacob. Give me what I want, and I'll give you what you want."

25

Might Be the One

Dear Dr. C.,

Let me keep it real. My name is Enid Pinner and I don't care who knows. Maybe a few of the brothers I'm talking about will read your column. I just had to write in to say I'm tired of dealing with broke-ass men. Why are you in the club but you don't have a car? If you have a car, why do you have rims on it, but you have a roommate and you're over thirty? Why were you in the strip club buying twenty-dollar lap dances but can't take a sistah out to a decent restaurant once in a while? I don't even care about the college degree anymore, but I do care about your financial sense. I'm sick of brothers who wear Air Jordans and put them on their kids, but don't have health insurance. I'm tired of men asking me if I can cosign for them to buy a plasma television. What the f*&% is that? Why is that when sistahs decide we want to raise our standards, and date only men who can afford to do a little something for us, we are considered gold diggers? Got brothers making songs and whatnot.

If that's the case, then we need to start calling women who don't do this cattle keepers because all they are doing is dealing with bullshit.

I Don't Care If You Call Me a Gold Digger in Charlotte

Dear EP,

I hear you loud and clear. I printed your letter because it was sad, funny, and most of all true. And believe me... I ain't saying you a gold digger...

Yours truly,

Dr. C.

It had been four months almost, since he'd seen her last. It didn't matter; he still felt the same way about her. So many times he'd seen her face, until the dreams were starting to seem real. The moment the students had left for the day, he began to gather up the last of his things. There were only three days of school left in the year, and because he wasn't returning, Jacob had packed all of his belongings. He was donating most of what he'd acquired over the years to other teachers, but he was still responsible for gathering it.

When Jacob saw her emerge from behind the boxes and storage bins that were stacked near the door of his classroom, he didn't believe his eyes. But this time it was no dream. "Hello," she said as she walked in and closed the door behind her.

Jacob's eyes filled with water and he nearly broke down in

tears. He couldn't move. Elise walked toward him. He reached out for her. He couldn't believe she was there in front of him. "I love you," he said.

"I love you, too."

He looked down at her stomach and she was bulging. "So . . . we're having a baby?" he asked.

She looked into his eyes and tried to read him. "Is that okay?"

Jacob nodded. "It will be if you marry me."

The tears then belonged to Elise as she nodded. "I missed you so much." They hugged. "I always loved you. I just didn't want you to get into trouble. She was going to get you locked up," she said over the tears.

"I know. I know. It's okay. You're here now."

"Can we leave? Can we go to your place?" she asked.

"Yeah, of course."

Jacob grabbed his things and they left the building. "Where's your car?"

"Indianapolis. I flew out here."

They got into Jacob's car unnoticed and drove off. Elise recounted the whole situation from the day Alicia had come to her job and questioned her about her involvement with Jacob up to where she'd begun fishing for information about Diego. Elise hadn't known much other than that he was writing a column for *Girl Talk*. Soon came the threats as Alicia claimed to want Jacob for herself.

As they cruised along Elise turned to Jacob and asked, "So what did you do to get her to change her mind? She seemed to want you so bad. She was like a psycho."

"She didn't want me so much as she wanted to hurt Diego."

"So what did you do?"

Jacob's face twisted. "Will you accept the answer that I give and leave it at that? Can you do that?"

"Yes, I can."

They drove farther and she asked again, "So what did you do?"

"I did what I had to do. I'm not happy about it, but she had me in a bad position. It was one that I couldn't get out of, and Diego *had* done her wrong."

Elise nodded and said, "Okay."

Two days later, on the last day of school, I stepped out of my classroom and heard a huge commotion in the hallway. Then I saw Lisa come bolting down the hallway. Huffing and puffing, she said, "Diego, there's like twenty police down that motherfucker."

"What's going on?"

"I don't know, but they have your boy on the ground out in front. They said something about a robbery nearby. Ms. Knight wants everyone to keep the kids that are here inside the rooms."

"What?" I said, in shock. "Hold up. Watch my kids for a second." The sixth graders had graduated the week before, leaving Lisa with nothing to do. I left her there and headed up the hall. At the end of the walkway I looked out the window and saw all the police cars. It looked like a drug-zone raid.

I walked down the steps and out the door. I was stopped by an officer and forced to identify myself. I looked over and saw that the exterior door to the boiler room was being guarded by two officers.

Ms. Knight was now standing next to me. She looked as if she was about to have a heart attack. "Diego, I don't believe this. How could this happen? How could he do this and involve our school, put our students at risk in such a way?"

She was talking so fast I had to slow her down. "What's going on—"

Before I could even get the question out she blurted, "He's the one who's been robbing all the stores and banks around here, during lunch hour. He was going out robbing places and running back here. Right under our noses."

I couldn't believe it. "Are you serious?" I asked. Then I saw four officers emerge from the boiler room with a duffel bag, carrying it as if it contained a bomb.

We walked outside and I figured that the "he" she was referring to was Grump and that I should never have put it past him. I thought about all the times he'd come back into the school after a lunch break sweating like a hog. I asked, "Didn't we have a background search done on him before he came here?"

"Diego, he's been here for almost twenty years," she said as we walked. "I don't even think they were doing background checks when he started."

"Twenty years?" I was puzzled. Then, as we made our way to the edge of the parking lot, I saw *him*. Mr. Waverly was in handcuffs as he was being lifted into the rear of a SWAT van. I couldn't believe it. "Mr. Waverly?"

"Yeah. He's been robbing stores for the last five months. They found a gun and some money in the boiler room. This is going to be a mess. Lord, I have a huge migraine coming." She then turned around and left me standing there watching the man who'd been like a distant uncle, a mentor at times, being hauled off to jail. I couldn't believe it. It was like watching a movie. Instantly, I thought of Jacob and what I'd done.

Alicia had come between him and me. She called me from his house phone and left me a message that he'd fucked her. According to her, better than I ever had. I found it hard to believe—both parts. But she promised that she could deliver proof, via her camera phone. And when I called Jacob, he denied it, but then tried to explain why he hadn't mentioned her coming to his house.

He called me later and tried to convince me that it was a lie, but I didn't want to hear the story. I was too hurt. He got tired of me cursing him out and began to curse back. He was my best friend in the world, but no matter how many times I tried to figure it out, I couldn't understand how he'd break code like that. He, more than anyone else on the planet, knew how I felt about Alicia. I had nothing else to say to him, yet I wasn't finished with him.

The news cameras were there for the arrest. When they hauled him off, a few students watched in shock. He tried to keep his face down as the cameramen moved in closer, but it didn't work. The image was clear, and when the four o'clock news rolled, everyone who knew him was shocked to hear the headline: *Jacob Marsh, band instructor and teacher at Lyndon Johnson High School, in Greenbelt was arrested today for an alleged sexual relationship with a former student.*

I watched with bated breath and the whole thing seemed surreal. In a fit of anger, I had turned in my best friend. Now that I'd watched the whole thing as it unfolded in front of the world's eyes and my own, the feeling in my stomach told me that perhaps I'd gone too far.

26

It Don't Hurt Now

Dear Dr. C.,

I recently met a brother online; it was my first time trying one of these dating services, and we exchanged numbers. When we talked, he seemed really normal. I don't know if I was expecting him to tell me he had a few dead bodies in his basement, but at any rate we made plans to go out.

It turns out that we know some of the same people. He went to Howard U. I went to Hampton U. I was so happy to hear that the people I knew who knew him spoke highly of him. We have started to see each other regularly and I enjoy every minute of the time we spend together. This past weekend he told me that he wants our relationship to be committed. My thing is this. I have always had problems with guys once the relationship starts. I can't take the way things change. It's like I get depressed when the honeymoon is over and immediately want to end the relationship.

I'm not trying to play games with this man; I just want to stretch out the good treatment. What should I do?

Loving the Attention in Atlanta

Dear Attention Lover,

What you need to do is this. Make a list of everything that you have to have in order to feel good and satisfied in a relationship. Then make a list of the things that he is doing right. Then be honest with him. Tell him up front that if he won't be able to keep up the standard that he is setting, you will most likely become dissatisfied with the relationship. You have to be realistic, though. A new relationship absorbs both parties to a degree that few can maintain over a long period of time. You can't be a nut, believing that he can spend every minute of every day making you feel special and appreciated. That's not a relationship, that's a job. And one that will constantly be vacated due to exhaustion.

Just be up-front. Few women do this. They just go with the flow and watch men slip gradually from the prince who swept them off their feet to the frog that's sitting on the couch hogging the remote.

So if you want to get what you want and keep it . . . speak up. The squeaky wheel gets the grease.

Yours truly,

Dr. C.

A week after I turned my best friend in to the police, it'd seemed I'd jumped out of the frying pan and directly into the fire. Something as routine as getting a piece of ass had turned into a disaster. There didn't seem to be any getting out of this situation without either getting killed or going to jail.

My life or his? I pondered. This man had crashed down my door and had a shiny, silver revolver in his hand. I wondered if the brother was prepared to kill as he'd promised.

Just then he peered up the stairs and spotted me. As he asked the words in a deep James Earl Jones voice, my whole life passed in front of my eyes.

"Where is my wife?"

I stood there silent. I asked myself *how*. How did it come down to this? I thought about everything that I'd done from the beginning to get here. A chain of events began to play out right there as I traded stares with my lover's husband in the middle of the night.

I thought about all the things that had made me act the way I did. My upbringing, my selfish desires to have it all, right or wrong. It might have been the fact that I was so good at hiding who I really was most of the time that women were always falling in love with an illusion. From the time I was eight, women, my teachers and aunts, had all called me charming.

I was light-skinned when it was the shit to be just that. I grew into a handsome and confident brother. I was intellectually inclined, with a strong sense of street savvy. Women loved me, not only because I knew what to say to them, but because sometimes I even knew how to listen.

It was all about to blow up in my face, though. It looked like I was headed to jail or to the morgue. I couldn't hear him talking anymore even though his lips were moving. He moved toward me and I was startled as his wife yelled out from the top of the steps.

"Pleeeease stoooop." Her voice pierced my state and almost snapped me out of my trance. My hands trembled and I thought about all the letters I'd responded to, all the advice I'd given.

I heard the words that I'd read that day. *One day, Diego. You'll get yours.*

Then I thought about all that I had to live for. Things were going to be different for me. As the dirt I'd done all began to flash in front of my eyes, it became so clear to me. It had never been worth it. Then just like that, I heard the boom, the echo, and then I lost my balance. It was over just like that.

As I lay on my back and closed my eyes, I thought of her. I thought of Heaven, my daughter. At that point, all the women that I'd used, trying to heal and hide from the pain—they didn't matter. Early in my life, I'd kept count and treated my conquests as a symbol of who I was. As of late, I'd come to realize that I did this because . . . like so many men, it's all we know. And because sex was the first thing that women were usually willing to give.

Now I was simply hoping to have a chance to see another day. I finally realized that I didn't *need* to be here. On my back, at the mercy of this man.

I opened my eyes when I heard him crying. He was on his knees. The gun was still in his hands, but he was weeping like a baby. He had fired a shot well over my head, with no intention of hitting me. He was simply hurt. As I sat up I looked into Paige's eyes and her face was filled with shame. She walked down the steps to her man and began to weep with him on the floor. Then I heard her begin to say that she was sorry.

"How could you do this to me?" he asked hysterically over and over. "I love you. Why, Paige? Whyyyyy?" he cried. It was weird hearing this deep voice sounding so pained.

"I'm so sorry. I am. Please forgive me."

He was bawling like a baby at the top of his lungs. I was waiting for the snot bubbles.

"Can you forgive me, please?" she begged. Then she said something that I was sure stunned him. In the middle of probably the worst moment of his life, she said, "I forgave you."

It was like he'd been shot with a tranquilizer gun. He stopped crying and looked into her eyes as if she were no longer his source of pain. Then she said, "We have to go. I'm sure someone called the police."

He gave me a menacing look as he moved hastily out the door. Less than ten minutes later, I was at my kitchen table helping the police fill out a report and trying to explain what had happened and why this man had burst through my door. They'd seen it all before, and once they'd finished the report, gathered some evidence, and taken a few pictures, they advised me to get a restraining order and promptly left.

Once they were gone, I called my insurance company to report my catastrophe. They told me that they would send someone out within the hour to board up my door until the morning, when I could have it fixed.

I went and sat in my living room, turned on the television, and waited for the employee to arrive. As nervous as I'd been, incredibly I was able to close my eyes and start to drift off. That's when I heard footsteps and looked up, startled.

"What are you doing here?" I asked.

"I came to apologize. That was wrong what I did . . . I called Paige's husband and told him all about you two. I thought he'd come over here and kill you."

"How did you know? How did you find him?"

"It's a small world."

"Well, he almost did kill me. So you hate me that much?"

"I thought I did, but I don't. In fact, I still love you."

When Alicia said those words, my heart melted. "What about all that stuff with Jacob?"

"I lied. He didn't touch me. At least not in the way that I'd wanted him to. I did want him to fuck me. But not because I loved him. Because I loved you and wanted to hurt you, like you hurt me. I even threatened to turn him in to the police. I did a lot of mean things in the cause of trying to use him. He ended going into a screaming fit, totally unlike Jacob. Then I understood why. He told me that he was having a baby with the girl, Elise, and the look in his eyes told me that he would do anything to protect what he had with her."

"So what did you do?"

"I decided to leave him the hell alone. He told me that if I wanted to hurt you, then to do it, but to leave him out of it."

When she said that, I had to take a seat. Jacob was sitting in a jail cell and I'd put him there. I couldn't believe that this was happening. There she was in front of me again.

"So why did you do all of this?"

"Diego, you made me crazy. Everything you did made me crazy. But through it all, I never stopped loving you."

I closed my eyes and thought about it all. The entire year went spinning through my head. All the hurt I'd felt and caused. The wedding. Gina and the baby. The column. The show. Lanelle and

Paige. Finally, what I'd done to Jacob. Now that Alicia stood before me, I realized that it was all because of her that I'd done the crazy things I'd done. Then, as I stared into her eyes, I stood and moved toward her. In a low whisper, I said, "So . . . after all this . . . you still love *me*?"

"Yes," she said. My thoughts shifted to my friend. I was going to have to straighten out the whole mess with Jacob; however, it would have to wait until the morning.

With that, I took Alicia by the hand and led her upstairs to my bed.

One Year Later

In the end, it seemed I got exactly what I'd always wanted. Alicia and I were married three months after the night she'd walked through my crushed-up door. We eloped and tied the knot in Hawaii in front of my brother, Lee, and his wife. Jacob had been invited, but the whole thing was too awkward. Although we were friends again, our relationship had been strained by what I'd done to him, and the advances on him that Alicia had made had left me feeling uncomfortable.

The day after Alicia confessed everything to me, I had gone to Jacob's principal first, and then the authorities, to revoke my statement. I claimed that it was a love triangle and that I'd been a scorned lover, which in effect had been true. I was then charged with filing a false report and they decided to investigate Jacob's involvement with Elise anyway. They dug, but nothing came up. Though they were forced to drop the charges, it was a real mess. Jacob and Elise basically brought the whole thing to a close when they married the day after her eighteenth birthday. By law, she couldn't be forced to testify against her husband in any case, and since he had resigned from his job with the county, there was nothing for them to do.

He managed to keep his recording deal even after the negative publicity; after all, it was 2006. Without a criminal record, a scandal, or at least a brush with the law, who was he but another Goody Two-shoes? He'd had sex with a student, knocked her up, and married her. That was *hot* by today's standards.

As another show was winding down I looked at the clock and smiled. With just a few small exceptions, my life seemed to be on track. My show had been launched and was noted number two in the D.C. area. I wanted that number one spot.

"You got questions, he's got answers. Ladies Listen Up." The sexy voice chimed out as the theme music and the slogan echoed over the airwaves. The phone lines began to light up for the last segment of the show. "We're going to take one more call before we take it home. I've got Anna on the line people. Go on, Anna."

"Hey, Dr. C."

"Hey you. Anna, you sound young. How old are you?"

"I'm eighteen. A freshman at the University of Maryland."

"Okay, go ahead," I said.

"I have a dilemma. It's kinda complicated."

"Go on, shoot. I got answers."

"Okay. Well, I'm in love with someone, but she's married."

"Whoa."

"Yeah, she's actually married to our former teacher."

When I heard this, my senses began to go off. "Say what?"

"Yeah, she married my former teacher. But I really care about her and I think she cares about me in the same way. The thing is, I know that he's been cheating on her, but I don't want to tell her because . . . well . . . it's going to cause a whole bunch of trouble."

"How do you know he's cheating?"

"I followed him . . . and you know what makes it so bad?"

"What's that?"

"It's with his best friend's—or should I say . . . his former best friend's wife."

"That's sounds serious, but it looks like we are out of time," I said as my heart began to beat fast. Then I said, "Caller, you stay on the line."

Anna let out a very devilish chuckle and said, "I thought so."

Author's Note

In case you all didn't know, some authors, including myself, equate writing a book to be something like having a baby. It's an exhausting, exciting, and sometimes painful process. Ultimately, you've created a piece of you that you send out into the world to be a reflection of all your labor and love. I only pray that I touch, inspire, and move those who are gracious enough to support my work. Most of all, I try to entertain all who read as I try to fulfill my purpose here on earth.

In writing *Ladies Listen Up,* I wondered if I would leave any socially redeeming literary footprints. I feared that I might be adding just another "drama book" to the tables and shelves that are full of them. After reading it in its entirety, my fears were put to rest. I think the messages throughout are clear and abundant, if only you pay attention. I admit, they are sprinkled in amongst much drama and shocking prose. Still, they're all the things I learned as I lived, or watched what happened around me. Don't get me wrong; this is not an autobiography, but I did come to a soul-stirring revelation. This book is the *closest,* yet at the same time, the most *distant* from my actual life as I've written thus far. Some of the memories and content were disturbing, even to myself, as well as to some of my closest friends. Yet as a writer I had to be true and put it down the only way I knew how—authentically.

Last, I want to send a note to the women whom I've shared love with. I want to thank you for the growth and for being a reflection of the things that were the best and worst of me at that time. It was *our* experiences that placed this book in my heart before I even knew I'd be destined to write it. This book is not meant to cheapen any of it. So please, never think that. Even if you think you see yourself in this book . . . chances are great that I'm talking about someone else. And if by chance I'm talking about you, don't trip 'cause . . . *I'll mourn forever. Shit, I got to live with the fact that I did you wrong forever.*

Acknowledgments

Once again and always, I have to give thanks to the Almighty. He always carries me to the other side and restores and builds my faith. After that I want to give another dedication out right here to two of my friends and test readers. Chad Cunningham, you are like a little brother to me and I really appreciate you having me on *your* team. I remember watching you run across the yard with that plastic football helmet on, now look at you . . . coaching me as I bang out these chapters, making them the new *hotness.* Next, I want to thank my newest muse, Enid Pinner. Your energy and enthusiasm helped me put it down in a big way. By the time you read this I will be able to say thanks for all the love and hospitality at the CIAA. Seriously, I really appreciate your attention and passion for this book.

First, I got to thank my number one fan, my mother, Doris Patrick, the reason I was even able to become a teacher, so for this one, you really get some credit. Aunt Nancy, I want to thank you so much for coming to the rescue and allowing me some crucial time to knock this out, you are the best, and to my sister Tanya, I just love you the most, girl, welcome home. Much love to Chuck, Ted, Marcus, Damien and all of my family, near and far.

India, no matter how things wind up, I want to thank you for everything you've done to help. I love you always.

Tressa Smallwood, God saw me down here struggling and he sent you to come help a brother out. You are the best, even if you call me out on the regular. It's rough out here, thanks for being the best partner in the world.

Rockelle Henderson, if I can call this thing I do a *job*, I want to thank you for making it a dream job. I know that I bug you and drive you crazy . . . I'd always heard that authors did that, but now I know it's true. But you always have an ear, a laugh, and some time for me. You're my friend, my editor, my publishing everything, and I appreciate you and you are definitely earning your check with me. Dawn Davis, I'm working on my craft so that one day soon, I'll have you eager to snatch up one of my manuscripts to work on. It's an honor to work with you. Gilda Squire, I gotta say "Wow," I have a super publicist in you. You are the best; thanks for making sure everything is up to par for a brother and never taking any shorts. All of the Harper/Amistad family; thanks a million for the confidence and support, and for making me feel like a star. Morgan, Laura, Tanya, Mary, Michael, and Andrea and everyone who I haven't met, but has a hand in taking me on my journey, I thank you from the bottom of my heart. Special thanks to my editorial team.

Josie, I had picked you for that cover and couldn't be happier. You're a star and a pro. Fulani S. Hart, great job also. Les Green, thanks for the work on the website as always. Thanks also to Joshua Sheldon and to Ed Walker for the photography.

ACKNOWLEDGMENTS

Thanks also to Karibu Books. Especially Lee, Sunny, and Trina. Congrats to Yao and Simba on the new store in Baltimore. You two are the trailblazers of black bookstore commerce. Much love to every one of the other store owners and vendors out there doing it for me. Thanks to the crew at A&B. To Tamara Cooke, my accountant, thank you a thousand times for always taking care of me. Sheryl Hicks, still us . . . here after all these years, they come and go, but I'll always have you. Thanks to Yolanda Marie, Lynn Thomas, Lori, Vangie, Ma, and Zero at 4 Star's Hair Salon. There are so many lovely women in my support system. Thank you all for all your endless support. I'm on a roll but I can't name you all; I'd certainly run out of paper. But if you've helped me, past or present, please know that I truly appreciate you.

Some of you I have to love from afar, and some of you still creep into my dreams even after all this time. Sadly, some of you just don't understand me, and maybe you never did, but I still love you. On the flip side, some of you just haven't got a clue . . . and it's clear now, more than ever, that it was your loss.

Tikeya, stop being so rough on a brother; I am not a loser, even if my niece calls me one! She's only four, what does she know? Shout out to the Chase twins. Lisa Lamar, you are now immortalized. Thanks for all the memories. Much love to Tracye Stafford, we got to keep it moving. It's so good knowing you have my back to the fullest. To Lisa Richardson and Angela Oates, looking forward to getting back to work.

Kelli Martin, I still hear your editorial voice, much love, always. Patty Rice, you are always remembered. Stacey Barney, look forward to working with you. Much love to all my old colleagues at Woodridge.

DeWright Johnson, much respect and love you always. To all my friends, past, present and future, what can I say . . . I need ya'll.

ACKNOWLEDGMENTS

Shaka, you know what? I should call my brother. Anthony, Mike Davis, Rufus, Lowe, Eric Patterson . . . man, you are one of the wildest dudes ever, Black, Butter, Daren, Carl, and my brother Jim Chaney.

Nothing but love to some of my fellow authors out there. Victoria C. Murry, Karrine Steffans, Zane, Shannon Holmes, Lolita Files, Danette Majette, Zach Tate, Candace Dow, Wahida Clark, K'wan, Crystal Winslow, and so many others I've met out there who are so down-to-earth, it's a real pleasure. There's a lot of haters, snakes, and thieves out there, but don't let 'em wreck your flow. Even if you don't lift a finger they get pushed back and around and still don't wind up happy; it's funny to me.

Thanks to all the radio stations, book clubs, and magazines. Especially my sweetheart Justine Love, and my homey Todd B at WPGC, and my girl Natalie Case at Magic 102.3.

Much love and gratitude to Nina Graybill. To Manie Baron: here's to the future, show me what you know.

If you feel like I left you out, don't. Sit down and try to list everybody who has lent you a serious hand in life, or this year even, you'll understand. I got nothing but love for you.

Last but definitely not least are the most important—my readers. To any Darren Coleman fans, and to the readers who aren't fans yet, thank you from the bottom of my heart for giving me a shot. Spread the love and send a friend to scoop up a copy.

Till the next episode, I love ya'll. I'm out.

Dr. C

Reading Group Guide

1. This book tells the story of Diego, who is able to give no-nonsense advice, yet unable to make almost any wise decision regarding his own life. How do you think he got to be that way?

2. At the outset of the book, Diego was reflective of his behaviors and how he got into a horrible predicament. After reading the story, do you feel that he was truly sorry for anything he did?

3. Is Diego's attitude toward women indicative of how you feel most men are? In what ways?

4. Jacob seemed to be the most sensitive and the most sensible of the pair, which made what happened with him and Elise all the more shocking. Do you think his fall from grace was realistic, believable, and understandable?

5. In the end, do you think it was possible for Jacob to really have found love with Elise? Could it last?

6. Although the author uses humorous situations to depict Lee's problematic situation with his wife, he recognizes that domestic abuse is very serious. Roughly 40 out of 100 domestic abuse cases involve women against men. While women have been encouraged to report it, virtually nothing has been done to encourage men to come forward. Do you feel that this trend is acceptable, and if not, what should be done?

7. Jacob's story is a classic tale of a cover-up spinning out of control. He contemplated trying to talk to his superiors earlier but changed his mind out of fear that he would lose it all. Do you think things worked out best for him?

8. Diego used sex as a medication to numb himself during tough times. Do you think he was a typical man, or a sex addict?

9. Was Diego qualified to write the column based upon all of his experiences with women?

10. Did it seem realistic that Alicia's pain would drive her to do the things she did?

11. Which character was your favorite/least favorite? Which one, if any, could you relate to the most in your life, past or present?

12. Could you ever imagine that school teachers behave like Diego, Jacob, and even Willie, who drank and smoked marijuana on school grounds daily?

13. Which letter to Dr. C. did you most relate to?

14. What was your favorite part of the story and why?

15. Ultimately, what did you take away from this book? What do you feel the author's motivation was for writing it?

An excerpt from the *Essence* bestseller

Don't Ever Wonder by Darren Coleman

1

Once Upon a Time

Aubette was already packed at seven p.m. People piled in for happy hour after work, and on the weekends they stayed until three in the morning once the party started. I hadn't come for mingling or party atmosphere this time though. I came for one quick drink and a little conversation. On my cab ride over to 27th Street, my fingers were crossed that my meeting wouldn't turn ugly, even though I had been assured that we were adult enough to handle this.

Once inside I made my way past the bar and headed toward the rear of the lounge. Aubette was filled with a mix of folks dressed in business attire and around-the-way girls already dressed for the club. As Twista's "Slow Jams" was coming to an end, I had to weave through a few dancing couples to get to the table. I looked over to my left and spoke to my favorite bartender, Terri. She waved and shot me a smile. As soon as I cleared the bar I saw her sitting at a small table off to my right. A mix of emotions flared up and I swallowed hard as I made my way to her. Our eyes were locked and she stood up as I reached the table. She extended her arms and gave me a tight hug. The warmth was familiar and when she pulled away she was sporting a smile as wide as the Hudson River.

"Mr. Dandridge. How nice to see you after all this time," she said both sarcastically and seductively. Anthony Hamilton's "Float" was coming through the speakers and for a second I remembered our first dance together. It was hard to believe that one innocent dance could have led to all of this.

I smiled at her. "It's good to see you too. You look lovely." I couldn't help but notice that she was looking exceptionally beautiful. Not that I had expected anything less from her, but when you don't see someone for a while you tend to forget some of what you loved about them. She was wearing a copper strapless dress that showed off some serious tan lines and had on the necklace that I had gotten her from Tiffany. She had obviously been on vacation. "Nice necklace." I mentioned and then added, "Nice tan too."

"Oh thanks." She was grinning. "An old friend picked it up for me a while back. As for the tan, I picked that up in Puerto Rico at my family reunion."

I knew about the reunion because my wife, Shelly, had contemplated for weeks whether or not to attend. She had decided not to go once her mother had confirmed that Nina would be there. We sat and the waitress came back for our orders. I pointed at Nina and asked the waitress to take her order first. "I'll take a glass of white zinfandel and the adobo-roasted chicken for my entrée."

"I'll take a vodka martini and the shrimp dish right here," I said, pointing to the menu.

The waitress took the menus and headed off. There was a moment of uncomfortable silence that I tried to fill by observing my surroundings. I was interrupted with, "Cory, are you okay?" My hands were on the table and she reached for them. "If you are uncomfortable, we don't have to do this. You can leave."

I lied. "No I'm fine. I was just thinking about work. I have to stop doing that." I paused. "So what did you want to talk about?"

"Whoa. I wanted to have a drink and chill with you first, been a long time, right?" She released my hands. Her touch had been so subtle I had forgotten that she was holding them. "I must admit that I am surprised that you even agreed to meet me."

I nodded my head in agreement because I was surprised as well and it *had* been a long time. But I guess that deep down inside I had wanted to see her months ago just to be sure she was okay. I granted her request and relaxed a bit while we ate and ordered our second and third drinks. It was a quarter past eight when my phone rang. I excused myself and went down the steps and into the restroom.

"Hey, sweetie." I said to my wife on the other end.

"Hey, do you think you can pick up Amani from the sitter's? I told Mrs. Lamar that I would be there by eight and Rockelle and I are still out trying to pick up a few things for Christina's baby shower tomorrow." Shelly had been planning a baby shower for her college roommate, who lived in Brooklyn.

"Why don't you call and ask Mrs. Lamar if she can stay a little later. I am in the middle of something and probably won't make it there for at least two more hours. I have a really important assignment and this deadline . . ."

"Fine." I heard the disgust in her voice as she cut me off. Then she hung up. Shelly's combative behavior whenever she didn't get her way, or if I didn't jump through hoops, was becoming a routine. If I went to the gym, or, heaven forbid, got a drink before coming home, she bitched. I was getting so sick of it that the makeup sex no longer seemed worth it. I knew I was headed for attitude city by the time we met up at home, so I decided to loosen up and enjoy my time with Nina.

Nina's face looked a little flushed from the wine when I got back to the table. All my apprehensions had faded and now I wanted nothing more than to sit and talk for at least another hour with my sister-in-law, who happened to be my ex-fiancée. As a matter of fact, I was feeling way too relaxed for my own good. I was relaxed enough to give my wife the impression that I was probably still working on some important project. And thanks to the alcohol, I was relaxed enough to let the truth come out of my mouth: "Nina you are so beautiful. I am so sorry for hurting you the way I did. If I could take it all back I would."

After coming out of left field with the first statement, I began rambling. "I didn't even realize how much I loved you. I have to admit that I think I made the biggest mistake of my life." She looked down at the table for a second, dodging my eyes. "I don't expect you to forgive me, I just want you to know that . . ." I shook my head in disgust at myself for spilling my guts like a loser. I went on. "I just want you to know that I am sorry and have been miserable without you."

While I spoke I hadn't noticed that her eyebrows had raised and that her lips had parted, exposing her shock. She would have interrupted me if she could have but I had stunned her with my confession. She placed her hands over her face, stood up, and rushed off to the bathroom.

I waited in confusion for about ten minutes, wondering what was going through her mind. Was she embarrassed, angry, or was she feeling the same way? While she was in the restroom the wait-ress came back and I paid the bill and continued to sit patiently waiting for her. Feeling drained, I closed my eyes and tried to tune out the crowd's chatter.

"How much do I owe you for the bill?" I looked up and saw her standing right next to me.

"C'mon now. You know better than that." I motioned for her to sit down and she shook her head no. My heart was sinking fast as I asked, "Are you are ready to leave?"

"Yes." Her demeanor had changed. Her body language commu-nicated that she was no longer relaxed. Her arms were folded and she was clutching her purse as if I was going to steal it and she looked like she had been crying.

"Let's walk then." I said as I led her toward the door. The spot had gotten packed. Everyone was piling in trying to get the last taste of summer before September and the fall weather rolled in. We hit the street and moved toward the curb. "I'll get you a cab."

"No, wait. Walk a little up the block with me. I want to respond to what you said in there." We started walking. The air was warm and people were moving about on both sides of the street. We made it halfway down the block before she turned and said. "Cory." I was still. Hands in my pockets. My heart began pumping wildly. I looked directly at her. "I want you to know something."

"I'm listening."

"I was wrong too. Not just you . . . the whole thing was wrong. I should have never dated you. A crush is one thing because believe me, brother, you are *fine*." She punched me in the chest softly and laughed. "What we did though was wrong. You and my sister were together and made a child. I still think that she is ignorant as all hell for keeping you in the dark for five years about the child you two had together. That will never make sense to me and I hope that it never makes sense to you either."

I digested what she had said but wasn't sure if she wanted a reply. It was obvious she didn't because she went right on. "But two wrongs don't make a right. I should have been better than that and so should you."

I cut her off. ". . . But baby girl . . . *you* are so damned fine. How could I resist you?" I pinched her cheek, lightening the mood, and we both laughed. "You're right. No doubt about it. I have lost many nights of sleep over the way I have handled things."

"As well you should have."

"But what does it mean to be here now? Everything that has happened can't be undone. These feelings can't be turned off." I looked down at the sidewalk. "I do still love you though." The words just slipped off of my lips.

I felt her fingers touch my chin. "Poor Cory," she said. "You'll love me today, then Shelly tomorrow. Whoever ain't there . . . that is who you will love, Papi. With you it's never the here and now. You are a faraway love."

"What?"

"You're a faraway love. No good at loving up close and in the present. That's the funny thing about men. Something most women will never understand." She sensed that I was all ears. "When a sistah leaves your ass, you all of a sudden gain all this clarity. But by then it's too late. She has picked up the shattered pieces of her heart and moved on."

"So it's too late." At that moment I was thinking that I could end my marriage to Shelly and make everything right. Thoughts of my life as it was cruised through my mind. Not many people get a chance to go back and try to re-create a magical feeling that once meant everything. I had taken that chance with Shelly and found out that sometimes the past is better left right there, in the past. She still found it necessary to argue over small things and hold grudges. As far as I was concerned Shelly was still spoiled, and to listen to her tell it, I was still selfish.

Looking deep into her eyes and almost through her, I was half-listening and half-wishing that Nina and I could move somewhere far away and be happy, never worrying about anyone judging us because we fell in love. The idea of it sent a wave of happiness through me. Realizing though that Nina would have probably figured me crazy, I didn't share my thoughts and instead remained silent.

"It's way too late," she said, backing toward the curb. She turned and hailed a cab.

"So how long are you in town for?"

"I leave on Sunday."

I pulled out a card and wrote my cell number on the back of it. "Call me tomorrow. The afternoon will be best."

"I'll think about it." A cab stopped and she opened the door. "I won't make any promises," she said nonchalantly. Her tone stung a bit.

"Hey."

She looked back. No smile.

I couldn't believe myself as the words slipped off of my lips. "Do you still love me?"

As she backed into the cab she said, "Once upon a time." The door shut . . . and just like that Nina was gone again.

2

The Honeycomb Hideout

He was in the fetal position, sleeping like a baby. The sheets were all twisted up between his chocolate legs and saliva dripped slowly out the corner of his mouth. As usual only the aroma of bacon, eggs, and fried potatoes were enough to stir him from his slumber. Like clockwork Janette came into her bedroom with breakfast on a tray.

"Wake up, baby." She nudged his slow-moving body so that he could sit up.

"I'm up." Nate stretched and propped the pillows behind his back. "Where is the remote?" Janette pointed to the covers next to him and he nodded his head, letting her know he wanted her to hand it to him.

"So are you going to come down to the office today and join me for lunch." Every day she asked and every day he gave her the same answer.

"We'll see." Nate flipped the channel to ESPN. "I told you I was going to go down to Run n' Shoot today to renew my membership.

While hiding out in Charlotte he had gained fifteen pounds. He seemed to meet one great cook after another, but Janette was a triple threat. She fried, broiled, and baked her thick ass off. Although he would never admit it she was the only woman whose cooking topped his grandmother's.

"You said the same thing last week and the week before." Janette was in the closet deciding which shirt to put on. "I don't know why you think you need to go to the gym. No woman wants a man that is skin and bones. You look great."

Compared to you I look great, he thought to himself. "Nah, this isn't me. I don't feel right. I have never weighed over two hundred pounds." He had a mouth full of food and was talking at the same time. "And you *are* going to stop making me all this fattening food. I know what you are trying to do."

"And what is that?" Janette said, sticking her head out of the closet.

"You want me all fat so nobody else will want me." He was spreading Country Crock on his toast.

"Negro, please. I'm a thick sistah and brothers are constantly pushing up on me."

"Yeah, that's because you are a two-hundred-pound goddess." He puckered his lips up to get a kiss. Janette walked toward him and gave him a smooch on the lips and turned away to continue getting ready for work. "And that CL600 you pushing don't hurt either." He started laughing. Janette walked back over toward Nate and punched him softly in the arm and snatched a piece of bacon off his tray. "Hey, now. Don't mess with a dog's food while he's eatin," Nate growled.

"And don't bite the hand that feeds you."

"Speaking of biting, come here." Nate placed the breakfast tray on the floor. He reached for Janette and his hands caught hold of her waist.

"No, sweetie. I am going to be late for work. We don't have time." She didn't try hard enough to pull away.

"Work. I got all the work you need right here." Nate slid his Calvin Klein boxer briefs down to his ankles and kicked them off. His dick was halfway hard and when Janette took a look she couldn't fight the arousal that washed over her body. From the first time she had laid her hazel eyes on Nate she had wanted him. The tricky part had been getting him to do more than sex her. Her weight was distributed mostly on her hips and ass. Although they sagged a little, her 40DD breasts made most men drool and she kept them encased in the most beautiful brassieres money could buy. All of this is to say that Janette had no problem with her size, nor any problem enticing men with her appearance. She did however harbor deep fears of a man straying and wanting a smaller woman once she had become attached and decided she wanted him all to herself.

Nate had noticed Janette heading to her car after a jazz concert at Marshall Park on a Sunday afternoon. He had been intrigued with her walk. He had never seen a full-figured woman move with the grace of a runway model. He had no intention of stopping to talk to her until he moved past her car and saw her smile at him. He smiled back at her and then he heard her laugh and ask him if he was scared to stop and talk. Janette was confident and beautiful. Her hair, nails, and feet were always done. She was showing off at the concert with a tight pair of capri pants and a linen shirt with no bra underneath it. He had ended up standing at her car talking and putting his mack down until every car had emptied from the parking lot.

They had spent the next few days talking on the phone before

Nate had decided to give thick loving a try. He had not regretted it. Janette ended up breaking him down with a massage that left him weak as a lamb. Before he met her he hadn't slept soundly since leaving D.C., almost a year back. After Kim's suicide Nate had succumbed to guilt and shame to the point that he had nightmares and anxiety attacks that left him short of breath. Eventually the cooking and pampering that Janette provided softened Nate, and he was able to fight off the guilt and depression that haunted him almost every night. As time wore on he became dependent on Janette and had all but abandoned his old ways of womanizing and running the streets. Although he was officially living in his Aunt Marion's basement, he slept at Janette's almost nightly. He'd put on weight like a pregnant woman and had stopped getting his hair cut regularly. It was as if he simply no longer cared about his appearance. The stress of Kim's death and the guilt for his role in it had begun to wear him down. He was lost in feelings of regret for his treatment of her. Secretly he longed for some relief from the despair, but he'd never had to ask anyone for help. He didn't know how, and now it was beginning to cost him. The man he'd always been was fading into something far less appealing. It would have been apparent that he was a broken man to anyone who truly knew him. But to Janette, he was a cuddly dream come true.

She took a glimpse at her clock and knew she would be late for her first patient. Still she leaned over and took him in her mouth. As she began sucking Nate, she thought long and hard about getting married one day. She had an idea what it would take to keep a husband happy and this was her version of it. Nate's head instantly fell back and his mouth dropped open. She was sucking him so good. He knew that she was trying to take him out fast so that she could get to work. He wanted to slow her down so that he could show her that he was the boss. He attempted to pull himself up but her hands slid up his chest and pressed him back into the bed. With the other hand she began to pump his shaft while making loud slurping and purring noises with her mouth wrapped around the tip of his manhood.

"Oh, Nett. Oh, Nett." He moaned out. "No, baby, not like this."

She knew she had him. She started bobbing her head up and down using her tongue and the roof of her mouth to drive him over the edge. She had one hand on his nipples, pulling and caressing them. With the other hand she gripped his balls and massaged them, never stopping the suction she had going on.

The room began spinning. Nate was flat on his back trying to watch in amazement as Janette used her tongue like a weapon of mass destruction. Just as Nate was about to reach his orgasm, he regained his composure and caught her head on the upstroke. He pushed her head back and rolled away.

"Take those pants off," he demanded. Her face showed disappointment that she hadn't made him erupt but she knew her body was in for a delightful pounding. She grabbed her Nextel and smashed a button.

"Liza," she said into the phone.

"Hey, Janette. What's up?"

"Are you at the office?" Nate was standing behind her sliding her pants off. She stepped out of them. He then grabbed her thong and began sliding it down as well.

"I just got in."

"Okay, I am running about a half hour late. Call Mrs. Tucker and see if we can push her down to three-thirty. What is she getting anyway?"

"Fillings. Two of them."

"If she can't make it then . . ." Janette stopped when Nate's fingers found her button and penetrated her at the same time. "Whoo." She said aloud. She mouthed "stop" to Nate but didn't mean it. "Just do what you got to do. S . . . s . . . see you in a little bit."

"Girl, you all right over there?" Liza had a feeling what was going on. Liza was Janette's first and only receptionist and she noticed that Janette had been running late more in the last three months than she had in the previous four years combined since she had been practicing dentistry.

The phone was already on the floor and Janette had leaned over the bed. Nate had slipped on a condom and was entering Janette an inch at a time. "Mmmm," he said. "Slippery when wet."

Janette's breathing quickened as Nate locked onto her hips and began banging away. Sometimes he hit it slow but that was more for him than her. She loved to be licked slow but fucked hard and fast. "That's right, daddy. Bang it. Bang it."

The bed was shaking as Janette used it to hold herself up. "You like that? You want it harder?" Nate quickened his pace and was pulling all the way out and slamming back into her. He worked nonstop on her, hitting it from the back like a madman for five minutes straight as sweat began pouring off of his chest.

Janette's eyes rolled up into her head and she thought about how lovely life had been since Nate had been around. Any women who said size didn't matter obviously had never been hit by a Mandingo like Nathan Montgomery. She was bouncing back against him, enjoying the feeling of him thoroughly working her middle. "Ooohhh, baby. Don't stop." She felt electric sparks start in her toes and creep slowly up past her ankles. Her thighs began to tremble to the point that she feared she wouldn't be able to keep her balance.

Nate felt her orgasm nearing and decided to send her over the edge. He took the thumb that was gripping her right cheek and let is slip into her ass. When he did this Janette growled like a grizzly that had been shot with a dart gun. She tried to stand as the tides of her orgasm crashed through her body but she was too weak. "Are you cumming, Nett?"

Why he had to ask she never knew. "Yes. Yes. Yessss." And she let out a series of short screams. His breath quickened and she knew what to do. She summoned all the energy in her body and pulled away from him, spun around, and dropped to her knees. In one motion she had the condom off and Nate in her mouth.

"Oh yes." His body stiffened and the veins in his neck seemed to pop out at the same time he released into her mouth. She took him all in until she was sure he was finished. *This is how to get a man and that food I cook is how to keep one,* she thought as she swallowed his juices. "Girl, you so nasty," Nate said as a smile slowly formed out of the fuck face he sported moments earlier.

Janette wiped the drops that had run on her chin and licked her fingers clean. "You love it. You love it." She repeated.

"I can't get enough of it." He began laughing. He pointed down to his penis, which was still hard. He walked into the bathroom singing, "It's the remix to ignition coming hot out the kitchen. . . ."

He could see that Janette had picked up her cell. "Liza. Cancel and reschedule all my appointments. I'll work late all next week." He stood in the door of the bathroom and shook his head.

"Girl, you are crazy."

"Nasty, crazy, whatever. Just come eat me."

ALSO BY
DARREN COLEMAN

DON'T EVER WONDER
A Novel

ISBN 0-06-059486-1 (paperback)

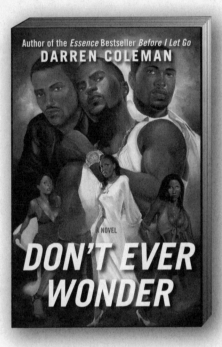

Nate, a "reformed" womanizer, is still recovering from a tragedy and swears that his days of being a player are over. Have his new faith and new woman really tamed him, or is he just biding his time until he reenters the game? Brendan is the type of man every woman wants—until she gets one. But, since his heart was broken, Brendan has vowed never to commit again. Cory, a successful businessman, has it all on track. Or does he? Will his affair with his sister-in-law come back to haunt him?

Each man must confront his own ideal of manhood and intimacy as he embarks on an emotional roller-coaster—one that will keep you on the edge of your seat, as well as give women an inside look at what brothers really want.

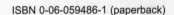

IRRESISTIBLY AMISTAD

NVISION PUBLISHING ORDER FORM
Buy any Nvision Publishing title or Darren Coleman book from Nvision Publishing!

DO OR DIE
$15.00

LOST & TURNED OUT
$15.00

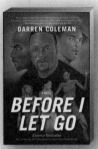

BEFORE I LET GO
(Amistad Edition)
$14.95

DON'T EVER WONDER
(Amistad Edition)
$14.95

LADIES LISTEN UP
(Amistad Edition)
$14.95

PURCHASER INFORMATION

Name _____

Register # _____
(applies if incarcerated)

Address _____

_____

City _____

State/ZIP _____

Which book _____

# of books _____

Total enclosed $ _____

Send to
Nvision Publishing/Order
P.O. Box 274
Lanham Severn Road
Lanham, MD 20703

Make check or money order payable to
Nvision Publishing. Checks must clear before
orders are sent. (Not advisable to send cash.)

Add $4.00 for shipping via U.S. Priority Mail for
a total cost per book of $19.00.

Nvision Publishing deducts 25% from orders
shipped directly to prisons. Cost is $11.25 plus
$4.00 shipping for a total cost per book
of $15.25.

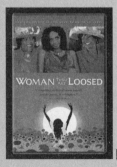
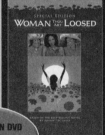